ROCKET REPO

C.P. JAMES

vinci
BOOKS

BY C.P. JAMES

The Reassembly Series

Rocket Repo

Trawler Trash

Ship Show

Xeno Xoo

Fleet Feat

Dark Dodgers

The Cytocorp Saga

Dome Six

Into the Burn

Out of the Seam

For Mom and Dad. Thanks for always trying to understand.

Vinci Books

vinci-books.com

Published by Vinci Books Ltd in 2025

1

A CIP catalogue record for this book is available from the British Library.
Paperback ISBN: 9781036701307

FSC
www.fsc.org
MIX
Paper | Supporting responsible forestry
FSC® C018072

Printed and bound in Great Britain by Clays Ltd, Elcograf S.p.A.

CHAPTER 1
THE GASH

Geddy Starheart peered deep into the hot gash and thought of Tatiana.

If only she could see the final piece click into place. The singular dedication he'd shown to this chore would've impressed her. The years he'd spent mining the ore. The modifications to the smelter. The precision with which he cast every piece of his ship.

Of course, after she was done being impressed, she'd drive her stiletto heel into his forehead, because he was supposed to be dead.

The first of the bots appeared through the crack in the tunnel, its tukrium skin still glowing red from heat so intense it warped the air around it. The metal tracks whined and whirred, churning sparkly clouds of silicon-rich volcanic dust as it turned up the well-worn path, heavy with ore. Then came the second and the third, the luminous metal fading as it cooled. They lined up behind the first in a rickety little caravan.

One salvage bot could make two trips into the fissure before something conked out or melted. Anything more was pressing his luck. He'd lost four already. They weren't designed for mining at all, say nothing of extreme heat, and reprogramming them was a hassle.

Even from across the old lava tube, the heat radiating from the hole in the rock pushed his thermal suit to its limits. Just fifteen minutes left him feeling like a well-done pot roast, sweat running down the small of his back and into his ass crack like au jus. Even the water in his reservoir became too hot to drink after a while. He lumbered across the sandy floor and fell in behind the bots as they climbed back up to the main tunnel.

The deep tracks they left in the sand suggested a good haul. With a little luck, it would contain enough shinium, as Eli called it, for the final piece of the ship's outer skin. Running it through the smelter and casting it would carry him well into the evening. Two, maybe three days and Earth 2 would be behind him forever.

If he could, he'd hang his arm out the window and give it the finger.

Even the recycled air of a starship would be preferable at this point. Doubling up on filters barely cut into the smell. On a good day, it reminded him of burrito farts the morning after a cheap-beer bender. A bad day, however, was like the devil's smegma.

No wonder it was now known as The Deuce.

Yes, technically it was his fault, but the geothermal plant would've tapped the pocket of hydrogen sulfide and methane eventually. It sure cleared everyone out in a hurry, though. The last transport left six months to the day after the gas first reached the city.

Tatiana showed up two weeks after the completion of Geo 2, which was to replace the aging Geo 1 plant. He could tell she was important, but not until she addressed the crews on the floor did he learn she was Ivan Semenov's daughter and sole heir, whom he'd put in charge of energy production.

And oh, what energy she produced. He could still see her, ice-blue eyes peering out between long black lashes, platinum-blond bangs slicing across her forehead like a razor.

Every Monday morning, she would show up and tell them they were worthless bottom feeders who were being replaced by robots. Good god, it was hot. Geddy wished to know her intimately. Getting tight with the Semenovs would cement his future, erase his debts, and potentially keep his past from catching up with him.

Her father practically owned Earth 2 and had a reputation for being a hard-ass, but no ass in the sector was harder than Tatiana's. He had to have her. *Had to.*

A friend of a friend got him a gig tending bar at one of Ivan's legendary parties. When she came slinking up in a painted-on dress, he turned on the ol' Starheart charm.

"Dry Martini," she cooed. "If I taste vermouth, I'll have you sacked."

"You got it," he'd said with a wink, his pants suddenly tight in the crotch. Nothing about her was dry.

Geddy was a beer and whiskey guy. He wasn't entirely sure how to make a dry martini, which went a long way toward explaining his empty tip jar. While she leaned against the bar, ignoring him, he surreptitiously jumped into the net and found the recipe, completing her drink half a second before she turned around. She sipped it, frowned, and gave a shrug.

"Well?" he asked. "Do I get to live?"

"For now." She studied his face like it was a curiosity. A museum piece. But she didn't leave or call security, which put it in the W column.

"Hey, I wanted you to know how much I enjoy your pep talks."

Her eyes narrowed, the corners of her luscious lips downturned. "What?"

"In Geo 1. When you said bots could do twice the work in half the time, it really inspired me. And when you had us all point and laugh at Dennis for losing his arm in that drilling accident? I mean, wow. Chills. *And* he learned an important lesson."

"What's your name?" Her eyes bore into him like the drills that made the tunnels.

"Geddy."

She returned several times for more martinis, and at the end of the night, he took her home. What followed was the most depraved and wanton experience of his life to that point, during which he lost enough electrolytes to give him a minor seizure. Man, what a night.

Six weeks later, they were engaged. Everything was falling into place.

One day, however, he was en route to the plant when he launched into a violent sneezing fit, snot spewing from his nose like the syrup dispenser at a continental breakfast. He'd never had allergies before. It went away, but that night he heard it for the first time. An androgynous voice in his head.

— *Hello?*

He whirled, unable to pinpoint its location.

"Who's there?"

— *You can hear me?*

He was completely alone at the time, checking pressure gauges in the sublevel. He couldn't tell if it was male or female, but it was pleasant and non-threatening.

"What?"

— *I've tapped directly into your auditory cortex. Only you can hear me. Don't worry, you're not going insane.*

Considering the source, that wasn't as reassuring as it was

meant to be. Too much booze and sex, he figured. But the voice remained. Not even headphones could drown it out.

— *I need your help.*

"Where are you? *Who* are you?"

— *I am an energy-based entity in a durable form. You inhaled me. Who I am is a difficult question to answer, but I've waited a long time for you.*

The next time, he only thought his reply.

— I've inhaled a lot of shit. Nothing ever talked to me.

— *Better get used to it. We've got a lot of work to do.*

CHAPTER 2

APRIL 10, 2427

Its name was unpronounceable in English, but the first part sounded like Eli, which it agreed to be called. Geddy resisted, rejected, and railed against the fact of his new and inescapable companion for weeks. Eventually, resistance gave way to acceptance, and that was the path forward. They'd since settled into a comfortable equilibrium. Hell, he needed the company.

Most of Geddy's life had been transactional. Go here, spy on so-and-so, report back. Find this one guy, break his legs if necessary, and extract what he owes. Everything came in tidy little packages.

Building the *Penetrator* by smelting an unknown metal out of the rock was nothing like that.

Geddy had flown a thousand starships but didn't know jack about building them. That was where Eli came in. He didn't have to create literally every part from raw materials, but it was vital the ship's exterior be completely clad in shinium, for it was the only material that could pass through the barrier around his home world.

There was a good reason he'd never heard of shinium. Eli

explained it was formed by violent celestial events billions of years ago — Big Bang-level cataclysms under very specific gravitational and magnetic conditions. Thus, it was exceedingly rare. Even if its existence was discovered, the techniques for smelting and working it were only known to Sagaceans, Eli's kind, who Geddy also hadn't heard of.

If it existed on Earth 2, it would be very deep.

His work at the plant customarily took him into the service tunnels, which made it easy to conduct his exploration and core analyses in secret. After a few months, Eli hoped they might discover a vein of the precious ore by exploring a little-known system of lava tubes and uncharted caves nearby. To know for sure would require a smidge of explosive and several metric tons of willful ignorance. The first he managed to acquire with little difficulty. The second he already had in spades.

The blast opened a pathway to the ore, but it also cracked open a weak spot in The Deuce's unsettled bowels, triggering a massive collapse that blocked his return and released an ocean of smelly gas. When they couldn't find him, authorities assumed the worst.

By grace or by luck, he followed the caves until they dumped him out on the other side of the stubby mountains west of the city. By then, though, the noxious cloud had reached Laguna, and an emergency was declared. He was on his way to find Tatiana when he spotted a news crawler on a holo-board proclaiming the tragic accident claimed the life of a worker named Geddy Starheart.

The original plan was to build the ship in secret, but as he monitored the situation from a distance, he realized all he needed to do was wait. A week later, he watched the last transport leave from a lonely perch on the hillside and got to work that very afternoon.

Fortunately, Earth 2 already had a smelter because of the

crust's high concentration of bauxite, whence came aluminum. The process of extracting and working shinium, however, required extensive modifications that took the better part of a year. Designing around the available components, another year. On and on it went.

Yes, he wanted Eli out of his head — all this was on his account — but he also wanted off this stinking, lonely planet. Isolation kept his past from catching up to him even better than marrying Tatiana would've, but enough was enough. There were other, better places to lay low, which he could only do once Eli was out of the picture. Places with women, and beer, and entertainment, where he could be anonymous, save his money, and retire to Pretensia with all the other old crooks.

A drop of sweat tumbled off his nose and landed on the hot die, sizzling as it evaporated.

He cracked the die open and gave it a little tap. The final part came out cleanly, a thumb-sized cylinder with staggered rings running down its length.

"What's this thing do?" Geddy asked aloud, turning over the freshly cast part in his gloved hand. Mostly he shaped and cut panels in the *Penetrator's* outer skin. Anything exposed to the barrier had to be made of pure shinium. Eli continually stressed the importance of this.

— *It's the key.*

"I suppose we'll spend all next week making a hood ornament?"

— *No, this ought to do it.*

He carefully picked it up with the tongs and plunged it into the water, releasing a burst of bubbles and a puff of steam. Once it cooled, he removed his gloves and inspected the part more closely. Another day or two and he'd have the burs filed down enough to give it a go. A quick test flight around Trebek, the nearest moon, and it would finally be time to say sayonara to this dump.

— *You must protect the key. You're the only one who should ever fly it.*

He slipped the still-warm key into his pocket, removed his face shield, and shut down the forge for the last time. "Fair enough, pal. In the meantime, I'd say we've earned ourselves a little celebration. There's a bottle of Old Earth with my name on it."

— *Not to rain on your parade …*

"Lemme guess. You forgot a cup holder."

— *No, nothing like that.*

Geddy hung the face shield on its hook and tossed the thick gloves on the table as he emerged into the hazy, reddish light of their two suns. Soon, hopefully, he could amend his current definition of fresh air. It was only slightly less putrid outside. It got a little better at altitude, which was half the reason he lived in Tati's old penthouse in Semenov Tower.

He closed his eyes and took a deep breath, barely believing he was so close to the end. Whatever Eli had to say couldn't spoil this moment.

"Can it wait 'til tomorrow?"

— *Today is April tenth.*

A blanket of dark anxiety settled over him. It couldn't be April again already, could it? "You're shittin' me."

— *I do not shit.*

He heaved a sigh. "Then I guess we've got an extra stop to make."

The contents of Earth 2's mausoleum, cremains, and Old Earth digital archives had made the trip to Earth 3 with everyone else. The spring after the last transport departed, Geddy returned to the old house at the military base and erected a little shrine to his late parents.

The last two vehicles that still held a decent charge in all of Laguna, the planet's only city, were a maintenance truck and a motorcycle. He used the truck exclusively to shuttle parts to the spaceport, where the *Penetrator* was housed. The bike was just for fun. He wasn't entirely confident it would make it from the smelter out to the old base and back. If not, he might have a long walk. But it was either that or not go at all, and this was his last chance to say goodbye.

Reducing a city of one million to scrap was slow business. Seven years on, autonomous equipment still carried out the tedious work of chopping everything up for salvage. Two autonomous "crews" had begun at the far end of the manmade lagoon in what used to be known as the rough part of town and were working their way toward downtown. Each had to chew through about six kilometers' worth of city.

The two destructors — basically colossal lawn mowers with whirring wrecking balls instead of blades — could level a fifty-meter swath from the lagoon to the edge of the city in about a week's time, then turn around and work their way back to the water. Excavators with metal claws followed behind, loading the debris into trucks that hauled it to the space elevator.

He figured he had a year, give or take a month, before they reached downtown. Of course, he'd be long gone by then.

Giving the wrecking crews a wide berth, he took the long way to the base, much too far for any sensors to pick him up. At this point, there probably wasn't any reason to be paranoid about being discovered, but why take the chance? By the time he reached the main gate half an hour later, the bike's batteries were down to ten percent. Now he had to stay long enough to charge them to at least twenty-five off the still-functioning solar array.

Either the bots were programmed to leave the base alone or they were saving it for last. It probably still had value as a military outpost. Whether the old Planetary Defense Force was being rebuilt on Earth 3, he didn't know. A great deal of money had been spent on defense during the Ring War, but they never joined the Alliance or the fight.

Ivan Semenov, Tatiana's father, discovered there was much more money to be made cleaning up after a war than fighting it, thereby multiplying their fortune. What began as a humble refuge for the last humans quickly became a sprawling, overwrought paean to the very excesses that put them there. In that regard, the base was a welcome throwback to the earliest days of Laguna settlement, utilitarian and simple.

No matter how many times he visited the old bungalow on C Street, smack in the middle of the housing afforded to officers and their families, he still struggled to place himself there. His father, Lucas, who he idolized, was a sergeant major in the PDF and its most gifted pilot. His mother was a docent at the Museum of Space Exploration out at the spaceport. She knew a thousand stories about Old Earth. It was a peaceful, joyful time, and he had lots of friends.

But on April 10, 2402, everything changed.

Geddy returned from school with all the other PDF brats to a gloriously empty house. It was his parents' twentieth anniversary, and his old man had something special cooked up. He'd talked his superiors into letting him take a military shuttle north to see the Ice Castles, skyscraper-sized crystals pushed up through a deep crack in Earth 2's crust by its hyperactive geological forces. The idea was to have a picnic, spend the night, and watch the suns come up.

For Geddy, having an entire night to himself was a rare treat. He ate a dinner of cake and ice cream, played video games, and went to bed with a stomachache. To a thirteen-year-old on a military base, it hardly got much better. The next day, he ate the leftovers for breakfast, eliminating all evidence of his sweet indulgence.

Later that morning, a PDF colonel named Pritchard — his dad's commander — and two airmen knocked on the classroom door and held a muffled conversation with his teacher. When she pointed out Geddy, glassy-eyed and pale, he assumed the worst. And he was right.

Pritchard sat Geddy down in an empty classroom and explained that there had been an accident, and that both his parents perished. Both the ship and their bodies were unrecoverable. The news tore him in half, and numbness became a stand-in for acceptance. There was a full military funeral, with honors, and praise was lavished on them both.

With no close relatives, Geddy was placed in the care of a foster family. They were nice enough but didn't share Geddy's determination to learn exactly how an ace pilot like his father was brought down by a no-brainer joyride to the Ice Castles. The PDF's investigation concluded it was an equipment malfunction, and that was that.

For whatever reason, he never believed it. He pressed his foster parents to challenge the PDF's account, but they advised him to process his grief and move on. The resentment that followed built to the point where Geddy decided to stow away on a freighter during a refueling stop the day after he turned fourteen. He didn't care where it wound up.

Clearly, he should've. Seventeen years on Kigantu rotted him on the inside. If he hadn't left when he did, he'd be an irredeemable lowlife like everyone else in that godforsaken ball of sand.

But even though he'd come back here each of the seven years he'd been alone on Earth 2, it was always hard to go inside. He sat on his bike outside the cookie-cutter home for a few minutes screwing up the courage to do it.

— You don't have to. I just thought–

"It's okay. I would've forgotten."

After a time, the steady metallic rumble of destructors in the distance, he climbed off and went inside.

There wasn't much to the shrine, really. Just an old screen on the kitchen table playing a series of home movies in an endless loop, powered by a solar cell on its last legs. As for the house, any number of PDF families had come and gone since he was a kid. It was just a shell around a fading memory. He'd park himself at the head of the rectangular table and watch the looping video from start to finish, then raise a glass of Old Earth northward and toss it back. There was only one swallow left in his dad's old bottle.

Early on, the practice elicited tears. He'd pushed away thoughts of his childhood for so long that seeing it play out again was almost like watching some movie that firmly established its characters' happiness so the tragedy to come would seem that much worse.

With each passing year, he felt more and more disconnected from this version of himself, as though he and his parents had merely been actors in this sad tale.

After an hour, Geddy abruptly shut off the display and flipped it face-down on the table, then rose to stretch.

— *What are you doing?*

"This shit's bumming me out."

— *Would you like to talk about it?*

He retrieved his jacket from the hook by the front door and slipped it on. "Nope. That's enough trips down memory lane. Today's about the future."

— *What about your drink?*

"There's an unopened bottle at the museum with my name on it. Right now, we're gonna say goodbye to Cherie, get shit-faced, and start fresh tomorrow."

— *You're sure you don't want to–*

"Yes, Eli, I'm fucking sure, okay?! They left me alone, and once I get you home, I'll be alone again. Finally."

He marched outside, leaving the door wide open.

— *Aren't you going to close it?*

"What's the point?"

Geddy threw his leg over the bike and flipped up the kickstand, then slid on his sunglasses.

— *At least make yourself a copy of the video. I really think you'll wish you–*

"Enough, Eli! My god, you're like the mother-in-law I never wanted. If I didn't know better, I'd think you didn't even want out of my head."

Eli paused.

— *I'm only trying to help.*

"I appreciate your concern, but I'm fine."

He gunned the motor, squawking the tire as the foul wind tugged at his hair. Eli didn't say another word the whole way back to town. He was an ostensibly immortal and indestructible passenger who could see the world through Geddy's eyes. He could no more read his mind than make him feel.

Yet, amid the crowded headspace occupied by his parents, the PDF, and practically every life choice that led him to this weird point, he had carved out a generous space for Eli, his only companion. That was more than he'd ever afforded anyone. And as he drove, he could almost feel that little space fill with hurt.

Maybe he wasn't so indestructible after all.

CHAPTER 3

COME HERE OFTEN?

Laguna Luxe Mall sat at the edge of a perfectly circular manmade lake, practically a city unto itself encircling the base of Semenov Tower. Geddy shuffled along the empty halls, more or less retracing his previous steps through the patina of dust on the floor.

A scanner at the entrance used to read your account balances to see whether you could even afford to enter. He'd never actually seen the inside until Tatiana took him shopping for engagement rings, making him feel as though he'd won a contest. Even now, he didn't quite belong.

Seven years after it was abandoned, most places in Laguna still had power. The geo plant was offline, but the solar arrays still gave the batteries enough juice to keep the lights on.

He paused at the tall glass doors that opened onto the veranda outside the lagoon entrance and peered across the water. A cloud of dust and debris indicated where the machines were tearing ragged bites out of the city. They were close enough now that he could clearly see "Semenov Planetary Systems" emblazoned on the side, perhaps a kilometer away. By the time they reached the tower, he'd be well on his way to Sagacea.

Geddy turned aside from the entrance and continued through the mall, his pace quickening until he arrived at the Intergalactic Concierge Kiosk. He unconsciously smoothed his hair.

— *Seriously?*

— Don't judge me. You said you'd never judge me.

— *Your priorities are confusing. That's not a judgment — it's a fact.*

He stepped into the circle, and a holographic woman materialized from thin air. Today's randomly generated outfit was a tasteful, yet sexy black dress that hugged every curve. Her lush, gravity-defying red hair tumbled over her bare shoulders in impossibly silky waves. Horn-rimmed glasses called to mind a hot librarian — one of his favorite looks. Did the algorithm know this was his last visit and pull out all the stops?

"Hello there," she cooed in a faintly British lilt, cocking her head playfully. "Your name's … Geddy. Is that correct?"

"Yes." He brushed a bead of sweat from his upper lip as his cheeks flushed.

"Welcome back to Laguna Luxe, Geddy." Her teeth flashed blinding white. Did he glimpse a tongue stud? My god. "I'm Cherie, your–"

"Personal guide to the wonders of the cosmos," he finished. "I know."

Cherie, the red-headed librarian. What a sendoff! For all he knew, he might never see a woman again. He undid his zipper.

"My records indicate you've come here many times."

"Oh yes," he said. "Many."

"What can I do for you today? You can ask me for directions, arrange travel, or order merchandise from practically anywhere in the universe. The sky's the limit. Or should I say, the stars."

She beamed her perfect Cheshire smile and placed a dainty hand on one hip while the other absently fluffed her hair.

In the early days, Cherie could reference their previous interactions. Since she started glitching a couple years ago, however, all she ever remembered was that he'd been there before. He couldn't have said whether he preferred the familiarity or the novelty.

"So, Geddy, now that we're friends and all, tell me how I can help you."

"You already are."

"Quite a beard you've got there, mister. Did you know Laguna Luxe Mall has two salons?"

"Yep."

She studied him up and down, noting the pants that had fallen around his ankles. "Uh-oh ... it seems you've had a clothing malfunction. Perhaps I could interest you in some new trousers?"

"Whatever. Take your time."

"Hmm," she mused. "Looks like you're a size 34. Perhaps something in Grelorian wool? It has a beautiful drape."

"Knock yourself out," he panted in return.

Geddy ordered six pairs of pants in different colors, two watches, cologne, and booked an afternoon tour of the Haunted Caves of Eicreon. The system wasn't connected to anything. He just kept ordering stuff for as long as it took using Tatiana's account.

"I'll have those delivered to your door. Are you still at 1607 Miranda?"

The sound of his old address always brought a smile to his lips. No one ever lived there after him. The evacuation was already underway by then. Still, it was odd the order seemed to actually go through. In the past, his visits to the kiosk ended with Cherie saying it couldn't be completed at this time.

Must be another glitch. He shrugged it off, pulled up his

pants, and refastened them as he turned to depart. "Sure, sweetheart. If I'm not there, just leave it outside the door."

Geddy removed the key from his pocket and set it down on his nightstand, then continued stuffing food and supplies into the plastic crate. The ship's cockpit was so tiny, even it would be a tight fit, say nothing of his pack and a change of clothes. Eli said he wouldn't need any of it, which was supposed to be comforting but only made him wonder if it was really a one-way trip.

It would be worth it to get Eli out of his head.

— *Help me understand why we can't perform our test flight today.*

"Because I need to get properly drunk, that's why. I've worked my ass off for seven years and there's a bottle of OE with my name on it."

— *You celebrate by poisoning yourself?*

"That's how humans roll, baby. Why are you antsy, anyway? You drifted through space for eons. What's another day?"

— *I guess I'm just excited.*

"All the more reason to get squared away now. We can jump right into preflight checks first thing in the morning."

Geddy set the crate on the hand trolley then looped the strap of his duffel around the handle and wheeled it out into the wide hallway. Once the last transport left, the one carrying Tatiana, he'd moved into her old place. She had the only penthouse to match her status, occupying the entire top three floors of the tower.

After descending in the elevator, he crossed the polished marble floor of the ornate lobby and exited where the maintenance truck awaited. He loaded his stuff into the back and headed toward the spaceport.

Before he inadvertently turned Earth 2's atmosphere into history's biggest fart, it had become a premier tourist destination. Ships sometimes had to circle for hours to get landing clearance. There had even been talk of building another spaceport on the fringes of the city, but it never materialized.

As he turned up the winding road to the spaceport, Geddy stopped to watch the distant circular platform of the massive space elevator rise skyward with a full load of scrap. It only made about four trips per day. Though fully automated, it reminded him there was still a whole universe out there. It accelerated slowly before disappearing through a thick layer of low, jaundiced clouds. Before the accident, they were wispy and white.

— Welcome to The Deuce. Come for the shit-smelling atmosphere but stay for the piss-yellow sky.

— Gee, never heard that before.

Getty ignored Eli and chuckled to himself as he urged the truck up the winding road.

Earth 2's sole spaceport was largely carved out of a mountain. It had a typical setup, with two gigantic circular platforms for transports and several smaller ones for ordinary ships. Under the deck was traffic control and the hangar, leaving the ground level and mezzanine to the Old Earth Museum of Space Exploration. When the road split, Geddy veered right toward the employee entrance. Once, his mother came here every day on the train, which was dismantled before everyone left.

Strictly speaking, he could've built the ship downtown, but the museum had lots of room, good light, and most importantly, a high-end purification system that still worked. He inhaled deeply, appreciating the much sweeter air. Plus, the same elevator that shuttled ships down to the hangar continued to the ground floor. That meant he didn't have to build *Penetrator* in the cold, echoey expanse of the hangar.

Geddy parked by the cargo doors and secured his gear to the trolley. As the door rolled open, he felt his first true flutter of excitement. By this time tomorrow, he'd be up among the stars for one last adventure.

Once inside, he made a beeline for the back of the domed atrium where the *Penetrator* waited on the elevator, sleek and refreshingly old-school. Technically, there wasn't a good reason to name it anything at all since it wouldn't have a transponder and would only make one voyage — two if you counted the return trip, but that was hardly a guarantee.

— It's beautiful, Geddy. You did a great job.

"No, *we* did, Pal. You and I."

The ship's design was dictated by the available parts. It was narrow and sleek, with a steeply raked window and a retractable shinium shield. Aside from the small cockpit, it was all engines — specifically a pair of lovingly refurbished MPD drives from a junked twin-engine Kemik AS-322 the repair bay had stripped down for parts. They were made for a much bigger fuselage, so this puppy would really move.

Geddy opened the cockpit door and tilted the crate at an angle to fit it into its place behind the seat. Then he shoved the duffle underneath.

"I could've done with a little cargo room."

— You don't need much. I will take care of you.

"I still don't know what the hell that even means. Unless the center of the universe is, like, less than twelve hours from here, I'm gonna need food at least. Or did we put a vacuum toilet in for nothing?"

— I keep forgetting you need food.

"Hmph. Typical."

Eli survived alone in the vacuum of space for eons. He could be forgiven for forgetting about stuff like food, but still.

Every time Geddy talked about what came after dropping him off, Eli changed the subject.

Anything that got him off this cursed planet and its sewer-scented air was worth a bit of uncertainty. And honestly, if he wound up dead, it would just mean his past could never catch up with him. Besides, the only people who might have missed him had long since moved on.

— *Guess it's time to drink yourself into a stupor.*

"Correctamundo."

Geddy cracked his knuckles and strode toward the inevitably named Space Bar, the little bar at the back of the museum. Keeping the last bottle of Old Earth bourbon inside the old beer cooler was probably sacrosanct, but he liked his whiskey cold. He turned it over in his hands, studying the label. It depicted Old Earth as sort of a cave drawing with hand-scrawled letters.

Most of the booze at the museum bar was cheap swill from Knetos, but he happened to find one unopened bottle of the good stuff at the back of an employee locker. As a testament to his willpower, he managed to save it until this very moment.

— *You seem very impressed with yourself.*

"You have no idea what it took to leave the planet's last bottle of good hooch alone."

Booze didn't affect Eli at all, but it made him easier to ignore. At one point, Geddy considered drinking himself to death just to have some peace.

Were it not for Eli's intervention, though, Geddy would've either wound up married to Tatiana or dead. If Geddy died here, so would Eli, because after the accident, rain fell as acid with a pH low enough to blister skin. It would dissolve his body and Eli with it. For better or worse, they needed each other.

And so they became united in their purpose.

CHAPTER 4

TRAVELING EXHIBIT

Halfway into the bottle of Old Earth, Geddy felt light as a feather. The museum's PA system, which once carried droning announcements about closing time or paged parents to collect their lost children, now blared rock music as he danced around, occasionally bumping into the railings protecting the exhibits.

Its central focus was the history of human space travel. The centerpiece was the one-fourth scale model of the Saturn V rocket that stretched nearly to the ceiling. A replica of the space shuttle *Discovery* hung at a jaunty angle as it maneuvered a section of the International Space Station into place. A whole corner was dedicated to the development of ion propulsion. Others to First Contact and the settlement of Earth 2.

Presently, Geddy set his sights upon his personal favorite piece — Neil Armstrong's actual suit from Apollo 11, or so the placard read. A looping hologram described how it had been lovingly preserved over the centuries thanks to the support of donors, and why it was now housed in a thick cylinder, in a vacuum and at a constant temperature, to preserve it for future generations.

"Hey," he slurred. "If this thing's so special, why didn't they take it to Earth 3?"

— *Perhaps it's not the real one.*

"Oh, it's real all right. Mom said so."

— *So, everything else in this place is a replica except for a four hundred fifty year-old suit? Think about that.*

"I don't wanna *think*, Eli. I wanna *dance*!"

Geddy took a pull from the bottle and danced — or at least, contorted his body roughly in time with the rhythm — until he attempted a spin and tumbled on his ass, the back of his skull cracking into the floor.

"Ah, shit!" he rolled onto his elbow, relieved to find he hadn't broken the bottle.

— *Maybe it's time to head back. We've got a big day tomorrow.*

"You head back, ya killjoy. I'm just getting started."

He got up, rubbing the back of his head as he caught himself against the railing that encircled the space suit. He turned around and narrowed his eyes as he studied it. It never once occurred to him it might not be the real thing. Before the accident, people flocked to see it. Were they all bamboozled?

Geddy set his bottle down and cracked his knuckles.

— *What are you doing?*

"I'm gonna see if it's real."

— *Ged, no. Come on. You've had your fun. Let's get some rest, eh? Big day tomorrow.*

He awkwardly threw one leg over the waist-high railing, then the other. You could tell the cylinder was thick and tough just by looking at it, but as for the temperature and vacuum thing, who knew? Now that Eli planted the seed of doubt, he had to know for sure. He placed his palms on the cylinder and pushed. As expected, it didn't budge.

— *Did you really think that would work? Maybe we should call it a night.*

"The people deserve to know, dammit!"

— There are no people. If it was real, they would've taken it.

But Geddy was undeterred. If he stretched out a bit, he could put his hands on the cylinder and still reach the bottom of the railing with his legs. And after seven years of mining and building, he was as strong as he'd ever been. Just one big push. If that didn't do the job, he'd let it be.

He took a deep breath and shoved, and the cylinder moved. Not much, but enough to raise the bottom edge off the base. There was no hiss of air to suggest a vacuum had broken.

"Ha!"

— Told you. Let's bounce.

Gritting his teeth, Geddy moved his hands a bit higher gave it all he had. It tipped, and he kept pushing. With a final grunt of effort, the whole display toppled over and landed on the far railing with a heavy, plasticky clunk as he collapsed forward onto the now-empty platform. The metal frame displaying the suit broke off its base, leaving the suit resting against the cylinder.

— Happy now?

"Not yet. This proves nothing."

He got up and rolled the cylinder until it tumbled fully onto its side on the floor, then pulled the suit free.

The placard said it weighed fifty kilos. This thing maybe was half that. He held it up to himself.

"I think it's a fake."

— You don't say.

"It's about my size, right?"

— Oh, brother.

Geddy turned the suit over in his hands, baffled by how to get in the damn thing. He found a sturdy zipper at the back, pulled it down, and slid the legs on while sitting on the ground. Then he rose and pushed his arms through the holes, finding he didn't have nearly enough mobility to grab the zipper. At least it was faithful to the original design, which would've required multiple people to get the astronauts in.

"Can you give me a hand with this?" He barked a laugh.

There was no need to take the helmet off because his head already fit through the metal cuff that held it in place. With it around his neck, the suit couldn't come off even though the back hung open like a hospital gown.

At that moment, Geddy's excitement to wear an old-school spacesuit overcame the fact that it was merely a replica. He should've known better anyway. The good stuff was kept under lock and key at the Old Earth Historical Society and had been taken to Earth 3 with everything else.

— *Can we go now? I need you sharp for tomorrow. I think we should conduct the test flight first thing in the morning.*

"Fine. But the suit stays on."

— *You shouldn't drive.*

"Relax, Bro. I'm a muthafuckin' astronaut."

CHAPTER 5

AN EARLY MORNING SWIM

— W*ake up.*

Eli's familiar voice faded into Geddy's recurring dream like a tinny radio, but it didn't register. He was in too deep and still half-drunk.

In it, he was thirteen again. The moment Colonel Pritchard's eyes fell on him, the whole classroom began to shake, a deep rumble that rattled his skull. Geddy dropped to the floor and assumed the position, but no one else did. Even as cracks opened in the floor, steam and magma oozing through, nobody moved. They just stared at him. His teacher motioned for him to come to the door, but he couldn't. He wouldn't. The whole world was collapsing under him and no one noticed.

— *Geddy, WAKE UP!*

With extreme effort, he cracked open one crusty eye. Only the faintest light came through the window, but it was as bright as the sun. His head throbbed. What was causing the floor to vibrate? Also, he had no memory of returning from the museum. Hopefully the truck was still in one piece.

"What's that? What time is it?"

— *Ten fifteen. I think they're here.*

"Who's they?"

— *The destructors.*

That simply wasn't possible. He'd been watching them do their thing for years, and he knew how fast they moved. A kilometer would take them five or six months, probably longer.

"It's just a little quake, Eli. They happen all the time."

Only it didn't feel or sound like a quake. It sounded like the *whing! whing! whing!* of the big machine's wrecking balls slicing through the air, leveling anything in their path. And close, too. A bank of glass windows exploding nearby could've been right outside the veranda door.

His whole body gave a start. "Holy shit!"

Geddy pried his other eye open and rolled out of bed, stumbling over the spacesuit crumpled on the floor as he hurried out to the veranda overlooking the lagoon. To his left, a cloud of gray dust completely obscured the adjoining mall. On the other side, a similar cloud billowed up from restaurant row, where the second destructor was. They would converge on the tower in minutes.

How did they get here so fast?

It only took a glance across the water to see how. They'd simply bypassed the last kilometer of untouched city just to bring down the mall and the tower. But why?

— *You have to go.*

"No shit! Where are my clothes?"

— *You're still wearing them.*

Sure enough, he was in the same stretchy pants and long-sleeve tee he'd worn the previous day. He only made two quick steps toward the elevator before Eli stopped him.

— *The key!*

He dashed back and dove across the bed to grab the *Pene-*

trator's thumb-sized key off the nightstand. Meanwhile, the destructors sounded like they were in the damn room.

Geddy's eyes frantically swept the room for anything else he'd forgotten, but thankfully, everything he needed was already in the ship. He scrambled for the elevator.

— *Forget it, there's not time!*

As usual, Eli was right. Plus, if the machines cut the power while he was inside, they were dead. The fastest way down — the only way down — was the swashbuckling way. He gulped and swung the foot of the heavy bed aside to give himself the longest possible runway. The lagoon was plenty deep for kids to dive off the little fake cliff along shore, but that was only about five meters. This was a hundred and fifty.

The first destructor cut into the base of the building, sending shockwaves up through his feet. He had seconds. He dashed back to the elevator, about-faced, and planted his foot against the wall, zipping the key into his cargo pocket.

Boy, nothing sobered a fella up like a collapsing high-rise.

— *Run!*

Geddy sprinted toward the open veranda door as the horizon started to tilt. Just short of the railing, he sprang off the floor with his right foot and planted his left on the railing itself to leap out over the lagoon, legs still pumping as though something was under them. For the briefest of moments, the old thrill of weightlessness returned.

But gravity and wind took over, and his legs wound up above and behind him. The rush of air pounded on his eardrums as he tried to orient his legs toward the water. It didn't work. He would enter in a dive at high speed. Reflexively, he shot his arms out in front of him and shut his eyes tight.

The water might as well have been concrete. The moment his arms pierced the surface, they acted like a hinge, his legs whipping overhead as the small of his back slapped down. As he tumbled through the water, a submerged rock rushed toward him through a fog of bubbles, and everything went black.

Geddy ran his tongue around his mouth and tasted grit. Water lapped at his feet. From nearby came the sound of the excavators chewing up what was, until quite recently, the tallest structure in the city.

How in hell was he alive?

— *Can you hear me??*

— Eli? Is that you?

— *It's okay. You're okay.*

He frantically unzipped his cargo pocket, shoved his hand inside, and heaved a sigh of relief when his fingers closed around the *Penetrator's* key.

But *holy shit* did his back hurt. The backs of his legs thrummed with pain from slapping the water like a beaver tail. At least he could move his toes.

— How did I get to the beach?

— *I don't know. When you blacked out, I couldn't reach you.*

He'd never swan-dived off a two-hundred-meter high rise. Who knew what that kind of fall did to your noggin, especially when it was still drenched in Old Earth? Maybe some unconscious survival instinct kicked in while he was unconscious.

Geddy winced as he rolled over and got on all fours. The destructors were now working outward from the pile of rubble that had just been Semenov Tower. Meanwhile, the excavators' claws ripped out hunks of girding and dumped them in a waiting truck.

Why the hell did they rip down the tower only to reverse direction and continue?

So much for sleeping off his drunk. The sooner he got out

of there, the better. When he clambered to his feet, he found he couldn't stand fully upright without compressing something in his back, so he started off like a stooped old man with his weight out over his toes, coughing painfully from his likely cracked ribs. A gap had opened up between the excavators and the destructors near the remains of restaurant row, so he angled for it.

Both the truck and the bike were parked in front of the tower, meaning they were buried under a mountain of rubble. Walking was off the table, so he needed another vehicle. Unfortunately, only emergency and maintenance vehicles in Laguna had a manual mode. The nearest ones were at the old hospital five or six blocks away, and last time he checked, their batteries barely held a charge.

Winding through the debris-riddled pedestrian mall, he continued out past the so-called garment district until he reached the hospital, where two dusty ambulances were parked under an overhang on their charging pads.

He got in and checked the battery level, shocked to see it still had a little juice. After disabling autonomous mode, he pulled out and zipped off toward the spaceport, the excavators receding behind him.

"You're unusually quiet."

— *I'm giving your pain the space it needs.*

"What the hell does that mean?"

— *Of all the tools that shape us, pain is the sharpest.*

"Gee, thanks, sensei. I feel better already."

Geddy ripped down the long, ramrod-straight road toward the mountain with the accelerator pressed all the way forward, glancing nervously at the darkening western horizon.

— *What is it?*

"The rain."

— *Doesn't this thing go any faster?*

"We're lucky it goes at all."

On the other side of the spaceport sign, he jerked the stick right, and the wheels expanded to counter the skid. He charged up the hill at full speed, the motor whining in protest, as the first fat raindrop went *splat* on the windshield. Then another, and another.

The wall of acid rain slammed into the ambulance like a crashing wave. Almost immediately, lung-searing fog began rising off the road. Geddy urged the vehicle on, its wipers quickly reduced to raw metal scratching against the windshield.

It was so hard to see, he almost plowed straight through the employee entrance, skidding to a stop just a couple meters short.

— *We're fine here. Wait it out.*

No. While it rained, they could run through the preflight checks. The second it let up, he'd raise the elevator to the flight deck and burn ass out of there before the destructors came this way. If the ship couldn't handle a little sulfuric acid, it sure as hell wouldn't protect him from the barrier around Eli's world.

He found a medic's jacket behind the seat, held it up over his head, and pushed through the door. The moment he got under the overhang he threw the jacket off to the side. Tendrils of smoke rose from it.

"Hey, it's a smoking jacket." He laughed at his own joke.

— *And you're an infant. Just get inside.*

A burning sensation pulsed angrily on the back of his hand. At the sudden appearance of blisters, he frantically wiped it on his pants, which also began to burn.

"Goddamnit!" He ripped them off, then opened the door and slipped inside, shaking his hand to distract from the intense pain.

Over the years, the rain had eaten away at the supposedly acid-proof roofs. Even the penthouse had a couple leaks in one bedroom. But with several floors still above him, there was no safer place.

He hurried down the hallway and into the atrium, turning left at the Goddard exhibit and angling toward the back where the *Penetrator* awaited. After his early morning ordeal, he slowed at the Space Bar.

— *Don't you dare.*

Smiling, Geddy curled around the display of *Voyager I*, then stopped in his tracks, his heart dropping clean through his stomach. A wave of panic walloped him so hard he had to catch himself against the wall.

The *Penetrator* was gone, and so was the elevator.

— *Um …*

"Don't panic. The rain probably caused a short or something. I'll bring it back down, no big deal."

He activated the display beside the elevator and saw it was on the flight deck, so he called it back. It chunkily hummed to life and he looked anxiously to the ceiling.

As he waited for the elevator to return, nervously shifting his weight back and forth, his still-addled brain was trying to work out why in hell the destructors suddenly decided to tag-team Semenov Tower in the wee hours of the morning. Turning the question over again and again, a narrative began to form. It should not, could not be possible, yet it stared him in the face, daring him to dismiss it.

A minute later, the elevator descended from the rectangular void in the ceiling. Geddy stood on his toes as a cruel hand curled its icy fingers around his pounding heart. Even then, he knew. To the depths of his rotten little soul, he knew. The motor wasn't straining at all. When it finally dropped to eye level, and then flush with the floor, the wave of panic crashed.

His only shot at leaving Earth 2 and helping Eli get home was gone.

CHAPTER 6

Q-36 SPACE ELEVATE, OR ...

Grief quickly gave way to rage. Geddy filled the cavernous atrium with every obscenity he'd ever learned, and a few he made up, until he went hoarse.

— *Are you done?*

"I think I know a few more in Spanish."

— *This is problematic.*

He stretched out fully on his back, wishing he was as dead as he felt. Meanwhile, the swirling wind drove angry sheets of acid rain into the glass. The barren swath of land between the mountain and Laguna was largely obscured by the toxic fog raised by fizzing sedimentary rocks. A few million years ago, while Eli was still drifting through space, the whole plain had been a shallow sea. At some point, cracks opened in the porous crust and drank it dry, leaving behind rocky soil that only became arable through extensive processing.

Apparently, the best planets were already taken.

— *Now what are we gonna do?*

"I dunno, but there's only one explanation."

— *You don't mean … ?*

"It couldn't fly without the key, right?"

— *Right.*

"So it could only have been hauled off. I never heard a ship, though."

— *You couldn't have heard the moon crashing into the lagoon this morning.*

He shook his head, biting hard on his lower lip. "This has Tati's perfectly manicured fingers all over it. I feel it in my bones."

— *But how could she possibly–*

"I don't know and I don't care. I just know we're getting it back."

— *But how? This is bad, Ged. Like, really bad.*

For all he knew, she'd tapped into the museum's camera feeds and was watching him right now.

It seldom rained, thank goodness, but when it did, it sometimes went on for days. If the machines came for the spaceport, the only protection was deep underground, likely in one of the very lava tubes where the ass gas liked to collect. He'd have to scavenge through the rubble for food and water. How long could he live like that? A few days? A week, maybe?

The *Penetrator* was his ticket off the planet. That only left one very unsavory option. He got up and marched back toward the empty elevator.

— *What're you doing?*

He tapped the display for the hangar. The lift engaged and began to rise.

"There's an old spacesuit up here. A real one. I used to play with it when I was a kid."

— *So?*

"So, there's only one way off this rock now."

Before the elevator even came to a stop, Geddy hopped up onto the floor of the cavernous hangar and made a beeline to the corner by the lockers, where an old black EVA suit and helmet hung from a peg on the wall.

— I know you don't mean the space elevator.

"You got a better idea?"

He lifted the old suit off the peg, leaving an indentation in the thick material, and inspected the fabric. Unlike the Neil Armstrong replica, it was heavy as hell.

— Forget the vacuum of space. That thing couldn't survive a vacuum cleaner. *It's an antique!*

"So are you."

— Touché.

But Geddy had faith in old things. The heavy, multilayer fabric was built like a tank. He didn't have time to inspect every square centimeter, but it seemed intact, as did the aluminum fittings at the articulation points. Stacked in the same corner on the floor was the backpack that provided air, pressure, and heat. He brushed dust off the ancient oxygen gauge. Half full, but he should be able to recharge it. Ditto for the battery. It only needed to work for fifteen, maybe twenty minutes, right?

The acid rain continued for much of the morning, during which he refilled the backpack's oxygen using the bottles from the old Kemik's life support system. The battery was kaput, but he found one with the same output and managed to solder it to the existing wiring.

It felt nostalgic to tinker around again. He's spent many afternoons up here watching the mechanics and engineers work their magic on ships of all kinds, some of which bore the scars of battle. Once in a while, they'd let him turn a bolt or plug things into sockets. That meant the world to him.

But Geddy wasn't so interested in working on ships as flying them. He knew how to patch a blaster hole or reroute a power coupling if he had to, but at the core, he wanted to be a pilot like his old man. Yes, he technically built an entire ship out of a virtually unworkable metal, but that was all Eli. As excited as he was to return him home, he'd been just as excited to rocket through the galaxy once again. It felt like a second chance.

By the time he carefully inspected the dusty old suit and tested the life-support systems, hours had passed, and the sound of the rain dissipated. A peek through the atrium windows revealed that most of the fog had cleared out, the suns cutting twin haloes out of the haze. In this dump, that counted for a sunny day.

As it tended to do, the rain had eaten the paint clean off the ambulance, turning it the color of burnished aluminum. Say what you wanted about sulfuric acid, but it sure spiffed up metal things.

He loaded in the suit, helmet, and the life-support backpack and turned the craft around.

— *We're really doing this?*

"Still waiting on a better idea."

As had been the case all morning, Eli didn't have much to say. He'd never admit it, but Geddy could tell he was sad, too.

He'd driven up to the rim of Herschel Crater now and then to watch the giant salvage elevator come and go, but never with the intention of riding the damn thing into space.

The work of cleaning up after failed civilizations or downed cruisers — sometimes entire fleets, depending on how things went — was big business, but also spectacularly expensive. The math rarely worked out in the salvage company's favor, which suggested the raw-material situation on Earth 3 was dicey. Probably one of the reasons it was their distant second choice.

He'd never been, but he'd heard stories. Eighty-seven percent water, crawling with apex predators the size of freighters. Winds that could pull hair out by the roots. No wonder it never caught on as a vacation spot.

The crater had been transformed into a vast scrapyard where the same bots he occasionally stole and converted for mining cut up and sorted through the debris brought in by the trucks. Every kilogram that went up into space cost big bucks, so stuck-on concrete and organic material had to be removed. A long conveyor carried clean scrap over the lip of the massive cylindrical cage, which slowly rotated to fill evenly.

The good news was, security wasn't a problem. As far as the bots were concerned, he was just some harmless local fauna. Of course, he'd never gotten very close.

— *How are we getting in there?*

Scaling the side of the cage wasn't an option. Not with all the gear and definitely not in a spacesuit. That left the conveyor, but the timing had to be perfect. Too soon and the system might detect him and stop. Alas, there was no way to know when the elevator had reached capacity, since it went by weight.

"You're the ancient, all-knowing being. You tell me."

— *We drive the truck in, run up the conveyor, and jump inside.*

"Very funny."

— *What do you mean?*

"That's not a plan. That's not even a first draft of a plan."

— *The simplest solution is usually the best, right?*

"It's not that simple."

— *Of course, you'll need to wait until it's almost full.*

"But I can't run with the suit, which means I can't even put it on until I'm inside. Will I even have time before it reaches the upper atmosphere?"

— *Hard to say.*

"As always, your counsel is invaluable."

Geddy ran through a couple other scenarios in his head, including somehow jumping the ambulance into the elevator as it lifted off, but dismissed them as even more ridiculous than Eli's solution.

"Just tell me what to do."

— *We watch this one carefully, note the timing, and work backwards.*

When it came to math and logic, Eli had him beat. Geddy ran mostly on gut instinct and bravado. In that sense, they made a good team.

He waited on the crater rim, making note of the timing. The container took about thirty-five minutes to fill. Once it reached the weight limit and stopped rotating, it only took eleven seconds to begin its skyward climb to the processing ship. About fifty minutes later, it returned empty and the process started over.

While it did, Geddy shoved all the gear into a corpse-sized duffle stuffed with medical supplies. It was heavy as hell, especially with the life support pack, but he could use the handles to wear it like a backpack.

He took a short run up and down the rocky black slope to test his agility. Not great. But, in theory, the conveyor should be much easier. With any luck, he could just ride it up like an escalator.

As the level of scrap in the elevator neared the top, Geddy climbed in the truck and powered it on, noticing the battery was down to just three percent. He should leave now in case it conked out.

"Ready?" Adrenaline surged into his veins, sending his heart on a fast ride of its own.

— *Ready or not, here we go.*

He shoved the stick forward, kicking up a cloud of gray volcanic dust as he sped down the slope toward the scrapyard. At first, he rolled past little work crews of bots sifting through the piles of metal without any of them seeming to notice. But the moment he came within about ten meters of the sorting bots, they pivoted toward him, red lights flashing, and closed ranks around him as he stumbled free of the truck.

— *So much for stealth.*

"Time to boogie."

Geddy threw the duffle straps over his shoulders and hauled himself onto the waist-high conveyor while it was running, the extra boost of speed helping him dodge one of the four-armed bots as it grabbed for his ankle.

So much for the escalator theory. His legs burned with effort as he jumped over hunks of girding. Window frames. A piece of handrail. About halfway up, the platform stopped rotating and the conveyor ground to a stop, but he still had thirty meters to cover. He kept motoring.

Suddenly, his feet were yanked from under him and he face-planted on the conveyor. The damn thing was going in reverse! He popped back up and gave a war cry as his legs kicked even harder, the top just a body length away, but the conveyor seemed to match his speed. A chunky sound came from under the platform like a clamp engaging. It was leaving.

— *Go! Like it contained the last porn in the universe!!*

A thin sliver of the conveyor's frame sat to the side of the belt itself. Geddy sidestepped onto it, the tread of his shoe slipping off the very edge as he closed the distance with two lunging steps. With a final, mighty leap, he pushed off and jumped.

With the extra weight, though, he just barely caught the top edge of the cage with his arm as it lifted off the ground and accelerated toward the clouds. The duffle was so damn heavy!

— *Gotta hurry, gotta get the suit on …*

"Aarrrrhh!" Geddy grunted and swung his right leg over the edge, pulled himself up to the top, and tumbled over onto the pile of jagged metal, ripping open a gash in his leg. "Shit! Aw, man, that hurts!"

— *It's nothing. Hurry!*

It was astonishing how quickly the air freshened as the platform climbed. Up here it was a lovely spring day. But as it accelerated up the cable with a metallic whine, the temperature plummeted. By the time he got the suit out, it had pushed through the cloud layer into the upper atmosphere. Ice coated his nose hairs.

The scrap continually shifted and settled under him, making it extraordinarily difficult to pull the legs and boots on. Glancing upward, he noticed the first pinpoints of stars in the rapidly darkening sky, partly obscured by a gargantuan, ship-shaped void directly overhead.

Frantic, he threw the upper part of the suit on, cinched the waist in place, and pulled on the helmet. His breath froze instantly to the inside of the face shield, making it impossible to see the life-support pack.

Sometimes, he could feel what Eli was feeling. This was one of those times. He was terrified.

No time to get the pack on. His shaking hands found the coupling near his right hip as he gasped for air. It clicked into place just as the last layer of atmosphere dissipated, and he switched the unit on. A rush of warm O2 washed over him like a shower on a cold night, and stars filled his vision.

Geddy flopped onto his back, panting from the effort as his lungs filled with delicious pure oxygen. Lights beneath the processing ship illuminated as the circular door of a cargo bay opened on the underside like an aperture. As the platform slowed, he felt himself rising inside the cage, his earlier momentum carrying him up with the other junk, but a force field across the top kept the scrap from flying away.

Just before the elevator entered the ship's cavernous hold, he saw the words stenciled on the side.

SEMENOV PLANETARY SYSTEMS
Your ruined civilization is our bread and butter.

CHAPTER 7
SPACE JUNK

The moment the platform rose through the cargo door, it reversed direction and the force field over the top disappeared. Geddy and many metric tons of jagged scrap floated to the ceiling. The platform then retracted back through and the aperture closed tightly around the fixed cable. A moment later, artificial gravity engaged, and everything dropped like a stone. Geddy narrowly missed being impaled by a metal sculpture of a spear-wielding tribesman.

The impact jarred his bleeding leg, delivering a jolt of pain. Even from inside the suit, he could feel the hot blood soaking his pants. For sure it was infected. Earth 2 had more than its share of nasty bugs. But he had bigger problems now.

Leave it to a Semenov to profit from both Earth 2's rise and its unceremonious fall. Getting to the bottom of this necessarily meant tracking down Tatiana, but for now, he was happy to put that off and deal with this novel situation.

— *We're not out of the woods yet.*

— No shit.

The scrap-processing facility was long and wide, the ceiling crisscrossed by machinery suspended from the ceiling. Automated saws cast fountains of sparks as they cut Earth 2's bones into even smaller pieces. Mountainous piles of metal dotted the perimeter separated by stubby walls.

The whine of a powerful motor came from the longer end of the receiving area. Geddy spun around in time to see an unmanned plow rumbling toward the pile he was laying in. Before he knew what was happening, he was swept up in a wave of sharp metal pieces tumbling over each other toward an empty spot along the wall.

It was basically a meat grinder.

He grabbed the backpack and rolled free of the pile just as the plow gathered and pushed it the rest of the way, the earsplitting scrape of metal-on-metal echoing through the chamber as it slowly filled with air. With his helmet on and the backpack's coupling safely attached, he got to his feet and put his arms through the straps.

The facility was aft, meaning any escape pods or shuttles would be toward the crew area. He headed that way as fast as he could, though his range of motion in the suit was as comically limited as a cartoon mummy.

Halfway to the big, sliding doors, they opened, and a pair of hulking, toothsome Gethenian workers strode through, animatedly engaged in conversation. Geddy ran-limped awkwardly into one of the scrap bays, pressed himself tightly to the stub wall, and hoped like hell they hadn't seen him.

"… so I say to this dude, 'show me what you got, tough guy.' He hauls back and throws this punch so weak, it damn near moved backwards. I felt kinda sorry for him. I mean, in front of his girl and all."

"What'd you do?"

"What *could* I do? I cracked his skull open against the bar and ritualistically consumed his brain while she watched."

"Ha! Classic Jimbo."

He held his breath as they passed. The crewmen continued

together to the rear of the facility and through the other set of doors.

As soon as they closed, Geddy stole the rest of the way as fast as his injured leg would allow. Sweat immediately soaked his clothes, and the ancient life-support system still hadn't melted all the ice from inside his face shield. His O2 gauge was already down to fifty percent, so he closed it off and removed his helmet.

A long hallway opened before him with recessed doorways the whole way down. Probably berths for the rank-and-file. Hopefully they were all on shift or asleep. He'd hardly ever been around enough legit business operations to know what they'd do if they found him. Pirates, smugglers, and mercs were more his crowd, and there wasn't much question what they would do.

Halfway down the hall, a dark-skinned Doxx-Morran man exited his room with a towel slung over his shoulder and headed their way. Geddy ducked into a doorway, thinking about what the hell he'd say if discovered. He peered around the corner just in time to see him disappear down the hallway, presumably toward the showers.

Geddy kept moving through the next set of doors. If his hunch was right, pods and shuttles would be in between the crew and officer quarters.

The moment he approached the door, it slid open, and he was face-to-face with the skull-bashing Gethenian crewman.

"What the–"

Geddy swung the helmet in a lightning-fast arc, catching him hard across the chin and knocking him to the floor. His eyes darted about, searching frantically for signs pointing to the pods. Didn't these commercial ships have signs?

Another hallway broke to the right. Geddy hustled through an open door at the end, then whirled and used the panel to seal it from the inside. It closed just before the crewman reached it, blood trickling from a small cut on his cheekbone.

Geddy popped it hard with his elbow, frying the circuits. It sparked and buzzed, sending up tendrils of smoke, and Geddy gave his adversary the finger he never got to give The Deuce.

"Well, now you hurt my feelings." Came a gruff voice through the door.

He backed away to assess his situation and immediately realized his error. It smelled worse than Earth 2 on a bad day. This wasn't a room — it was a trash bay. And he was the trash.

Geddy reflexively lurched for the door but pulled back. Flashing orange lights blazed overhead as the short airlock sealed before his eyes. He had seconds, if that.

He threw his helmet on, struggling to get it to seat properly. The door continued down.

— *Geddy …*

— Dude, I know!

It clicked into place at the last moment. As he fumbled for the switch to his life-support system, the outer door opened and compressed air launched him, ass over tea kettle, into space.

Geddy closed his eyes against the interminable spinning. Barfing inside a spacesuit wasn't his idea of a good time. Mercifully, his gloved digits managed to find the backpack's on switch. A brief hiss and the flow of air and heat returned, dispelling the fog from his helmet.

The gauge suggested he had twenty minutes of air, give or take a couple. As he rocketed away from the ship, however, he became aware of a cooling sensation on the elbow he'd used to smash the controls. He cracked open one eye long enough to see a finger-length geyser of moist, life-giving air seeping out through a pinhole in the ancient suit. Not a bad leak, but more than you wanted to see drifting alone through space.

— *Well, this isn't ideal.*

— About time you chimed in. What should I do here?

— *I'm not sure.*

Geddy had long ago made peace with death. You couldn't do all he'd done without accepting it. But now that it had come for him, he found himself overwhelmed with regret. He would die, and Eli would be trapped inside his frozen corpse until the end of time. All the work they'd done had been for nothing.

Despair briefly gave way to a fantasy about using the pinhole as a tiny thruster or throwing the backpack to send him moving in a more useful direction, like toward one of Earth 2's six moons, but that was ludicrous. Even if such a move sent him on the proper trajectory, it would take weeks or months to get anywhere. Stupid space. Why'd everything have to be so damn far apart?

— This isn't how I saw things going.

— *Me, neither.*

— I really wanted to get you back to your home world.

— *I know.*

— You want to know something funny?

— *Sure.*

— This is my worst fear.

— *Hurtling helplessly through space?*

— Yep. Number one.

— *What if the suit suddenly filled with spiders?*

— Yeah, I guess that would be worse.

— *See?*

Ten minutes passed. He didn't need the blinking red light on his O2 gauge to know it was getting low. Drowsiness was already creeping in. Soon, he'd just sort of pass out and never wake up. Not bad for a guy who expected to go out in a violent explosion or a hail of blaster fire.

— Hey Eli?

— *I'm here.*

— Are there more of your kind?

— *Oh, yes. Throughout the universe. Even now, I can feel them.*

— I wish I had that.

— *Had what?*

— A connection to something. Anything.

— *Silly boy. We are all connected.*

Geddy allowed that beautiful thought to wash over him, turning it over and over in his mind. But even now, at the end, he couldn't quite let himself believe it. How pathetic was that?

— How long do you figure we have?

— *Five minutes, give or take. Your brain is starving.*

— It always kinda was. You know, I never asked you what you thought about out here. Seventeen million years is a long time to ruminate.

— *I mostly thought about the other Sagaceans who were drifting like me.*

— Yeah, but what about you?

— *What do you mean?*

— Didn't you think about your situation?

— *My situation was not worthy of thought.*

— You didn't worry about where you'd land, or if you'd land?

— *Why would I do that? Worrying about an outcome you can't control is pointless.*

As he'd done a million times before, Geddy was projecting his well-worn human insecurities and fears onto a being that transcended such things. Eli didn't perceive time, or death, or anything else in quite the same way as he.

The next few minutes passed slowly. He wished he could arrest his off-axis spin so he could at least focus on something as he slipped away. The Deuce or the enormous salvage vessel would do. Anything solid to hold on to. But opening his eyes, even for a moment, made him instantly dizzy. Would he someday be a totem? The legendary Spinning Man? Would nerds track his progress through the cosmos?

Stars. The Deuce. Stars. Processing ship. Stars. Trebek, the nearest moon. More stars. A trawler.

A trawler?

Trapped in his dizzying rotation, Geddy only caught a glimpse of it at first, immediately dismissing it as a hallucination. But he kept his eyes open long enough to see it again. His head swam, his stomach turned. Perhaps his final act would be to fill his suit with vomit after all.

But a couple of mad rotations later, he spotted a little group of drones moving toward him, spreading out a square of metal mesh between them. The kind trawlers used to haul in junk a hundred years ago.

— *What's happening? Geddy?*

By then, his vision had narrowed to a tiny circle. The last thing he saw before consciousness slipped away was the ship's name, inexpertly stenciled on the side. Whoever put it there hadn't given themselves enough space, the letters bending down toward the front right corner.

For Sale Make Offer.

CHAPTER 8

FOR SALE MAKE OFFER

Voices stretched out from the dark, one male, one female. Fingers fumbled with his helmet, his head lolling back and forth as his lungs screamed. No way to know if any of it was real.

"How the hell do you get this thing off?" asked a young man.

"Ugh. Move." A woman. A hot one, if his instincts served.

"Let's just smash it with a hammer."

"His head's inside!"

"Well, I'm all out of ideas."

Hands clamped around his helmet and turned it, and cool air rushed in to dance on his grateful, sweaty face. His lungs drank it in hungry gulps, his vision still badly blurred.

"He's human," noted the kid.

"The Deuce is right there. What'd you expect?"

"Then why'd they eject him into space?"

"My guess is, they ejected that old-ass suit and he just happened to be in it."

Blinding lights flooded his eyes, his focus returning slowly. He brought his hand to his face, making them jump back.

Industrial sounds filled his ears, of humming ion drives and machinery large and small. An unsettling vibration traveled up through the floor.

As his vision resolved, he saw two beings leaning over him. The woman knelt at his side, her elegant white neck decorated with raised, parallel marks like scars that ended at her jawline. Her large, almost cartoonish yellow eyes crinkled kindly as she smiled down at him, tapered ropes of thick-stranded, blood-red hair like dreadlocks framing her delicate features. Temerurian. And she was indeed hot.

"Hey stranger," she said melodically.

"What kind of vibe are you getting from him?" asked the young male. Durandian, with puffy cheeks and a pursed mouth. If he was like others of his kind, he was cursed with a set of large, flat teeth that didn't quite fit, like a mouse with an overbite. Big, hopeful eyes reflected a life lived underground.

The woman closed her eyes and brushed his face with her fingertips, taking a deep breath. "He's not violent." She frowned and cocked her head. "He's been alone a long time, too, but also ... not alone."

"What's that mean?"

Her eyes gently reopened. "I don't know, but he means us no harm. Of that, I'm certain."

— She seems nice.

"Can you speak?" asked the male.

"Yeah," Geddy muttered dryly.

"Get him some water," she said. While the young man darted off, she smoothed Geddy's hair and dabbed at his face with a damp towel. "Space makes a guy thirsty." The kid returned with a bottle of water. "Here, can you sit up? Denk, gimme a hand."

She took Geddy's gloved hand and pulled him up into a sitting position while the kid supported him from the back. Once he was upright, she raised the bottle to his lips and he slaked his thirst, some of it dribbling down his chin. Typical recycled ship water, but at least it didn't smell like his taint after a day in the lava tubes.

She dabbed it away with the cuff of her shirt, a dark, leathery material edged with fat piping. "Better?"

Geddy nodded. "Thanks."

"You got a name?"

"Geddy."

"I'm Osmiya. Everyone calls me Oz. This is Denk. You're aboard the junk trawler *For Sale Make Offer.* We call her *Fizmo.*"

Now that he was upright, Geddy had a better view of his surroundings. Junk trawlers were bottom feeders in the starship food chain — scavengers who roamed the galaxy in search of salvage. Their cargo hold was a cross between a warehouse and a machine shop. It was also mostly empty.

Some of the crap on high shelves, halfheartedly covered in netting, had obviously been there for years. Tucked among the dusty chunks of fuselage and discarded appliances were a handful of cavelike berths where transient workers presumably slept. Trawlers sometimes employed broke travelers, vagabonds, and criminals in exchange for passage. People who didn't care where they went or didn't want to be found.

People like him, come to think of it.

He spied three rough-looking characters among the junk, all of whom were watching this little scene with great interest. Judging from the largely empty hold, there wasn't a whole lot for them to do.

"How'd you find me?"

"That Semenov ship throws away a lot of good shit," Oz said. "We jumped in three days ago."

"What's wrong with your tractor beam?" Geddy asked.

"We hawked it a few years back for novaspheres," Oz explained. "It's been a lean stretch."

"To tell the truth, we figured the suit was empty," Denk

said, his eyes bright. "Which you *have* to let us keep by the way. I know of a guy on Kigantu who'd give his middle nut for a vintage model like that."

— *Kigantu? Isn't that–*

Geddy knew exactly which guy that was, and he wanted nothing to do with him.

"It's yours, kid. Just keep me the hell away from Kigantu."

Denk's face lit up as he smiled, baring his giant front teeth. "Wow, thanks!"

"We'd sure love to know how you wound up drifting alone through space in an antique suit," Oz said.

"That's a very long story."

"Caloth's a long way. Come on, let's get you out of that suit."

So that's where they were headed. Caloth was hell and gone from Earth 3, but it was a transportation hub, and he knew someone there who might be able to help find him a ride.

Under Geddy's direction, Denk and Oz freed him from the suit, which had gotten rather gamey. Not as bad as the thermal suit, maybe, but still bad. Like everything else on Earth 2, it was saturated by the sewer-like air. So were his clothes. So was he.

"Dude …" Denk said, turning away as his eyes watered. "Ever hear of soap?"

"It's been a rough few days."

Denk dragged the suit and helmet to a chest-high shelf along the wall, tucking it behind a sheet-metal panel with DENK stenciled across. Once it was squared away, he pointed a warning finger at the lurkers among the junk piles.

"Anyone who touches my stuff gets floated. I mean it."

Denk was small and squat, with nary a muscle visible beneath his doughy body. Anyone rough enough to work a deep-space trawler in exchange for passage wouldn't take a threat seriously from this kid. Chuckles emanated from the half-darkness.

"Shut up!" hissed Oz, and they obeyed.

"I take it you two are regular crew?" Geddy asked.

"Pilot here," Denk boasted, pointing his thumb at his chest. "I know every wormhole and temporal anomaly in the sector."

"First officer," said Oz. "Security, weapons, and … guest relations. And I'm the closest thing we've got to a medic. Speaking of which …" She jutted her chin toward the blood seeping through his pant leg. "What happened there?"

"It's nothing."

"I'll throw a few stitches in once we get you cleaned up."

Geddy's eyes roamed around the hold, noting how dirty and worn everything was. "How old is this piece of shit?"

Denk gasped like a little kid hearing his first swear word.

"Old." Oz flared her eyebrows. "But call her a piece of shit again, and we're gonna have a problem."

Geddy chuckled it away as though she was kidding, but her face was a stone. He held up his hands in contrition. "Got it. Sorry."

Her eyes softened and drifted to the floor. "We've been through a lot, this ship and us. It's kind of cobbled together, but it's ours, y'know? She's tougher than she looks, and her sensors are tip-top. That's good enough for us."

"What about the rest of the crew?"

"Morpho's our mechanic." Her eyes searched the shelves and, for some reason, the ceiling. He's around here somewhere. And of course, Captain Bykite." Her jaw tightened as she said the name.

"It's his ship, I take it?"

"Until it sells."

"… which will be never," Denk finished.

"What about you, Mr. …?" said Oz.

"Starheart. I'm just looking for my ship."

"You lost a *ship*?" Denk asked, incredulous.

"It was ..." He trailed off, searching for the exact right word. Stolen wasn't quite right. All signs pointed to Tatiana, but she didn't exactly steal it, did she? She took it away like a parent takes away a toy. And likely for the same reason. "I suspect it's being held hostage."

"You know where?" asked Oz.

"I know where to start. But it's not your problem. If you can get me to Caloth, I'll be on my merry way."

Oz glanced sideways at Denk, who shrugged approvingly. "All right. But you jump when I say jump. In the meantime, let's take care of that BO. Come on, up you go."

He grabbed her hand, and she easily hoisted him to his feet. The ship's artificial gravity was weaker than Earth 2's gravity, so he felt pretty good. Once he steadied himself, she released his hand.

Geddy fell in behind Oz as she strode toward the bulkhead door separating the cargo area from the crew section. The moment he stepped through the threshold, he realized what she'd meant by "cobbled together." The front half of the ship and the cargo area were from different eras and origins and had essentially been bolted together. Their junk trawler was, itself, made of junk.

"Hold up." He stopped just inside the door, taking in the barrel-shaped crew quarters. "Is this an old Ghruk freighter?"

Her eyes flashed and she smirked at Denk, clearly impressed. "You know your ships."

"What the hell's a Ring War-era bird doing attached to a warehouse?"

"That, too, is a long story." She winked.

CHAPTER 9

XENOMORPH ZOO

The forward area was designed for Ghruk, not humans, so Geddy had to crouch awkwardly to fit inside the shower. A wrench clamped to a metal bar poking out of the wall served as the faucet. The yellow water suggested the recycler either wasn't working properly or never worked well to begin with, giving the impression his shower was of the golden variety.

The sooner he got to Caloth, the better.

— What do you think?

— That this water is mostly urine.

— I mean about our saviors.

— They seem harmless.

— Everyone seems harmless until they've got a knee in your back and a gun pressed to your skull.

— That's an oddly specific reference.

— I'm just saying.

He got out and pulled the curtain back as Oz entered with a fresh set of coveralls. Her eyes lingered momentarily on his naked body before she turned away, her smooth white cheeks flushing red.

"I brought you some clothes. We floated yours."

He took the pale green coveralls and kept toweling off. "Thanks on both counts."

"Okay. I'm going to go now." She awkwardly about-faced, bumping into the doorway as she left. The door hissed shut behind her.

— *She's adorable.*

— Yeah, well, Temerurians mate for life, so I'll be keeping my distance.

Geddy tugged on the coveralls, which were slightly too small and tight in the crotch. He arranged his testicles to either side of the seam and stepped out into the hallway, where he found Oz leaning against the wall.

"Feel better?" she asked.

"I think your recycler's on the fritz."

She gave a knowing smile. "Oh, I'm sorry," she said sarcastically. "You're welcome to use whatever water *you* brought."

He held up his hands in mock surrender. "Take it easy, it's not a complaint. Believe me, I've drunk enough piss water to give me mouth gout. Heh — that's fun to say."

"Mouth gout," she said, allowing a giggle.

"So, where's your captain? I'd like to thank him for scooping me up."

She nodded down the short hall. "On the bridge. Come on, I'll introduce you."

He followed her back through the crew quarters and a second bulkhead door to the bridge. Denk, seated at a greasy control bank, whirled toward them.

"Hey, you clean up pretty good." He took a long sniff and smiled. "I can hardly smell you from here."

A gigantic aftermarket chair at the center of the room turned dramatically around to reveal the captain. He was Kailorian, blue as the Old Earth sky, with four skinny, multi-jointed arms bearing three fingers each. His conical head was ringed with neatly trimmed white fur, with vertical slits in his orangey eyes.

Kailorians were all but wiped out by the Ghruk during the Ring War. Surprise must have registered on his face, because the captain smirked.

"Captain, this is Geddy Starheart. Geddy, meet Captain Bykite."

Bykite rose from the captain's chair, immediately bumping his tall head on the short ceiling. He rubbed it and fell into a deeply awkward crouch as he stepped down from his throne-like seat.

"How do you do?" He extended one hand, which Geddy hesitantly shook.

"Listen, thanks for picking me up. Not many people would've."

He shrugged. "The best way to know if something has value is to bring it in. Where you headed?"

"Oz said you're bound for Caloth. That works for me. I'm happy to earn my way."

His eyes darkened. "Unfortunately, we've had a stretch of bad luck. But I've got a feeling that's about to change. If so, we'll appreciate the extra help."

"Works for me."

The captain cocked his head. "I can tell you want to ask, Mr. Starheart, so just ask."

Geddy could imagine what his host meant. He glanced sideways at Oz, who gave a nod to indicate he could speak freely.

"Okay, I'll bite. How does a Kailorian wind up with a Ghruk freighter?"

He gestured grandly around him as he replied, clearly reveling in the tale. "When I was a child, a Ghruk destroyer leveled my village and everyone in it. Everyone but me. I vowed to hunt it down. Well, I never found it, but I found this.

Living well truly is the best revenge."

He gave the crouching captain a pained smile. If this was living well, it raised serious concerns about his standards.

"As it happens, I'm looking for a ship myself."

"What kind of ship?"

"Homemade."

Bykite arched his formidable eyebrows. "Impressive."

"Don't get your hopes up. I'm no mechanic."

He gave an amused chuckle. "You needn't worry about that, Mr. Starheart. We have the best mechanic in the galaxy. Morpho, don't be rude."

A shadow, just a flash of movement, flicked by overhead. It dripped from the ceiling as though melted, pooling on the floor beside Bykite before gathering itself into a black, gummy wad that looked like something you'd try to scrape off your shoe with a stick. It was roughly the size of a human brain, but clearly sentient. He'd been to every corner of the galaxy and never saw anything like it.

"Morpho, this is Mr. Starheart. He'll be traveling with us to Caloth."

The blob stretched itself out into the shape of a small hand. Geddy hesitated.

— *You heard the man. Don't be rude.*

He tentatively reached out. "How's it hanging?" Morpho gave it a light, sticky squeeze, lingering for a long moment before he returned to blob form.

"Morpho is a synthetic organism originally developed as a weapon. Sort of a … parasite that could pass through tight spaces and wreak untold havoc on unsuspecting ships. At least, that's our theory."

"You mean like breaking shit?"

"It could short circuits, remove bolts and cut wires, and if it cared to, take over a human host."

— *That's horrible! Though I am seeing the irony …*

— Stop it. You know I can't listen to you and him at the same time.

— *Sorry.*

"Sounds like something the Nads would come up with," Geddy said.

Bykite chuckled at the slur. Zelnads weren't a species, but a mysterious, cult-like group whose origins and purpose were unknown. Their technology was leaps ahead, leading some to believe they possessed divine knowledge.

"They're still around?"

Bykite narrowed his eyes. "Still? Have you been living under a rock?"

"Almost literally."

"Zelnads control most of the novasphere supply in the sector now. Their price is steep, too."

"That sucks. Hard to get around without them."

"Some time ago, we stumbled across a Zelnad destroyer, and it fired on us. Only it wasn't a torpedo but some kind of canister. We assumed a malfunction, but when it opened, Morpho here came out. For reasons we still don't understand, he fixed the hole it made. He's been with us ever since."

"How do you know it's a he?"

"He has a distinctly male energy," said Oz.

— *I picked up on that, too.*

— Sure, you did.

— *I do not understand the obsession with gender. I have no gender.*

— People get worked up about it for some reason.

An insistent beep sounded from the console in front of Denk. He spun around and killed the alarm as Bykite returned to his overstuffed chair. Geddy and Oz looked on worriedly.

"Report!" barked Bykite.

"One of the deep-space sensors picked up an explosion," he said excitedly. "Big by the looks of it."

"Distance?" Bykite asked.

"One point one parsecs. Just outside the Elenian Belt. It ain't exactly on the way to Caloth, but it only adds a day. It *just* happened, too."

"Your sensors reach that far?" Geddy asked, genuinely impressed. The average ship didn't have anywhere near that kind of range.

"Told you they were tip-top," replied Oz with a wink.

Oz stepped forward and put her hand on Bykite's shoulder. "Captain, new product would improve our prospects in Caloth. You know how much they like novelty at the bazaar."

"Very well. Denk, take us there."

Oz turned to tell Geddy to strap into one of the jump seats, but he'd already folded it down and was cinching the straps about his chest. She took her seat across from him, behind and to the right of the captain, and gave an appreciative nod.

"Someone knows the drill."

He returned her sweet smile. "Not my first rodeo."

"I look forward to knowing you better, Geddy Starheart."

This was the feeling he'd missed most. Rocketing away from one place and toward another. Tatiana robbed him of that by taking his damned ship.

"I love this part," he muttered. A heartbeat later, the *Fizmo*'s thrusters pinned him to the seat and his lips curled into a delicious grin.

"Approaching the belt, Captain," said Denk, dropping the *Fizmo* out of its burn.

The Elenian Belt was a dense ring of asteroids surrounding Elenia, an ancient planet that exploded eons ago, breaking it into chunks that now orbited its largest remaining piece.

Before then, the story went, Elenia sat at the end of a busy trade route. The entrance to a very useful natural wormhole lay just outside its atmosphere, so legions of sub-light ships coming or going from the outer sectors would stop there to relax and refuel. While the planet's demise didn't affect the wormhole, it was just this side of impossible to reach.

Geddy and Oz unclipped their restraints and stood shoulder to shoulder at the back of the bridge, which offered a better view.

"Holy hell," muttered Geddy.

He'd never been to Elenia himself, but the stories fell woefully short. Most asteroid belts eventually settled into thin disks, but the broken planet's gravity wasn't strong enough to align the pieces along an axis. Thus, they encased the planet like a shell, so dense in spots you couldn't see through.

"Where's our wreckage?" asked Bykite.

Denk tapped a few buttons and zoomed in on a small cargo ship in a lazy spin near the edge of the belt, a gaping hole blown out the side. Not unlike Elenia itself.

"Let's see ..." said Denk. "Transponder says it's the *XCV Sirwin*. Xellaran registry carrying live cargo. The registry doesn't say what."

"Where was it going?" asked Oz.

"Myadan."

She turned to Geddy. "There's a big zoo on Myadan."

Oz was right, of course. Everyone knew about the Myadan zoo, or xoo, as it came to be called on account of the myriad alien species.

"I don't care about the cargo," Bykite declared, scratching his elegant chin as he leaned in toward the screen. Coming off a bad run, it would've seemed like a pot of gold. "But other than that hole, the ship's almost new."

"Netting it would slow us down," Denk warned. "We're encroaching on you-know-who's usual territory."

Bykite grimaced and heaved a sigh, then squared his

pointy jaw. "I'm not leaving a mostly intact cargo vessel just sitting here, especially with you-know-who always hanging around. Let's bring her in."

"Whose territory? You don't mean the Nads," said Geddy.

"No, not them," said Oz. "A rival trawler called the *Red Raven*."

"And who's 'you-know-who'?"

She leaned in close and whispered, "His name's Beebit Tompanov. He and Cap used to be partners." Her breath tickled his ear.

"Business partners?"

"That, too. Bottom line, there's no love lost between us. He's got a knack for claiming the best salvages a few minutes before us."

"He's a mean, evil bastard," added Denk over his shoulder. "We're pretty sure his ship's powered by children's tears."

He deftly maneuvered the *Fizmo* into position in front of the disabled vessel, preparing to deploy the net. Meanwhile, Geddy was fixated on the hole in the side and deeply curious what made it. Clearly, the explosion was what put it into a spin.

— *I don't like this.*

— Tell me about it.

"Hey, it's not my place, but haven't you guys ever seen a space movie?" Geddy asked.

Bykite spun around in his chair, irritated. "As it happens, I'm something of a cinephile."

"Then you know that disabled vessels floating alone in deep space with a gaping hole in the side should be left the fuck alone. If I were you, I'd torpedo the damn thing and burn ass out of here."

The captain bristled. "You're absolutely right, Mr. Starheart. It's not your place."

"At least send in a drone to check it out and see what we're dealing–"

"Either keep quiet or leave the bridge." Bykite spun back around and nodded to Denk. "Mr. Junt, you have your orders. Beebit's not taking this one from us."

"Aye aye." He gave Geddy a sympathetic look and deployed the net.

A chunky metallic sound came from under their feet. Again, the drones floated out with a thin metal net accordioned between them. They spread out as they went, tiny thrusters keeping the net taut as it curled around the slow-spinning ship. As it settled into the net, the rotation stopped and the little drones reformed into pairs, gathering the ends together like a purse.

Denk pivoted the ship to face away, keeping a careful watch on the screens as the drones eased their way back into a tunnel on the underside of the ship. A light on the display switched from red to green once the net was locked in place.

"Retrieval complete, Sir," said Denk, smiling.

"Very good, Mr. Junt. Set our course for Caloth. As fast as you dare. And watch your scopes for the *Raven*."

"I always do."

He rose, wincing, as he bent his bullet-shaped head to keep it from racking the ceiling, and lifted his eyes to Geddy.

"Mr. Starheart, I was collecting valuable material from the deepest reaches of space before you were born. Question me again and you'll be thumbing a ride to Caloth. Am I clear?"

Geddy showed his palms in deference. "Your ship, your rules. I meant no disrespect."

Bykite turned to Oz. "Give him something to do. I'll be in my quarters."

"Yes, Captain."

Geddy and Oz watched him move painfully through the door to the bridge.

"Sorry about him," Oz said. "Just thinking about the *Raven* gets him worked up."

"This is a terrible idea," Geddy said.

"Then let's take your mind off it. Come on. I'll get you patched up and put you to work." She turned on her heels and strode back toward the cargo bay. "Know anything about coffee machines?"

CHAPTER 10

THE UNWANTED PASSENGER

Oz charged Geddy with cataloguing the *Fizmo's* most recent haul, a sad pile of dilapidated kitchen equipment ejected from a transport a few days earlier. Back on Kigantu, he dealt with big-ticket, black-market goods like rare weapons, armor, or artifacts. Now he was trying to figure out what specific model of broken coffee maker they'd snagged out of the trash and whether it could be fixed.

Oh well. At least no one wanted to kill him. Yet.

He ran the serial number through the database and learned it was a Hammond Perk City Deluxe. In good condition, it might fetch sixty credits. The only thing of value was the steel housing.

— *Take it apart. Maybe we can fix it.*

— It's not worth it.

— *You've got something more pressing? Come on, you just built a ship. This should be a snap.*

Geddy sighed and scanned the area around the bench for a screwdriver. There was a metal box overflowing with fasteners, but no tools of any kind. As he searched, he became aware of a presence behind him.

The hum of the ion drive masked the rough-looking man's approach. He was Dudiran and wiry, with short-cropped hair and bulging muscles. His shirt was rolled up and sticking out of his hip pocket, presumably to display his dozens of tattoos.

Great. One of these "my body is a canvas" yo-yos. Judging from his ink, he'd almost certainly been to prison. Maybe even the Stocks on Nirnaya Station.

"Something I can help you find, friend?" he rasped.

"A screwdriver."

He sucked in air through a set of shiny gold teeth. "Sorry. Only Oz and Denk get to use tools. See, in my hands, they're deadly weapons."

— *Why is there artwork on his skin?*

"You could turn a pointed metal implement into a weapon? Impressive."

He lifted his chin. "You like her, don't you?"

"Oz?"

"I wouldn't mind carving me a slice of that Temerurian tail." He smacked his lips.

"I've got a feeling you're not her type."

— *Careful. You don't know who you're dealing with.*

— Unfortunately, I do.

"You don't know me, Homes. See, ladies love Laszlo."

He pointed to an ornate *LLL* in the middle of his chest, tastefully perched atop a literal island of writhing, naked she-demons in a lake of what he could only assume was ejaculate.

"The trail of broken hearts must be long indeed."

He turned back to the coffee maker, wondering if he should try to find Oz or move onto another piece. Laszlo stopped him.

"Hey, look at me when I'm talking to you."

— Aw, hell.

— *What?*

— He's spoiling for a fight.

Geddy heaved a sigh and about-faced to find Laszlo

flanked by the other two hitchers, who were both as heavily tatted as he, but bigger. He was way, way out of practice and had no weapons. Two guys, maybe he could hold his own, but three? Even if they were lousy fighters, he'd get his ass kicked. His hangover hadn't quite subsided and his leg throbbed.

"Listen, pal, I'm just trying to get to Caloth, okay? How about we just stay out of each other's way?"

Laszlo sniffed the air and grimaced. "You know, it already smelled bad in here before you came. Now it smells like shit. What planet did you come from?"

"Earth 2."

He barked a laugh. "You came from the *Deuce*?! No wonder you stink so bad."

"Bullshit," said one of the others, a bigger Rastridean with long hair and arms the size of Geddy's thigh. "Ain't nobody been on The Deuce for years. It's as dead as ... something dead."

"Believe what you want. I'll work on this and you can work on your similes."

Geddy was about to keep trying to talk his way out of this when a sound from the back of the cargo hold stopped him. A skittering noise that disappeared as quickly as it came. If the thugs noticed, they didn't react.

"I'm just tryin' to have a conversation with you, Homes," said Laszlo, scowling. "Why you gotta lie?"

The sound came again, louder.

Geddy's eyes roamed over the back portion of the hold, searching for the source. Could it just be this Morpho thing? "Do you guys hear that?"

"All I hear is you disrespecting me when I'm just trying to knit together the fragile threads of friendship," said Laszlo, huffing.

At that moment, an explosive metallic clang came from the back of the hold. A dent, then a hole the size of a fist opened in the hull, jagged strips of metal jutting inward like flower petals. Instantly, the air was sucked toward it like a wind tunnel. Geddy reflexively grabbed the leg of the workbench, which was bolted to the floor.

Wind swept over him. Another punch, and the hole widened further. A shiny, gray-green set of mandibles poked through, hissing and snapping against the escaping air.

A ranse. One of the meanest, nastiest, hardest to kill creatures in the galaxy. They were native to Kigantu and could supposedly survive in space, though he'd never seen it first-hand until now. Some genius must have thought it was zoo material. It offered one explanation for the gaping hole in the side of the ship.

The three thugs fell over each other trying to grab something solid, but only the two behind Laszlo succeeded. The same fierce wind yanking at Geddy's coveralls pulled Laszlo across the smooth floor, his fingernails scraping on the smooth metal as he flailed for a handhold, eyes peeled in terror and screaming for help.

Oz burst through the forward door with Captain Bykite at his heels.

"What happened?!" she cried, the wind bending her hair around her face as she widened her stance.

"It's a ranse!" Geddy hollered. "It must've come from the cargo ship!"

She drew her blaster and was about to fire when Laszlo slid the rest of the way across the floor, slamming into the rear cargo door just below the hole. Another punch, and it opened wider. Oz inched closer, struggling to aim while Laszlo, dazed from the impact, tried fruitlessly to crawl away. As he did, his body rolled up over the hole, momentarily stopping the rush of wind.

A heartbeat later, the ranse exploded through the LLL on his chest like a turd from hell. It tumbled onto the floor of the hold in a tight coil that unfurled into a three-meter-long centipede covered in a thick exoskeleton. Laszlo's corpse puckered into a grotesque navel shape, again sealing the hole.

— *What the hell is that thing?*

— The end of the road if we don't get it out of here.

Oz fired her blaster at the pissed-off arthropod, the bolts leaving scorch marks as they ricocheted off its nearly impenetrable exoskeleton. It reared up, then fell forward into a ball that rolled toward her with eye-popping speed. She unloaded her pistol into it, but it launched itself at her like a live cannonball.

"Oz!" Geddy screamed.

At the last moment, she threw herself back into a limbo shape, touching the fingers of her free left hand to the floor as the ranse sailed just above her. Instead, it barreled into a very surprised Bykite with its spiky mandibles, knocking him to the ground, snapping at his face as he tried to throw it off.

"Aighhhh! Help!" he shrieked.

Oz rolled to a kneeling position and whirled to fire again, but Geddy stopped her and pointed at the rear door. "Shoot out the hole!"

Poor, dumb Laszlo's corpse had plugged the hole like a cork. Oz unloaded into his twisted body, and it sucked through, but not before the ranse buried its bloody head in Bykite's chest, teeth gnashing and mandibles grinding like the tunnel drills on Earth 2. She dropped to one hand again and swept her leg with whip-like speed, connecting with her boot and sending the hissing creature tumbling toward the back.

It collapsed into a ball again as it flew up to the sucking hole, partially blocking it once again. Its spiny, vise-like legs clung stubbornly to the edge, scratching the metal as its bloody maw thrashed back and forth, coating the door in Bykite's sticky blue blood that instantly froze.

Geddy scrambled to his feet and grabbed the coffee maker

from the bench, then gave a primal scream as he ran toward the hole. He heaved it as the ranse thrashed about, desperately trying to crawl back in. The machine rode the vortex straight into it, slamming into the vile creature with a sharp clang and knocking it back out into space. Held tight by the vacuum, it sealed the hole and the hold began to re-pressurize.

"Cut the wreck loose!" yelled Geddy. "Hurry!"

Oz dashed to a control panel beside the forward door and popped a red release button with her palm. A heavy clunk rang from under the floor as the net released.

Geddy stayed beside the plugged breach, carefully watching the coffee machine, ready to run in case the ranse burst through again. Behind him, Oz returned to Bykite, who was on his back, coughing wetly.

"Captain!" she cried. She looked pleadingly to Geddy. "There's a medkit on the bridge!"

Geddy was no medic, but gauze wasn't going to fill the gaping cavity in Bykite's chest. He didn't know exactly where Kailorian hearts were, but the volume of blood spurting from the wound suggested it was still pumping away. He burst through the door and found Denk in a panic on the bridge.

"What happened? Is everyone okay?"

"Bykite's in bad shape. Is the wreck clear?" Geddy asked.

"Yeah," he nodded, double checking his readouts. "Yeah, it's clear."

"Where's the medkit?"

Denk pointed to the wall by the galley. Geddy found the metal box and opened it to find two rolls of medical tape, a scanner with a dead battery, and a thermal blanket. He grabbed it anyway and ran back into the hold.

Oz had removed her jacket, wadded it up, and gently placed it under Bykite's head. He tried to speak but only gurgled. A final gasp, and he was gone. She sank back onto her heels, her head drooping forward in grief.

Geddy knelt beside her and placed a comforting hand on her back. "It must've crawled out of the wreck and up the net. I did say this was a shitty idea."

"Really?" Oz spat, her big, beautiful eyes glassy and red as her hair. "That's all you can say? 'I told you so'?"

He threw up his hands. "Well, I mean, it's not like I can say it to *him*."

CHAPTER 11

BYE BYE, CAP'N

After the ranse attack, Oz directed the two remaining thugs to weld a patch over the hull breach while Geddy helped Denk prepare Captain Bykite's body for a space burial. For want of a body bag, they rolled him up in the sheets from his bed and secured them with a few sturdy wraps of duct tape. A loose, but tasteful ceremony followed, then he was sent tumbling out of the trash ejector, reminding Geddy once again how lucky he was to be alive.

Morpho didn't appear until after Bykite had expired, at which point he dissolved into a literal puddle on the floor.

"I've never seen him like this," Oz commented, wiping away a tear. "He and Cap were close. Like, *really* close."

The machinery of Geddy's brain devoted a couple cycles to how a Kailorian and a nonverbal wad of chewing gum became *really* close, but it led down a dark path.

Shortly after, the four of them sat wordlessly around the metal table in the small galley, Oz and Denk listlessly probing their bowls of nutrimush while Geddy shoveled it into his face without so much as tasting it. He hadn't realized how hungry he was. All he wanted now was sleep, but it didn't feel right to get up and leave.

— *They're grieving. You should get them talking.*

— Not exactly my strong suit.

— *You've had no one to talk to but me and a sexy hologram for seven years. You could use the practice.*

He heaved a sigh and set down his spoon. "I've got an idea." They looked up hopefully at him. "How about you each tell me your favorite Captain Bykite story? You know, to honor his memory."

Oz and Denk glanced up at each other, weighing this suggestion. Denk gave a halfhearted shrug.

"Yeah, okay," Oz said.

"Got anything to drink?"

Oz popped up off the bench and retrieved a half-empty bottle of Kailorian gin, then fished three small cups out of the cabinet. She poured each of them a couple fingers and sat down.

"There. Now, after we memorialize him, we can raise a glass and say goodbye," Geddy said.

"I like that," said Oz. "Is that from Earth 2?"

He could still remember being at the officer's club on base after the funeral watching his father's pilot buddies do exactly that.

"Old Earth, actually." He forced away a thought of his mother.

"Denk?" Oz asked. "You want to lead us off?"

He sniffed and folded his hands on top of the table. "Okay, here's a doozie. A couple years back, we got a lead on a Zelnad wreck on Nichu. We've only got one novasphere, but figure it's worth burning it to check it out. So we park the *Fiz* in orbit and take the *Dom* down–"

"Sorry," Geddy interrupted. "The *Dom*?"

"Our dropship."

"Technically, it's an old Kailorian fighter," added Oz. "Cap took it when he ..."

"When he what?" Geddy asked.

"When he sorta ... bugged out of the Ring War."

Earth 2 never got lured into the War, thankfully, but dozens of other worlds did. As the Alliance began to collapse, many abandoned their posts, especially the last-ditch reinforcements. Without knowing the whole story, though, he couldn't judge.

The more interesting question was how a Kailorian deserter wound up jockeying a converted Ghruk freighter in the ass end of space. Bykite never got around to explaining that.

"So, you're on your way to Nichu ..." Geddy reminded Denk.

"Right. We check it out and find the wreck buried in the snow. Totally trashed except some kind of positronic drive core, almost intact. Anyway, we load it into the *Dom*, come back to the ship and have this little celebration because we're about to be set up for years, right?"

Geddy smiled, intrigued by this solid setup. Zelnad tech was coveted on the black market. "I'd imagine so."

"After about four bottles of gin, the prox alarms go off. We rush to the bridge and find ourselves face to face with a Zelnad destroyer."

He leaned in excitedly. "No way! The same one that shot Morpho at you?"

"Who's to say? They all look the same."

Geddy couldn't help but laugh.

Denk smiled. "What's funny?"

"A schnozz shot a wad of snot at you, and now it's your mechanic," he said, slap-happy from his long, deeply weird day. "It's funny."

"What's a schnozz?" Denk asked.

"English slang for nose. Because Nad destroyers look like …" He trailed off, noticing that neither of them were laughing. "Never mind. Sorry, I keep killing your flow. Please." He gestured for Denk to continue.

"Right. So no novaspheres, and we can't outrun 'em, but …" he raised his stubby, rough finger. "We've got one of their drive cores. They hail us and Cap has this crazy idea." He launched into an awkward fit of snorting laughter.

"Uh-oh, here we go," said Geddy, happily following this thread. "I love me a crazy idea."

"While I'm stalling them, he and a couple of the guys from the hold load the drive core into the airlock, then he barks at me to turn us sideways. As soon as I do, he pressurizes the ejector, blows it at them like a torpedo, and we do a full burn outta there. Aw, man, I can't believe we did that. Whew!"

Geddy leaned in, eager for the big finish, but Denk just stared at him. Oz wouldn't quite meet his eyes. After giving Denk ample time, he said, "Then what?"

Denk blinked, confused. "What do you mean?"

"Did it take out the schn– er, destroyer?"

"Did what take it out?"

Geddy rolled his eyes. "The drive core!"

"Oh, well, no. I mean, it was really more of a diversion. Honestly, they probably just hauled it in, but we were long gone by then."

His gaze drifted to Oz, then back to Denk. "Sorry, I'm a little confused. You burn a novasphere to score a piece of Zelnad tech in deep space that would set you all up for life. Nads show up and ask what you're doing there, and Captain Bykite … gives it back to them and runs away. What am I missing here?"

The fondness in Denk's expression dissolved. "Well, I mean, it's not like he *handed* it back. It came out of the ejector with a little, you know, pace. Like a brisk jogging pace, I'd say."

"But you had a legitimate claim, right? The moment they showed up, though, Bykite gave it right back."

Denk hung his head. "Well, when you put it like that ..."

An uncomfortable silence followed. Oz cleared her throat to break it. "Okay, I've got one."

"Great!" said Geddy, slapping his hand on the table. "Though Denk's was hard to top."

She sat up, tapping her slender fingers on the metal as she sifted through her memories. "All right. Well, a few months ago, Cap and I go down to Napnap for a little, you know, R&R."

"You mean you and the captain ...?"

Oz's eyes popped open. "What?? No. No, no, no. Very, very separately. I mean, except for drinks. And dinner. Well, and breakfast. But just as captain and first officer ..." She threw up her hands in frustration. "Why does everything I say sound like we were ... ? The point is, we were on Napnap, as friends, to get drunk and gamble."

"Why didn't you just say that?" asked Geddy, smirking.

"Anyhow, this one night, we start off in the touristy part of town. Hours later, we're at some townie bar, drunk off our asses, and Cap gets himself into a game of uguinok."

— *What's uguinok?*

— Sort of like liar's dice, only more murdery.

— *What are dice?*

Geddy clapped his hands together and rubbed them excitedly. "Now we're talking. How many great stories start with a game of uguinok, eh?"

Oz shook her head trying to show she was unamused, but her upturned lips said otherwise.

"Right out of the gate, Cap wins five straight games. He's

up three or four thousand credits, so I tell him he should quit while he's ahead. Of course, he doesn't, his luck sours, and next thing I know, he's into these guys for almost ten grand."

Denk giggled, but Geddy had serious doubts about where her story was headed.

"Okay ..."

"But Cap was stubborn, y'know? He keeps going double or nothing, and he keeps losing. Pretty soon he's down *forty large* to the Napnaps."

"Wow. That's a chunk of change."

"Well, I finally convince him it's time to go, only I know he can't cover his losses. I look away for like two seconds and when I turn back, he's already out the door. I had to fight off three guys and grab one of the *Dom's* skids as he was taking off. I barely got inside before we left atmosphere. Suffice it to say, we haven't been back to Napnap since." She chuckled, shaking her head. "That was some crazy night."

"A scrap over a Napnap flap," Geddy joked, clearing his throat. "I'm sorry, was that it?"

She gave an awkward shrug. "Yeah. I mean ... yeah, pretty much."

"So, just to recap, Bykite got wasted and welched on a bet he couldn't pay. Then, he left you to fight for him while he tried to take off, alone, in the fighter he stole when he deserted the Kailorian army in the middle of the Ring War."

Oz opened her mouth to refute this summary but stopped herself. Instead, she exchanged an uncomfortable look with Denk.

Geddy sighed. "Sorry, I didn't mean to dig anything up. He clearly meant a lot to you guys."

A long, heavy silence ensued, during which he had no idea what to say.

"He was actually kind of an asshole," Oz said.

"The worst," Denk immediately agreed, nodding.

She heaved a sigh. "But he was our asshole."

Geddy raised his cup high. "To your asshole."

Denk and Oz clanked their metal cups against his and drank, wincing. Kailorian gin tasted like industrial solvent, but beggars couldn't be choosers.

"What about you?" asked Oz.

"What about me?"

"We haven't heard your story."

He eyed them warily. "If it's all the same to you, I'd prefer to keep it that way." She and Denk stared at him, waiting. Guess it wasn't all the same to them.

— *Now who's the asshole?*

"All right, fine. What do you want to know?"

"What were you doing all alone on The Deuce?" Oz asked.

"I was born there. I left for a long time, but I came back."

"Wow, Starheart," she said drolly. "You really know how to spin a yarn."

"It's still better than most of mine," Denk admitted.

He heaved a sigh. They did save his life. Plus, after he found his ship, he'd never see them again. Might as well open the ol' kimono a tad.

"You might say I'm a deserter, too." His focus shifted to a long scratch in the metal table. "My parents died when I was a kid, and I didn't deal with it very well. I stowed away on a freighter bound for Kigantu."

"Kigantu ..." Denk said, deeply fascinated. "The Double A."

"What's the Double A?" asked Oz.

"The Aquebba Auction," Geddy explained, surprised she didn't know. "You know those stories about bigwigs making deals in smoky back rooms that affect the balance of power in the universe? That's the Double A."

"Sorry," she said. "I killed your flow. Please continue."

Geddy laughed in spite of himself. "Let's just say I got

involved with some pretty bad people. I didn't just want to run away — I wanted to disappear. No better place to do that than Aquebba."

Oz sat up. "Okay, but why didn't you go to Earth 3 with everyone else?"

"Because they thought I died in the accident."

Denk gasped and spoke in a reverent whisper. "The fart heard 'round the galaxy."

Geddy chose to omit the part where he caused it. "I had some unfinished business."

"Your ship?"

He nodded. It was clear by the looks on their faces that his answers were as cryptic as they sounded to his ears. After only talking to Eli for the past seven years, the give and take of a conversation felt unnatural.

"If you didn't have a ship, how'd you get into space?" asked Denk.

"I hitched a ride on the elevator."

His eyes widened. "You rode an elevator into space in an eighty-year-old spacesuit?"

Sensing the opportunity to score a couple points back, he gave a crooked grin. "Well, when you put it like that …"

Oz studied him, sizing him up, and finally chuckled. "You were all alone on The Deuce for what, then — *five years*?"

"Seven."

"Huh."

"What?" he asked.

"I don't know. For some reason, I got the sense you weren't."

"Weren't what?"

"Alone."

— *Aww, she senses me. It's nice to feel seen.*

He gave her his most charming grin. "To be honest, I did

carry on a long and passionate affair with a lady hologram at the mall."

Oz and Denk threw their heads back and laughed, and he couldn't help but join in. He hadn't done much of that in the last seven years, either, but in that moment, it fit like an old glove.

CHAPTER 12

CALOTH

"Approaching Caloth," said Denk, waking Geddy from his half sleep.

Caloth was one of many planets with the conditions to support life that never quite got over the primordial hump. Its surface was a mix of sand and fanged peaks that didn't exactly scream "welcome," but it was ideally located along several shipping routes and therefore had a busy spaceport.

He worried about his prospects here. Hitching a ride to Earth 3 to see Tatiana would take more than the ol' Starheart charm even if it was at its sharpest, which it certainly was not. Unfortunately, he owed more money here than he could even hope to borrow from the one person who had any.

From the jump seat, he watched Denk's deft hands fly over the controls and bring up their entry vector, a glowing tunnel that indicated their optimal approach into Caloth's relatively dense atmosphere. Reflexively, he tightened the straps across his chest.

"*For Sale Make Offer*, you are cleared to land on platform 7A."

"Copy that," said Denk, then turned back toward Oz and Geddy. "Let's hope the shield holds."

"Come again?" asked Geddy. Without shields, a ship the size of the *Fizmo* would break apart in seconds.

"Hope everyone used the bathroom. This could be rough." Geddy couldn't tell whether he was kidding or not.

The liquidy warp shield sealed around the old ship as they descended through wispy clouds. Denk had a wonderful touch, keeping them squarely down the digital gullet. Veering outside it even a little could push the shield beyond its limits.

The whole ship shuddered and creaked like a boat drinking the ocean. Geddy's jowls were vibrating like the time he motorboated that dancer on Stemir. What was her name? Candy? Caramel? Some c-word.

"W-w-hat's wr-rong with the d-d-ampeners?" he stammered.

"One of the things we need to f-f-ix," Oz said.

Shortly after they plummeted through slate-gray clouds, Denk gave the stick a tap to lift the nose, and they settled into a controlled glide.

"Thank you, baby," cooed Denk, caressing the controls in an oddly sensual way. "You're so good to us. I just wanna love you up."

— *Is that normal?*

— Pilots. It's a thing.

Caloth's enormous spaceport lay dead ahead, near the base of mountains so straight and sharp they resembled the blade of a colossal knife, rusted and pitted. It was a colossal planet, but the only habitable area was the few million square kilometers that always had the sun. The rest was permanently dark and cold. A giant manmade shade called the umbra provided an artificial night.

It seemed like a lot of trouble to build here, but it was in neutral territory near two natural wormholes and a short hop from the galaxy's largest nebula, whence novaspheres came. They were made of exotic matter that could open jumpgates to anywhere in the universe. Geddy called them blue balls on account of their color.

Workaday scavengers like these endearing yutzes and their sentient snotball usually got this deep into the sector the old-fashioned way — by humping it through open space for weeks on end. Caloth's more affluent visitors stopped off for two reasons: To acquire blue balls — both kinds — and to enjoy its only attraction.

The Hau Bazaar.

Every junk dealer, trinket maker, entertainer, gambler, pickpocket, and disgraced politician within two parsecs had made some kind of bargain at the Hau. If you couldn't find it there, it probably didn't exist.

For rich tourists just passing through, buying some gaudy sculpture or ultra-powerful blender was just the pretense. What they really wanted was to *feel* close to danger without actually being *in* it. The only place you could see more aliens in one place was the Xeno Xoo on Myadan.

Back in the day, it was a regular stop on Geddy's route, but he hadn't been there for at least a decade. Showing his face there was risky, but fortunately, his thick beard and shaggy hair made him almost unrecognizable. Besides, there was only one person he wanted to see.

Denk swung the *Fizmo* around, deployed the skids, and settled gently onto the pad. When the engines spun down, the ship seemed to sigh with relief.

Denk popped out of his seat and headed toward the back. "I'll make sure our passengers disembark."

Oz turned back to Geddy as she unbuckled herself. "What's the plan, Stan?"

"There's someone I need to see."

"They can help find your ship?"

"At least they can get me to someone who can. What about you?"

"We'll load up our best salvage and find a space at the bazaar. Denk's hopeful your suit will score us a novasphere or two. With luck, we'll have enough to make a jump and do some more hunting."

"You should find yourself a couple crewmembers. You're a bit shorthanded now."

"We've always been shorthanded."

"Tell you what," said Geddy, scratching his chin. Some part of him wanted to forestall their final farewell. "My contact here might be able to get you the best price on that suit. I'll track you down after I meet with her."

Oz smiled warmly. "That'd be great. Thanks, Starheart."

The bay door opened, and Denk came back in. "All right, they're cleared out. Time to find some real food. Geddy, you up for a bite?"

"Thanks, but I've got some business to take care of."

"He's gonna try and find a buyer for the suit," Oz explained. "He'll find us later."

"Sweet," said Denk. "Thanks, man."

"No promises. Give Morpho a squeeze for me."

"Do it yourself." His eyes rolled up to the ceiling.

Morpho hung from a grate in the ceiling by one slender black strand like a spider. He lowered himself onto Geddy's shoulder and wrapped around his arm, spiraling his way down to form a hand shape between his fingers.

— *He's really very sweet.*

"Thanks, Morph. I'll miss you, too."

Hau Bazaar was so vast that, even from the upper levels of the spaceport, you couldn't quite see where it ended. Its crisscrossing rows formed a spiderweb of paths, packed dirt formed by millions of feet shuffling between the tattered huts and makeshift storefronts. In spots, they funneled into choke points prime for pickpockets. Space was at a premium, and vendors fought for it. Sometimes to the death.

This was all part of the appeal, of course.

At the center of the circular layout was the so-called Hell Well, a fighting arena comprising a floating platform over a steaming pit that supposedly went all the way to the planet's molten core. Like the rest of the bazaar, it was pretty much a free-for-all, offering desperate travelers a final opportunity to score novaspheres or money. Victors walked away with twenty-five percent of the take, which often climbed to six figures.

The thing with being dead was that your accounts got liquidated. Geddy didn't have a credit to his name, but his creditors were legion. People who would be very interested to know he was still alive. If he ran into any of them here, he could find himself in a world of hurt.

He pulled up his collar and hunched over before plunging into the bustling throng, wishing like hell he'd thought to ask Oz if she had an extra blaster. Hopefully his bushy, gray-tinged beard would be sufficient disguise.

Only suckers let the spaceport mechanics work on their ships. If you needed repairs, it was faster and infinitely cheaper to buy parts and do it yourself. Most of the mechanics got parts secondhand but charged clueless tourists the price of new ones, pocketing the rest. He'd even heard stories of mechanics who surreptitiously removed good parts from ships, traded them for bad ones plus a bit of cash, then fixed them when they inevitably broke. It was all one big grift.

Geddy's destination was the cluster of bars and food stands surrounding Hell Well. The crowds there were a mixed blessing. They'd make it easier to move around anonymously, but then again, there was a better chance of running into someone he knew. With luck, being out of the game for the last decade, including seven years of being presumed dead, would keep him below the radar.

"Antimatter repulsors, here!" shouted a squat Udsar from atop a neatly arranged pile of old wing-mounted weaponry, gold chains connecting his tusks to the tips of his furry, wide-set ears. "Best prices at the bazaar!"

A few stands down, a substantial crowd had gathered around a six-armed Doxx-Moran doing a demonstration from a little platform. She dumped a bottle of wine onto a swatch of cream-colored fabric then held it up so everyone could see it run harmlessly off into a bowl. Meanwhile, her other arms were assembling small boxes into a row.

"Behold as our patented DirtDodger ship-holstery laughs in the face of tough stains!" she barked. "Now, ordinarily, a full roll of DirtDodger fabric in your choice of designer colors runs six hundred credits. But for today only, the factory has authorized me to offer not just one, but TWO rolls of DirtDodger plus TWO Miracle Sponges, TWO of our unbreakable Ship-Shield bird entrail scrapers, and TWO EverSuck accessory hangers for the same six hundred credits!"

Geddy pushed past the cluster of eager buyers and out into a wider path that separated the regular stands from all the food. The smell of grilling, boiling, and frying made his mouth water. He passed a stand whose owner had his back to the hibachi and snagged a morsel of something delicious looking off the corner. Some kind of fish, it seemed. It was a bit salty for his taste, but melted in his mouth.

He rounded the corner just as a halfhearted cheer sounded from the Hell Well, just two rows away. The thin crowd suggested it wasn't much of a battle.

— *Who are we looking for, exactly?*

Geddy initially worried the stand wasn't in its same old

spot, but a bit of red canvas had merely been thrown over the top. Everything else was the same, including, to his great relief, the proprietor.

"Yervina Pyetnyev," he said.

The cantankerous old woman's egg-shaped body had widened to such proportions that she could barely maneuver between the fryer and the bowl of secret seasoning. Her pale, flabby skin dripped off her frame like wax. Was this what happened to Basoan females of a certain age? Yowza.

She glanced up from her labors just long enough to meet his eyes, her froglike mouth agape. He held a finger up to his lips hoping she wouldn't scream out his name for everyone to hear. It didn't work.

"Geddy Starheart??" she bellowed in her thick brogue, her four-fingered hand flying to her chest. "What the heevens. I thoot you were deed. How'd Iya know ye's not a goost?"

He smiled and gave her weathered menu a solid rap with his knuckles, sending it swinging back and forth on the two little chains.

"Alive and kickin', Yervina. Solid as an afternoon shit."

She shuffled laboriously out from behind the counter and hugged him, which felt like trying out a mattress.

"Well, let's have a look at ye." She eyed him up and down. "A bit scrawny, yah? Let's put some meeyat un yer bones." She returned to the fryer and cocked her head. "Ye still wunt the usual, I 'sume?"

"You know it," he said. "I like my egg sac crispy."

"Crispiest at the bazaar." She dredged the fat lizard in Zihnian yak milk. It smelled like a spignork carcass rotting in the sun.

— *What the hell is that?*

— A nyaptomurk. It's this lizard thing from her home planet.

— *Is it good?*

— Not remotely. I'm just buttering her up.

"So, how's business, Veenie?"

"Look around ye. I can beerly pay reent. Nehbody wants fried nyaptomurk anymoor."

"What's the world coming to?"

"Eh. Not like Iya got betta prospects. Reteermeent will have to weet. So how loong has it been, then? Six, seven years?"

"Since I've been here? Ten."

She finished seasoning the dead lizard and dropped it in the hot fryer, which sizzled a bit too vigorously. Now it would be super done on the outside and raw on the inside, like always. Ah, well. She'd only been at it most of her life.

"Yeesh. Where dooz the time go? What brings ye to the business end of space?"

"I need a ride to Earth 3."

"Earth 3? What would ye want with that watery heelscape?"

"Personal errand."

She gave him a wink. "Ooh, it's aboot a lass, innit? Always is."

Using a set of tongs, she lifted the now-overcooked nyaptomurk from the oil kettle, wrapped it in paper and plopped it onto an aluminum plate, then slid over a basket of condiments, which he was certain to need.

"Can you get me there or not?"

"How mooch ye got?"

"It's not how much, it's what."

"Goo on."

He leaned over conspiratorially. "A spacesuit. Last century, minor cosmetic damage. And it might need a good, you know, airing out."

She heaved a sigh and settled onto a short stool that looked like it might once have been much taller. "Eh, not mooch of a market for that sort a' thing anymoor. The odd collector, maybe. I think ye'd be loocky to git seven or eight hundred."

His heart sank. Denk seemed to believe the stupid thing was priceless.

"Damn. What are novaspheres going for these days?"

"Eight to teen. Sometimes more."

"*Thousand*? Holy hell."

Geddy thoroughly baptized the lizard in hot sauce and tore off a bite from the foreleg. It took everything in him not to gag.

Yervina looked expectantly at him. "Weel? As good as ye remember?"

"Your recipe's secret for a reason." He chewed joylessly from the very back of his mouth, unwilling to give the stringy meat the benefit of the doubt. Nutrimush was a thousand times better, and it tasted like silage.

"If that's the best ye got to trade, I don'a think ye'll be gettin' off Caloth, say nothin aboot Earth 3."

His face fell. "That's not what I wanted to hear."

"Sorry I can't help ye, Ged. Fer what it's worth, loonch is on the hoose."

— It should be *under* the house.

— *What are you going to do?*

— I'm thinking.

— *So* that's *what tickles.*

"Ye know, there's more than one way to get mooney in this place."

She nodded toward the platform suspended above the Hell Well, where two small aliens were slapping ineffectually at each other, both terrified of falling in. The handful of patrons gathered around the railing were chatting, ruefully shaking their heads that the epic battles of yesteryear had come to this. You could see at least some of the fight from virtually anywhere at the bazaar, though, so a good one could attract a huge crowd in minutes. Back in the salad days, when he had money to burn, it was a great way to spend a few hours.

One of the little aliens had to stop between bouts of comically inept fighting to catch its breath. When it did, the other shoved him over the edge, his thin voice fading as he fell. Hardly anyone noticed.

"I seem to remember bigger crowds."

"Eh, this generation has no sense of shoomanship. Lately, they either dance aroond like this or sail over the side with one kick. Guess moost folks agree to disagree now."

He grimaced distastefully. "What a shame."

Yervina heaved a sigh. "And that's during the dee. At night, this place is a goost town. Too dangerous."

Geddy could hold his own in a bar brawl but hadn't thrown a punch in years. Also, he was trying to keep a low profile. The fighting platform over Hell Well was the most conspicuous location on the planet. On top of that, he'd have no control over who he fought.

Unless …

"I might have an idea."

CHAPTER 13

HELL WELL

Nearly two hours after leaving Yervina, Geddy finally found where Oz and Denk had set up their shop — a narrow space in the farthest corner of the bazaar between a pair of Bonzoks hawking kitchen knives and a guy who was having a hard time keeping his flesh-eating potted plants from biting shoppers. Interesting business model.

Denk had artfully rearranged their scrap around the old spacesuit while Oz batted her eyelashes at patrons in a vain attempt to seize their attention.

She brightened when she saw Geddy approach and gave Denk's arm a slap. He raised his hand in greeting and came to the edge of the busy walkway as shoppers shuffled past, wrinkling their noses at the sad little display. They didn't look like a vendor — they looked homeless. It was bound to be slow in this hidden corner of the bazaar, but they might as well have been invisible.

"I was starting to think you took off," Geddy said. "I swear I covered every square inch of this place."

"Yeah, well, at this rate, we might be stuck here forever," Oz said, wiping sweat from her forehead.

"No luck?"

"One guy offered five hundred for the suit. His buddy offered a thousand for me," she said.

"Yet you're still here." He offered a sympathetic smile.

She jutted her chin at him. "How about you? Find your friend?"

"I did. According to her, the suit ain't worth much. But I may have a way for us to help each other out and breeze outta here with our pockets full."

She flared her eyebrows. "You have my attention."

"Walk with me."

Oz told Denk to keep an eye on things, then followed Geddy into the confused flow of foot traffic. He led her through the next couple aisles, then pulled her into a sort of alley between two tents. Privacy was hard to come by in this place.

He described his plan. That she didn't reject it out of hand said more about her desperation than the plan's quality. In fact, it was foolhardy and might get them both killed. But if it worked, it solved both their problems and then some.

"Think we could pull it off?" His eyes darted back and forth between the crowd and Oz. "I saw how you handled yourself with the ranse. You clearly know how to fight."

She hemmed and hawed a bit, arms tightly folded across her chest. "You trust her to hold up her end?"

"As much as I trust anyone, which ain't saying much. Can Morpho handle something like that?"

She gave a knowing chuckle. "I've seen him do shit you wouldn't believe. I'm more concerned about you."

"Why's that?"

She cocked an eyebrow. "Do *you* know how to fight?"

"I've been in my share of scrapes." It was hard not to sound cocky. "But it needs to look good or there won't be enough action."

Oz's lips curled into a mischievous grin. "Oh, it'll look good. What are novaspheres going for here anyhow?"

"Eight to ten."

Her eyes peeled wide. "Apiece? A year ago, you could get two for five with a coupon."

"So, you're in?"

Oz chewed on her lip momentarily, weighing her options, then nodded. "I can fake it as well as the next girl. And it seems I have no choice. Obviously, neither do you."

"Okay, then. Have Denk and Morpho meet me at Nyaptomurk Nook. It's the five o'clock fight."

"I'll be ready." He turned to leave, but she stopped him. "Where are you going?"

"If I'm gonna be on that platform, I need to hide my face."

"How come?"

"Because I'm supposed to be dead. And I aim to keep it that way."

Geddy hunkered down in the back of Yervina's empty stand and waited for Denk to arrive. He came along about 4:30 with Morpho riding on his shoulder as usual. After introductions were made, Yervina motioned them closer — no easy task in light of her girth.

"Okay noo, I spread the word that there's a real fight coomin'. The bookies alweez coom at the start, so it's gotta looks like a good, even metch. Savvy?"

"Understood," said Geddy.

"So then, who'll be the 'loser?'" She looked back and forth between the two of them.

"He will," said Denk obviously.

Geddy sucked in air between his teeth, wincing. That wasn't the plan. Who would believe a Temerurian woman got the best of him? They'd be on to the ruse and all this would be for nothing.

"Me??"

"That's the only way Morph'll do it. I happen to agree. No one would believe you'd win."

That stung. Once upon a time, nobody wanted to fight him. He could've breezed into Caloth and blown three or four grand with nothing to show for it but a hangover. Now he was expected to lose a fight to a girl in front of a couple thousand spectators while putting his life in the hands of an intelligent tarball, all just to get to Earth 3 and confront the conniving succubus who almost certainly took the *Penetrator*. A woman who would probably kill him for not being dead.

— *That seems pretty fair.*

— No one asked you.

He turned back to Denk with a roll of his eyes. "Is that it, or are there more indignities?" Denk averted his eyes and kicked at the ground. "Ugh, what now?"

"Well, Oz and I were talking, and since you need to cover your face anyway, we thought Morpho could do it."

"Do what?"

"Cover your face."

Geddy barked a laugh at the outlandish idea, but Denk didn't join him.

"You seriously think I'm gonna wear a glorified wad of Zelnad spunk on my *face*? Hard pass."

A movement from Denk's bulging jacket pocket caught his eye, and a tongue-like black appendage poked out. Morpho had heard everything. Well, shit.

"Ay!" exclaimed Yervina. "What the heel is that?"

"This is Morpho," said Denk, smiling. "He's an amorphous biosynthetic blob. I'm proud to call him friend."

Morpho gave a little salute.

— *Aww.*

"Well, noo I've seen everything. He's kyna cute, thoo."

Geddy sighed and rubbed his temples. "All right, Morph. Just stay out of my … you know, orifices."

"You'll hardly know he's there," Denk assured him, letting Morpho crawl into his hand.

Geddy glanced behind him, confirming no one was paying them any mind, though a few people were starting to gather around the Well. Yervina hadn't had a single customer since his return. He felt badly for her, but then again, she was getting twenty percent of the take just for arranging their escape.

"All right, let's get this over with."

Denk held Morpho up next to Geddy's face. He slithered on, prickly microscopic fingers gripping his pores. It was a deeply weird, but not unpleasant sensation, not unlike the odd-smelling beauty masks Tatiana used to wear at night. It only took a couple seconds for Morpho to stretch over his entire face, eventually covering his head and upper neck. It felt oddly comforting, like a friendly octopus hugging his head.

"Well?" Geddy asked. "How do I look?"

Yervina bemusedly studied his face. "Like yoor into latex."

"Yeah," chuckled Denk. "Or if you face-planted in a puddle of coal slag."

They shared a belly laugh. Geddy groaned and rolled up his sleeves. "Very funny, you leeches. It's only my life on the line."

Denk patted him on the back. "Just stick with the plan. Once Oz knocks you into the bottomless pit, he'll grab onto the sides or something and arrest your fall, no problem."

"Or something?"

Only now that he was mere minutes from his fake battle to a fake death did this plan strike him as exceedingly dangerous.

A commotion came from the direction of the Hell Well.

Denk's head swiveled toward it. "That must be Oz. Come on, let's get you lined up."

"Good loock, Starheart," said Yervina. "Iya'll be rootin' for ye."

Yervina would help Denk extract Geddy from the pit later that night and arrange for a ride back to the *Fizmo*. That entitled her to a share of the take, though twenty percent was potentially a lot.

He had a hard enough time trusting one person, let alone three — four if you counted Morpho. Why did he think this was a good idea?

Geddy's procession through the swelling crowd drew more than a few sniggers.

— *They're laughing. Don't they know people die here?*

— That's the whole point, Eli.

— *For the record, I did not sign off on this. Count me out.*

— Noted.

They pushed through the throng of violence enthusiasts to the far side of the ring. The distinct smell of sulfur wafted up from the pit, sparking an unwelcome flashback to The Deuce. Visions of sweating his balls off in the thermal suit flashed through his brain. A distressingly narrow ramp led to the floating platform, which no longer looked as big from this angle.

His heart thudded a warning in his chest. Even though it was just for show, he hadn't been in a situation like this for a very long time, maybe ever. Plus, he barely knew Oz and had only seen her throw a couple slick moves during the ranse attack. How exactly would this play out? They should've rehearsed at least.

He leaned close to Denk. "Any last-minute advice?"

"Try to stay conscious."

Geddy gulped as a man in a sequined jacket appeared on the far side of the ring and climbed up the ramp to the platform, waving at the cheering crowd. He couldn't make out the man's face until he reached the top and activated his microphone. It was Everett Hau himself, the flamboyant trillionaire who built the spaceport. He used to announce the really big fights back in the day, but Geddy couldn't fathom what he was doing there now.

— Aw, hell.

— *What? You know this character?*

— We go way back.

— *So, he hates you.*

— Oh, for sure.

Everett's highly arched eyebrows and glittering white teeth made him look as excited as he sounded, his highly inflected voice booming over the spectators. His job was to whip them into a frenzy, and it was working. The energy was palpable.

"Ladies and gentlemen, children and larvae of all ages, welcome to today's main event! I'm Everett Hau, and it's fight night on Caloth!"

The crowd exploded, drawing even more people in behind where he waited at the bottom of the ramp. It crossed his mind to run as fast as he could back to the *Fizmo* and take off, but that was something Captain Bykite would've done.

— *Only you could engineer a scenario where fake fighting for money was the nobler of two choices.*

— That may be true.

"Our first contender hails from Temeruria, but don't let that empath bullshit fool you. She's been the scourge of pirates from here to the dark sectors. A master of multiple styles, she has delivered at least seventy-one souls straight to hell. A pitiless fountainhead of pain who likes to relax with a good book. Please give a warm Caloth welcome for the Withering Widower, the Mistress of Murder, the Empress of Entrails, it's … the Crimson Queen!"

Geddy turned to Denk, incredulous. "This is all bluster, right?"

He shrugged. "Oh, no, she's the real deal. It started out as a way to make extra cash, but then she really got into it. She's got a perfect record, too."

Oz emerged from the crowd wearing a skin-tight red suit that left little to the imagination, accented here and there with silvery armor that might have been tukrium. Red paint streaked her face in perfect symmetry, her eyes dark and smoky. She strutted up the ramp, egging on the crowd as they hooted and whistled their approval.

"Wait, where did she …? Denk, what the hell did I get myself into?"

"Don't sweat it, man. She's just a big ham. So, what's your fighter name?"

A jolt of adrenaline seized his muscles. "Oh *shit.*"

Everett Hau's voice boomed through the speakers, quieting the rowdy fans. "Facing her today is the Man of Mystery, the … Dean of Destruction, the one, the only …" he turned dramatically to Geddy and pointed a shaking finger at him, his eyes wide.

"Uh …" Geddy stammered. "Gimme a sec …"

— The Masked Spaceman?

— The Cowled Criminal? Let's do a little free association. You start.

"Black … Face!" Everett said.

"Wait! No, no!"

Denk shoved him toward the ramp. When he stumbled, he caught the eye of a man nearby who scowled and shook his head, folding his arms in disgust.

"Black Face? I minored in Old Earth history, asshole!"

"He misspoke. That's not my–"

"Oh, he's *shy,*" taunted Hau, earning a wave of derisive

laughter. "Come on everybody, make some noise for Black Face! I think he needs a little encouragement!"

They did no such thing. Oz stood at the edge of the platform with her arms akimbo and her hip jutted out as though to say, *Really?*

— *Wow, they sure hate you.*

— I've got two words for you. Cowled Criminal.

Geddy trudged up the ramp in abject silence, glancing nervously down into the pit. Wispy smoke rose from the steaming depths, making it impossible to see more than a few meters down. Whose dumb idea was this?

Upon reaching the platform, he leaned in close to Hau. "It's not Black Face, it's … uh … Cowled Criminal."

Hau studied him briefly, then smirked. "All right. Sure." He swung back to the crowd and switched his mic back on. "Correction, everyone, Black Face has changed his name."

The crowd erupted into boos and jeers.

"Give it up for the Coward Criminal!"

Geddy glanced apologetically at Denk, who slapped his forehead with his palm and shook his head.

— *It's not too late to take a part-time job. You could wash dishes. Work your way up to line cook.*

— Let's put a pin in that idea.

Oz paced back and forth near the center of the platform, her expression twisted into a murderous sneer. The rocky intro made Geddy forget this was supposed to be a show. The better the show, the more money he'd have to get to Earth 3 and get his ship back — maybe with a little to spare.

"Now, you all know the rules of Hell Well," said Hau dramatically, his voice echoing through his namesake open market. "Once the ramps retract, our fighters will engage in hand-to-hand combat until one of them falls into *hell itself,* a one-way, six-minute trip of abject terror into Caloth's molten core!"

Again, the crowd erupted, thirsty for blood.

"Fighters, take your positions!"

Geddy shuffled to the nearest of two red circles at the center. Oz knelt in the middle of hers, whispering a silent warrior's prayer to some vengeful Temerurian god.

He leaned toward her and stage-whispered, "Hey, maybe pump the brakes on the whole–"

"Do not befoul my ears with your words, Black Face," she growled, glaring at him over the tops of her dark eyes, fathomless and empty as the pit itself.

"Again, that's not ... aw, man."

— If you don't find some mojo here, this fight's gonna be over before the betting starts. Now come on. It's time to pay the bills. Have fun with it.

As usual, Eli got it exactly right. These people needed a show, and the better the show, the better everyone made out.

Hau moved to the edge of the ramp, waving his arms and getting the crowd riled. "Who has the galaxy's best entertainment?!"

"Hau Bazaar!" screamed the crowd.

"I can't heeeear yoooou!!"

"Hau Bazaar! Hau Bazaar!"

He galloped down the ramp as he had a million times, and they retracted the platform leaving Geddy and Oz to fight to the death.

"Just so you know, I'm not pulling any punches," Geddy said.

She cocked one eyebrow and snarled, "You'll have to land one first."

CHAPTER 14
RED VS. BLACK

The moment the ramps retracted, Oz launched herself at Geddy, landing a series of machine-gun body blows before popping him in the corner of his mouth. Morpho absorbed most of the impact, but he still reeled back a step, more out of surprise than anything. She was lightning quick, dancing side to side like a video game character.

He'd been hit by more than his share of women over the years, including and especially Tatiana, but usually open-handed, and he never hit back. No getting around it now.

"That's just an amuse bouche," she teased. "Wait 'til you taste the appetizer."

Her voice echoed out over the maniacal crowd as though amplified somehow. Geddy glanced up to see a pair of tiny drone mics hovering over them, ready to pick up their blows and taunts. The audience had clearly decided he was the bad guy. Might as well have some fun with it.

Having Morpho with him felt surprisingly reassuring, almost like wearing a parachute. Could he stretch himself into one if he fell?

"You dare strike the *Cowled* Criminal??" he bellowed, stutter-stepping toward her.

He feigned a roundhouse. As soon as she went to block it, he aimed a kick at her abdomen with his left leg and connected, but only because she let him. Her eyes widened in phony surprise as she stumbled back, pretending to fish for balance near the edge. The crowd gasped, but she quickly returned to her wide fighting stance.

"You like that, bitch? I call that the Kigantu Rib Roast."

"Well, it's underdone," said Oz. "Back to the kitchen it goes."

She spun and leapt in a tornado kick that caught him utterly by surprise. He was so focused on the lead leg that he forgot the trailing one. Her shiny red boot caught him squarely in the jaw. Stars filled his vision as he stumbled perilously close to the edge. It was no act.

Geddy was more of a brawler than anything. He'd picked up a few dirty tricks here and there but rarely needed more than instinct and guile. Truth be told, most of the criminals and thieves he used to associate with didn't have the discipline to be real fighters. But Oz knew what the hell she was doing.

"You got lucky," he spat.

"I'll bet you haven't gotten lucky in a long time."

— *She's got your number there.*

— Stay out of this.

The crowd laughed in raucous approval. Geddy glanced down just long enough to see clusters forming around the bookies with people shaking credit squares. So far, there could be little doubt about the outcome. He needed to change that to maximize their haul.

A couple quick steps toward Oz, and he shot in for her legs. But she leapt over him and he went sprawling, far enough that his head crept over the edge. The pit yawned underneath him, its sides almost perfectly smooth. What the hell would Morpho grab on to?

— *Is this a fight or a comedy routine?*

"Not helpful."

Oz, standing over him, cocked her head. "What's not helpful?"

"Your face," he sneered, kicking himself for answering Eli out loud. Force of habit.

Red-faced men leaned over the railing around the pit, spittle flying from their mouths as they screamed for blood and death. He rolled over and sprang to his feet, giving a battle cry as he rushed Oz. Maybe she let her guard down and maybe he surprised her, but he got close enough to fake a jab and slam his forehead into her nose.

Again, Morpho absorbed much of the impact, but he could tell he hurt her and instantly felt terrible.

Oz backpedaled and fell on her ass, skidding to a stop near the edge of the platform. For a tense moment, the throng held its collective breath. In one smooth move, though, she kipped upright, and they burst into wild applause. She wiped the blood from her upper lip and licked it off.

"Impressive app," he sneered. "Time for the main course."

"Enough with the food metaphors."

"Eat me!" he gave a subtle wink.

Back and forth they went, stealing glances into the crowd to see how the action was looking. The spectators were nearly thirty deep in places now, sweaty handfuls of galactic credits being shoved toward the bookies.

He landed a few good punches, though he couldn't help but hold back. Oz, by contrast, drove right through with her long, muscular legs, landing incredibly precise kicks to his head with such force that Morpho couldn't absorb all of them. The fight had drained from him, he was getting tired, and the crowd was ready to see Hell Well claim another victim.

Time for the big finish.

Anticipating another spin kick, he ducked and dove, planting his shoulder in her abdomen. He didn't hit her particularly hard, but she stumbled as though caught off guard, and they tilted together toward the edge. He tried to stop and pull away, but she held onto him, pulling him with her. A blink later, they tumbled into the gaping mouth of Hell.

For a painfully long moment, Morpho did exactly nothing. Geddy gave a yelp as he fell, mostly out of surprise, but when Morpho didn't leave his face, panic seized him, and he clung to Oz.

"Now, Morph!" yelled Oz from under him.

In an instant, Morpho peeled himself from Geddy's face, making a little sucking sound as he stretched himself into a rope and snaked under their arms. Coiling himself against Oz, he sprang sideways and webbed out, latching onto a tiny outcropping on the wall. It took less than a second.

— This is going to hurt.

— *Yep.*

When the Morpho-rope went taut, they slammed into the wall like the crack of a whip. Morpho lengthened into a thin piece of living cordage a centimeter wide. Geddy could feel him under his arms, straining under the load.

"He's gonna break!"

"No, he won't," Oz assured him. "He might lose his grip, but he won't break."

"Is that supposed to be reassuring?"

They were hanging maybe seventy meters underneath the platform, swinging back and forth like a pendulum. The opaque chasm yawning beneath them was silent save for a faint treble hiss like white noise. You couldn't have heard it from up top. It was pretty hot inside, too, considering how far down it was to the core.

"Morph, get us to that ledge and you can take a breather," said Oz. "Right now, we need you to pull!"

In all Geddy's sordid past, he'd seen and done just about everything — or so he thought. But he had never, ever been rescued from a bottomless pit by a living rope.

Inch by tedious inch, Morpho contracted, little tugging pulses traveling from under his arms up toward his anchor point and their destination, a narrow ledge cut into the wall. The higher they rose, the thicker he got.

The Morpho-rope had squeezed them into an impossibly tight embrace, their heads on each others' shoulders as they eased slowly upward. Sweat dripped off his nose onto her back. He hadn't been this close to a female in a painfully long time, and it was starting to show.

"Sorry."

Oz giggled. "What do they call *that* on Kigantu?"

"A boner."

"I get it," she whispered. "This is a hot outfit."

— Quick, gimme something else to think about.

— Like what?

— Anything distractingly bad.

— Butt sweat. Dishes. Umm … Mrs. Tatiana Starheart!

— Okay, it's working.

"Not to change the subject," he said, breaking the moment, "but what the hell are we *both* doing down here?"

"Before I went back to the ship, I talked to one of the bookies. The odds of both fighters falling in at the same time were five hundred to one, so I placed a side bet."

"How big?"

"Big enough to repair the *Fiz* and get you to Earth 3."

"I thought you didn't have any money."

"Bykite left us a few credits. We put most of it on the fight."

"Denk knew, too?"

"Since we didn't have time to choreograph something, we figured it was best if you didn't know. Sorry."

Several minutes later, Morpho hauled them up the rest of the way but remained coiled around them until they were solidly on the ledge. Even with his back pressed tightly to the wall, the edge only reached halfway down his thigh, making it seem like he could tumble forward into the abyss if he didn't lean back. Not exactly how he'd imagined waiting for rescue.

Morpho briefly sucked back into his original blobby shape, then splayed out next to them in a viscous gray puddle to rest.

Geddy ventured a glance up. The opening of the pit was far above, a dim, hazy circle with the platform at the center like a bullseye. No way anyone could see or hear them. All they could do was sit and wait for the artificial night to fall, and trust that Denk and Yervina would rescue them.

"I thought Temerurians were pacifists."

Temeruria never joined the Alliance and, like Earth 2, stayed out of the Ring War. Other than the elite Star Guard, they had no reputation for fighting. If anything, they had a reputation for avoiding it.

Oz gave a rueful nod and peered down into the blackness as though drawn to it. "When I was a girl, the Zelnads tried to draw Temeruria into a conflict and take our tukrium. They assassinated the king and bombed the palace. Hundreds were killed."

He frowned. "How come I never heard about that?"

"They rebuilt the palace, and a new king took the throne. He decreed that no Temerurian would never take up arms except in self-defense. It was like nothing happened. It made me so angry that I left and joined the Xellaran resistance. They trained me to fight. But then the civil war ended, and I found out I was banished from Temeruria for breaking the decree."

"You haven't been back since?"

She shook her head. "Xellara's where I met Captain Bykite at the IASS show. He offered me a job on an old Ghruk freighter if I helped him convert it into a trawler. The rest is history. Denk came on board a few weeks later."

"That's a helluva story."

"So, what's her name?"

"What's whose name?"

"The woman you're going to see on Earth 3."

He cocked his head. "What makes you think I'm going to see a woman?"

"You're too desperate for it to be anything else."

A sheepish smile came to his lips. "It *is* to see a woman …"

"Ha! I knew it!"

Holding up his finger, he said, "… but not for the reason you think."

Geddy wasn't ready for anyone to know about Eli, and no one was ready to hear it. But he didn't see the harm in telling Oz about the ship. The broad strokes, anyway.

"Her name's Tatiana."

"Ooh, *Tatiana,*" she teased, gleefully rubbing her palms.

"Semenov."

The color drained from her face. "No shit?"

"Yeah."

"That must be the other presence I sense in you."

— *Uh-oh.*

"Oh yeah?" he asked nervously.

"Sometimes absence has a presence. You must carry her in your heart."

– *More like your pants.*

What he felt for Tati wasn't so healthy as love, but Oz didn't need to know that.

"Maybe."

— *Liar.*

He continued, "We were hot and heavy, y'know. Even got engaged. Her family had money, and it gave me some cover."

"Cover?" She raised one dubious eyebrow.

"I've got a bit of a past. But I was trying to put it behind me. Tatiana was my way out."

"So, what happened?"

"Earth 2 happened."

"Oh."

He gave a pained nod. "I was underground when it blew. By the time I found a way out, they'd already declared me dead."

"Which gave you another kind of way out."

"By then, you might say I had a change of perspective. I decided the only way to really start fresh was to start over."

"You didn't go back?"

Geddy shook his head. "I watched the whole planet evacuate. They didn't leave a single working ship behind, so I started building my own."

"How long were you alone?"

"Seven years."

Oz's eyes dropped to his crotch. "That explains a few things."

"It got stolen the night before her first test flight."

"Stolen? By who?" She read his expression and her eyes popped out of her head as she gasped. "Tatiana."

"The Semenovs had the salvage contract. Some sensor must've picked me up. I think she took it to let me know she's on to me."

"Sounds like a real sweetheart."

Geddy gave a rueful smirk. "You don't know the half of it."

"And now you're going to get it back."

"Come hell or high water."

"How's she gonna react when she sees you?"

"Not well. But not before she makes me feel about this big." He pinched his fingers down to the tiniest possible gap.

Oz patted him on the leg and winked. "You're definitely bigger than that."

CHAPTER 15

HAU NAU

Artificial night crept across the faint circle overhead like an eclipse, which it essentially was. Profound darkness enveloped Geddy and Oz, a thing of substance and weight. Only the sensation of the ledge under his legs and the warm, comforting pressure of Oz's shoulder anchored him in time and space. All the while, the barely audible white noise hinted at something roiling and violent deep below.

By then, it was quite clear that the walls of the pit were too smooth for Morpho to grip and the opening too far for him to stretch. That they found this mini ledge was pure luck. Without it, there was no telling how far they'd've fallen.

A short while later, a faint electronic whir descended from above, becoming louder as it approached. A light flicked on bright as the sun and they shielded their eyes. It was a thumb-sized drone, searching for them.

"Denk!" Oz exclaimed giddily.

On hearing her voice, the drone immediately dropped down in front of them and projected a hologram of Denk's face.

"Hey, guys. How's it hangin'?"

"Cute," Geddy said. "How're you getting us out of here?"

"Everyone's gonna pee into the pit until you float to the top." He chuckled to himself.

"Denk, my ass has been parked on a ledge the size of my hand for an hour and a half. Try out your new material later." Geddy's legs screamed for terra firma.

Denk gave his head a cleansing shake. "Right. Sorry. Sending the platform down now." He turned to someone off-camera and nodded as the drone made room.

A minute or so later, a puff of air greeted them from overhead, and the drone's light illuminated the fighting platform they'd fallen from earlier, hovering just under the ledge. Geddy helped steady Oz as she stepped aboard, then he joined her, pins and needles surging into his aching legs. Morpho bunched himself up and hopped wetly onto the surface. The drone came up with them.

Geddy inhaled deeply as they broke over the edge of the pit and into the clear, cool night. Whoever was at the platform's controls guided it to the railing, where the three of them hopped gratefully to the ground.

Denk appeared and the little drone folded itself down, returning to a skinny little green alien with tentacled eyes who could've been a cousin of a semi-intelligent species on Kigantu. He strolled up to them carrying a small control box into which the drone just flew.

Oz immediately wrapped Denk in a hug. "We were starting to think something went wrong."

"Yeah, well, it took a while for the party to move up to the terrace." Denk nodded toward the sprawling outdoor patio on the spaceport's ground level, where the distant sound of a band thumped into the starry night. Colored lights played across hundreds of drunken revelers. "You guys got everyone pretty riled up."

"Who's your friend?" Geddy asked.

"Oh, this is Perdar. He runs tech on the fights."

Perdar lifted his head at them. "'Sup?"

Geddy took Denk by the shoulder. "Can I talk to you a sec?"

"Sure."

They left Oz to talk with Perdar and moved off to the side. "Did you get the money?"

"Sure did. A hundred ten grand."

Geddy's heart leapt and he gave a soft whistle, beaming. His expectations had gotten lower with every minute his legs dangled over infinity. Maybe it'd be worth it after all.

"Damn, that's a good take."

"I only took enough to get us two novaspheres. The rest I left with Yervina until we–"

Terror seized him. "You did *what*?!"

At that instant, floodlights came on, casting the arena in garish light. Blinded again, he shielded his eyes and took a couple steps forward. Denk, Oz, and Perdar hung back.

"Geddy Starheart," boomed a voice through the blinding wall of light. It was Hau, now wearing a dark evening jacket trimmed with silver sequins. His slicked-back hair looked blaster-proof. "Or should I say … Black Face? Ha ha ha! I wish I could've seen your expression."

— Shit.

— *What? You know him?*

— We've met.

He rolled his eyes. "It's the Cowled Criminal, damnit! Considering I came up with it on the fly, that ain't bad."

Hau sauntered up to the edge of the Well flanked by a retinue of Saraks hefting electric staffs that made the air crackle green around them. In the flickering light, their shark-like heads twisted into sneers. They often handled security when big money was involved. Their brains had just enough horsepower to carry out orders and not a pony more.

"Last time I saw you, you were running up a very large tab you never paid," said Hau.

He shrugged. "That was a decade ago, Hau."

"Yes ... and you won't *believe* the interest." He looked past Geddy at their new little friend. "Perdar ... And to think you were high in the running for employee of the month."

"Screw you, Hau," said the hot dog-shaped alien in a high-pitched voice. "Your health plan is garbage! I'm with these guys now!"

— Umm ...

— *Just roll with it for now.*

"Where's Yervina?" asked Geddy. "I can almost hear her wheezing from here."

A shuffling sound came from behind Hau, and Yervina waddled into view with a large satchel slung over her shoulder and plump with their hard-won cash. She wouldn't have told Hau about the money — just that the fighter called Black Face was actually Geddy. With that kind of scratch, she'd be able to retire and rid the world of her shitty cooking. Not a terrible bargain, but still.

Something brushed past Geddy's shoe. He stole a glance down and saw Morpho follow a long shadow cast from one of the Saraks. He was a ghost. Time to stall.

"Sorry, Ged." The combined effort of walking and speaking briefly overcame her, and she paused for a labored lungful of air. "Turns out there's a price on your head in aboot a dozen sectors. Including thees one."

"Tsk, tsk." Hau sneered. "It seems your little drink-and-dash at my expense pales in comparison to your other crimes. Have you ever noticed that people really don't like you? I've never seen a fighter so obviously reviled by the audience."

"I'm an acquired taste. So how now, Hau?" Oz muffled a laugh, and it pleased him greatly.

Morpho's dark, fluid form crept along the ground behind Hau's retinue, gliding silently toward Yervina and the handbag hanging down the long and gentle slope of her midsection. As he crawled along, he elongated back into the rope, snaking around the Saraks' and Hau's feet.

Hau chuckled quietly, clearly enjoying this. "First, you will settle your outstanding tab, with interest. Then you and your thieving friends will return the money you stole from me. After that, I'll take you into custody and wait for the bounty to roll in. Who will the highest bidder be, I wonder?"

"In that case, I've got good news and bad news." Geddy folded one arm behind his back and flashed three fingers hoping his friends would know to get ready.

"Okay, Starheart." Hau's thin lips curled into a bemused ribbon. "I'll play along. What's the good news?"

"Yervina should have enough money now to stop cooking." He lowered his ring finger.

"Hey!" objected Yervina.

"Surely there's bad news."

One finger. "None of that other shit is happening. Morph, now!"

Fast as lightning, Morpho snatched the handbag off Yervina's shoulder, then pulling himself taut around their ankles before shooting tendrils out to the edge of the Well. One yank, and they went down like a bowling pins, Yervina included.

"Run!" Geddy yelled.

"Perdar, the platform!" cried Oz.

The little alien dude tapped his handheld controller, and the floating platform skidded over the edge of the pit before settling into a rocking hover. He jumped on, followed by Denk, Oz, and Geddy. Morpho sprang through the air and collapsed into a pile under the handbag.

"All right, Morph!" Denk exclaimed.

"Go, go, go!" commanded Geddy.

Perdar did, but instead of rocketing away, the platform merely glided away, as Denk might say, at a brisk jogging pace. By the time they disappeared around the corner, Hau and the Saraks had untangled themselves and were easily catching up on foot.

"What the hell's this thing use for power? Rubber bands?"

"It's a platform, not a ship!" said Perdar over his shoulder — or whatever his spindly arms connected to. "Its propulsion is limited."

"Limited?! We'd be faster if we all farted in the same direction!"

— *That's it, Geddy!*

— What … the farting thing? That was just a–

— *Rubber bands!*

— Holy shit, you're right.

"Hope you're still feeling limber, Morph, because I need you to do your rope thing one more time."

Morpho poked up from the handbag and elongated once again. They were on one of the four main walkways that sliced the bazaar up in quarters with the pit at the center. It was a straight shot to the spaceport and the *Fizmo*. Bright lamps illuminated the walkway, providing little cover for the few lovers enjoying an evening stroll away from the crowds.

"Stop the platform!" Geddy ordered.

"What?!" Perdar asked.

"Just do it!"

Perdar slowed the platform to a stop between two of the lampposts. Geddy leapt off with Morpho coiled in his hand and looped both ends of him around the posts, leaving him with a few meters of slack. It would have to be enough.

He jumped back on and shouted, "Now back up!"

"Back up?!"

"Are you one of us or not?? Trust me!"

— *You're gonna break his heart, y'know.*

— I'm pretty used to that.

The Saraks were no more than twenty meters away, lowering their electric staffs like charging centurions.

Perdar backed up the platform while Geddy held Morpho-rope tight to the back. By the time it pulled taut and stretched, the Saraks were so close, he heard the crackle of their spears. Hau emerged from the middle of them, surprisingly spry, and leveled a blaster at them.

"Okay, stop!" he yelled to Perdar. "Morph, do it!"

With all his might, Morpho contracted, and the platform rocketed forward so fast, Geddy would've fallen off if Denk hadn't grabbed the front of his shirt. Morpho released the lampposts as they passed and immediately disappeared into the handbag.

"Yeeee hahhh!" hooted Geddy as passers-by dove for cover.

The platform finally slowed to its original speed about a hundred meters shy of the hangar doors. Hau and the Saraks were already gaining on them again.

"Come on, run!" Geddy said, grabbing the satchel of cash.

Oz bolted out in front, followed by Denk, Geddy, and Perdar, who hesitated to join them. Geddy appreciated his help, but a little guy wasn't what they needed. They needed muscle. Still, he couldn't leave the poor fella to Hau and his goons.

He skidded to a stop and turned back as electric bolts whizzed past. When he reached Perdar, he opened up the bag and shook it toward him.

"Jump in!" he pleaded.

"No way, man! Nobody carries a– Aighhh!"

A green bolt slammed into his back even though he was by

far the smallest target. He fell limply forward onto the walkway at Geddy's feet.

— *Can you wear him like a scarf?*

Geddy rolled him over as a fresh barrage of bolts hissed by. The tiny eyes at the end of his stalks had begun to darken.

"Get up, man! I'm not leaving you."

"Not ... gonna ... make it." The skinny alien's thin voice wavered. "This is where my ... journey ends. Avenge me, Black Face."

— *Well, this is awkward.*

"Um ... sure, okay. But again, it's not–"

He didn't finish the sentence, because Perdar was already gone.

— *Aren't you supposed to close his eyes?*

— How?

"Geddy, come on!" cried Denk.

He grabbed the handbag and ran at a crouch, darting back and forth to make himself a hard target. Oz hit the button to the ship elevator before he even got there so he had to jump on as it rose. Pressed to the back of the elevator, the underside served as a shield, blaster bolts punching the floor like angry fists. Geddy leaned over just enough to see the Saraks turn and run for the stairs. Meanwhile, Hau marched to a terminal on the wall and started punching buttons.

"He's closing the bay doors," Geddy warned. "Hurry!"

By the time they reached pad 7A, the doors were already sliding together. The *Fizmo's* ramp cracked open as they dashed toward it.

"Denk, I think we can skip the pre-launch checks," said Oz.

"Ya think?" said Denk, panting. Oz hit the button to the ramp as soon as she reached the top, and it sealed at Geddy's heels. The three of them ran breathlessly into the bridge and Denk leapt behind the controls, firing up the engines.

"Hang on," said Denk. "This is gonna be close."

He pivoted the nose toward the bay doors and gunned the engines as the bolts glanced ineffectually off the *Fiz's* thick hull. But they weren't going to make it.

"Roll it!" hollered Geddy.

Denk rolled her nearly vertical and burst through the bay doors, metal screeching against metal, a moment before they closed. He punched it, and they exploded into the simulated night.

CHAPTER 16

WATER, WATER EVERYWHERE

Not until they were well clear of Caloth's outer markers did Geddy finally allow himself a few deep breaths. He cupped his hands under the stream of yellow water in the bathroom and splashed some on his face, still red from Morpho's grip, and looked up into the polished steel mirror, his wild hair nearly scraping the short ceiling.

The water dripped from a point on his scraggly beard, flecked here and there with grey. The lines on his brow had deepened, and the bags under his eyes stretched halfway to his jaw. Tatiana couldn't see him like this. Riffling through the little cabinets in the wall, he discovered a small set of clippers that still bore flecks of light brown hair, most likely from Denk. From which part of Denk, he didn't care to know.

He flicked it on and trimmed himself up as best he could, leaving a bit of stubble. Without the beard, his hair appeared that much longer, nearly reaching to his shoulders. It had been months since he gave it a trim, but he wasn't about to try now.

Virtually nothing about their trip went as planned. He hadn't thought about Everett Hau in a long time and certainly never imagined seeing the guy again. Under any other circumstances, he would've breezed in and out of there like a ghost. But now, one of the wealthiest and most connected men in the galaxy knew he was alive, and soon, so would a host of others.

He cleaned up after himself, returned the trimmer to its spot, and emerged back into the bridge. Oz smiled on seeing him.

"Wow. From hobo to hippie in minutes."

"Listen, I'm sorry about what happened back there. I never meant to put you guys in danger."

She gave a sly grin. "I can't speak for Denk, but I needed a little excitement in my life."

"Me, too!" agreed Denk.

"Yeah, well, I owe you guys. At least we've all got a little money in our pockets now. Wherever you're headed to next, I'll just jump out and buy myself that ride to Earth 3. Thegus isn't far."

Oz exchanged a look with Denk and scratched absently at her ear. "Well, about that … we were talking, and we've agreed to take you to Earth 3."

Geddy's heart swelled. Seven years alone on The Deuce hadn't left him with much faith in people, but these were pretty good eggs.

"Think she could handle the jump?"

"It's not the jump so much as the entry," noted Oz.

Their hasty departure meant the damage to the *Fizmo's* rear cargo door didn't get fixed. Whether the patch they'd slapped over it would withstand jump compression was an open question, especially considering the bone-jarring entry to Caloth that nearly tore the ship in half. But even that was a walk in the park compared to Earth 3's challenging approach.

"We'll take the *Dom* down, find the parts you need and do an EVA to shore up that patch. That ought to hold you long enough to jump away."

"Works for me," she agreed. "Denk?"

"You bet. Entering the coordinates now." A few moments later, he turned back. "Wow, I've got us a clear vector. Ten minutes out."

"Thanks, Denk." Oz pivoted back to Geddy. "What about you?"

"I've got my own patching up to do."

She frowned. "With Tatiana Semenov."

— *I'm sensing jealousy.*

"Only enough to get my ship back. Unless she murders me."

She folded her arms tightly, looking down at the floor. "It's too bad you can't stay on."

"All you really need is some muscle. Maybe a navigator."

"And a captain," Denk said.

Geddy gave a halfhearted smile. "That money ought to float you for the next three months, at least."

"Yeah," she muttered. "It'll be nice to have a cushion for a while."

"All right, campers, buckle up," warned Denk, following his own advice. "Morph, novasphere me."

Morpho appeared from inside the handbag, stickily jumping from seat to seat until he reached Denk, who maneuvered the ship into position. Meanwhile, Geddy and Oz tightened their restraints. As much as he loved a terrestrial takeoff, jumping never quite agreed with him.

Denk opened the novasphere port beside him, a puff of dust suggesting it didn't see much use, and Morpho dropped the glowing ball in. A natural wormhole would've been ideal, but none came remotely close to Earth 3.

A moment later, the ball shot out of the nose of the ship like a booger and burst, opening a swirling, purple-tinged, vagina-shaped slit in spacetime. Geddy didn't understand the mechanics. He never paid much attention in physics.

"Activating warp shell." Denk eased the ship toward the void. The faint green bubble enveloped them.

Garden-variety blue balls only opened a jumpgate for a few minutes, meaning the likelihood of being followed was slim. If what Bykite said about Zelnads controlling the supply was true, then he'd better pick some up aftermarket before the price got out of reach. He'd need them so he and Eli could get to Sagacea.

"Well, guys, it's been nice knowin' ya," said Denk, only half-jokingly.

A good jump felt like a low-speed collision — one attention-getting jolt and that was it. A bad one was closer to the back flop he took from Semenov Tower, and you just never knew which you'd get. Once in a while, you heard about a gate collapsing mid-jump, the ship never to return. It sounded plausible. At any rate, it was getting hard on Geddy's body.

At least whatever happened would be instantaneous. But he sure hoped he'd get to see his ship again.

Fortunately, the jump wasn't too jarring, and not half as terrifying as entering Caloth's atmosphere. Knowing that no one on Caloth could follow enabled Geddy to truly relax for the first time since leaving.

"All right." Denk turned in his chair with a delighted grin. "For once, everything's in the green after a jump. Must be a good sign!"

Geddy and Oz unbuckled and stood to either side of Bykite's ostentatious old chair as they took in Earth 3. The planet was three times larger than The Deuce but almost ninety percent water. Gale-force winds battered it constantly, leaving the upper atmosphere perpetually shrouded in mist.

Most everyone lived underwater in submerged "seascrapers" next to island chains that protected them from the wind and water by the largest seawall ever constructed in the galaxy.

Wave and wind energy were less dangerous than geothermal, but that was where Earth 3's appeal ended. The ocean's edible species had been nearly hunted to extinction by colossal dinosaur-like creatures called mogorodons. Their time would come soon enough.

"That's some biiiig water," Oz said.

"You guys have never been?"

"Never had a reason."

Geddy flashed a smile. "Technically, you still don't." She chuckled and returned it. "Ready to saddle up the *Dom*?"

Oz looked away, picking at her fingernails. "Actually, I think I'll sit this one out."

"I thought–"

"We left a lot of stuff behind on Caloth. Morph and I are gonna clean out the rest of this old junk and make room for the next haul. Isn't that right, Morph?"

Morpho hopped back across the chairs and consoles, settling on her shoulder.

Denk joined them at the rear of the bridge, patting Geddy on the arm. "Looks like it's you and me, my friend. I don't know about you, but I'm ready to blow off some steam." He reached into the bag and shoved a fistful of squares into his pocket. "Three thousand should be enough for a good patch." He winked and headed back toward the crew quarters. "Listen, I'm gonna change clothes. I'll meet you at the *Dom* in a few minutes."

"Great," said Geddy with a wave of his hand. Once Denk was gone, he turned back to Oz. "You sure you'd rather jettison trash than meet my crazy ex?"

"Very."

— *She's got it bad for you.*

— Wait 'til she knows me better.

Geddy had flown in all manner of ships, but never an old Kailorian fighter. It was shockingly nimble for its size and could seat eight Kailorians, which necessitated ample headroom. Technically, Denk explained, the *Dom* wasn't a fighter so much as a well-armed light personnel carrier.

But landing on Earth 3 even with such a capable craft was no picnic. Geddy never had occasion to do it himself, but his father had back when it was just a military outpost and an exotic getaway for people like the Semenovs. You had to go into a fairly steep dive to knife through the wind. Bigger, heavier ships like transports had an easier time of it.

Denk activated his comms. "Earth 3, this is the dropship *Dominic* requesting an approach vector."

A young man in military garb appeared onscreen looking confused. Apparently, they'd changed their uniforms. The light gray ensemble would've looked more appropriate on a concierge.

"*Dominic,* this is Landing Control. Your transponder signal's on an unusual frequency. What's your business here?"

He muted the feed and turned to Geddy. "What do I tell him?"

"That we're here to see Tatiana Semenov."

"Semenov?" Denk said, blinking. "As in ...?"

"Yes, *that* Semenov. Just tell him"

Denk rubbed his hands together, eyes glinting with mischief. "Aw, man, I'm so glad I came." He cleared his throat and unmuted. "We're here to see Tatiana Semenov."

"Names?" he asked stiffly.

"Denk Junt and G–"

"No!" Geddy cut him off. "Don't say my name."

He frowned. "Why not?"

Geddy hesitated. The foundation of his carefully built house of cards was about to topple. It hardly mattered now.

— *You have to do it.*

— I know, I know.

He rubbed his temples. "Because Geddy Starheart's not what she thinks my name is."

Denk's eyes sparkled conspiratorially. "I *see*." He winked. "So, what should I say?"

"*Dominic*, please respond."

"Eddie Kepler."

Denk smirked and reactivated the comm. "Denk Junt and … Eddie Kepler."

The young man entered their names into a terminal and flared his eyebrows. "Ah yes, Mr. Kepler. Right at the top. Mr. Junt is in your party?"

Geddy rolled his eyes. "No, we just met. Of course, he's with me."

The young man bristled, tugging down on his ridiculous jacket. "Sending your approach vector. You're cleared for platform 3C. Watch the crosswinds."

"Thanks, Control. See you soon." The screen flicked off and Denk turned to Geddy. "Aw, man, I feel like I'm in a movie!"

"Pay attention so we don't get ripped apart, please."

He cocked an eyebrow. "You want to take her in?"

"How do you know I can fly?"

"I know a pilot when I see one. Come on, let's see what you got."

Just like that, he switched primary flight control to Geddy. It had been a long time since he had a control stick in his hands, and he was being thrust into one of the galaxy's trickiest entries. But all Kailorian ships flew pretty much the same.

At the edge of the atmosphere, he nosed her down to nearly seventy degrees, down the throat of the onscreen tunnel representing their approach. The ship's power caught him a bit by surprise as he accelerated into the dive. The denser air slammed into them, and the whole ship shuddered, but it was tighter and far more reassuring than the *Fizmo*.

"Damn, feel that wind!" Denk leaned gleefully forward.

"This thing's like a damned toy!" It took two hands to keep control of the stick.

A few seconds later, they broke through the clouds and the vast blue-green ocean filled their vision. They screamed earthward, accelerating to supersonic speed as the water rushed up to meet them. Waves the size of mountains frothed white at the top as they raced across the surface, crashing into the colossal sea wall in a furious white froth.

Geddy eased back on the thrusters at the same time as he nosed up. The fierce gale cradled them, smoothing their rapid deceleration. His spine compressed, his chest tightened. But the ship stayed perfectly within the digital tunnel as it leveled out despite the buffeting wind.

"Damn," Denk gave his head an appreciative shake. "That's some smooth flyin'."

Up ahead lay the massive spaceport, each of its four main branches boasting six levels. The seawall encircled the colony, its perforated design somehow collecting the power of the waves while turbines along the top harvested the wind. Mist exploded over their whirling blades as merciless trains of water pummeled it over and over.

Low-profile domed buildings were just visible below the surface. To the east and west stretched a short chain of rocky islands, likely along an ancient fault line in the seabed.

Calm water sparkled within the seawall, plunging them suddenly into a lovely tropical day. The husks of ships that couldn't pull out of their dives or were bested by the relentless wind littered the shallow sea floor like corpses.

"Good flying, *Dominic*," said the young man in the tower. "Welcome to Earth 3."

CHAPTER 17

TOTS

Considering the difficulty of entry, the spaceport was busier than Geddy expected. Mostly engineers and tradesmen by the looks of it along with a smattering of salespeople. Earth 3 was the newest colony in the whole sector, so it had only begun to catch on with tourists.

The platform marked 3C had no other ships around it. Two soldiers and an officer awaited their arrival.

"Military escort?" Denk asked, his voice tinged with concern.

Geddy recognized the officer right away as Jeret Jacquemard, formerly a member of Ivan Semenov's personal security team who always had a hard-on for Tatiana. How much did he know, and what was he doing here?

The *Dom* settled on the deck and shut down. Geddy rose, meeting Jeret's smug eyes through the window. He wore a slightly fancier version of the concierge uniform he'd seen earlier. The shit-eating grin he wore suggested he was looking forward to their reunion, which was more than Geddy could say.

"I assume Oz filled you in on the sordid details." Geddy blacked out the screen to check his hair.

"Yeah, but she never said your ex was a Semenov."

"Don't sound so impressed." He squared up to Denk, who was unreasonably excited. "Look, I don't want to spend a second longer here than I have to. I'll do my thing, you do yours, and I'll find you in the Vegas bubble for a farewell cocktail. With any luck, I'll have my ship, you'll have what you need to patch up the *Fiz*, and we can clink glasses before going our separate ways."

Denk feigned enthusiasm. "Yeah, okay."

The ramp hissed as it lowered it to the ground. Distant announcements drifted up as the salt air met his nostrils. Jeret drew himself up to his full height. He'd put on a few kilos.

"Geddy Starheart — or should I say Eddie Kepler?" The words squeezed through his clenched jaw like a ribbon of pappardelle. "I said I'd have to see it to believe it, but here you are. Back from the dead."

"I see you've filled out a bit, Jeret. Did that other ball ever drop?" One of the soldiers stifled a laugh, but Jeret silenced him with a glare. "We don't have any bags, but thanks anyway."

He stiffened and gritted his teeth. "I'm here to escort you to Miss Semenov's office."

"Office?" Geddy said, pretending to be impressed. "When I knew her, her office was a pool cabana."

"Oh, that's right ..." Jeret ignored the slight. "You don't know."

"Know what?"

"Ivan passed a couple years back. Aneurysm. Miss Semenov runs the show now."

It was painfully difficult to imagine Tatiana being in charge of anything, let alone whatever monopoly her father had established here. Then again, it had been a while. As for Ivan's passing, Geddy was just relieved he wasn't immortal.

"Ol' Ivan let himself die like some *commoner*, eh? Tough break. Well, lead the way. Denk, stay out of trouble."

Denk threw him a wave and took off in search of parts. Jeret nodded to the soldiers and led Geddy into an elevator that dumped them into a large, clear tube along the ocean floor. They loaded into a small monorail and glided along the chain of tiny islands, branching off here and there. Brilliantly colored coral decorated the sandy floor, but there was hardly a fish to be seen.

"Kinda dead out there," Geddy noted. "What's the point of living in an aquarium without fish?"

"The seawall allows small ones through, but the mogorodons pretty much hunted them out."

He smirked. "Fifty credits says she keeps one as a pet."

"Are we really doing this?" Jeret's face pinched.

"Doing what?"

"Pretending like it's not messed up that you're here. Alive."

"It's not weird for me. I've been alive this whole time."

"You broke her heart, y'know."

Geddy rolled his eyes and guffawed. "I doubt that very much."

"You never deserved her."

After passing several junctions, the pod slowed, pivoted toward one of the islands, and continued.

"Thanks for saying that. I'm still in recovery."

The tube dead-ended at another elevator. "This is you."

Geddy swung his eyes up. The rippling outline of an enormous house was just visible through the cloudy water. Clearly, Tatiana and the other fat cats snatched up the only available land for themselves. Everyone else was consigned to the seascrapers.

He climbed out and the pod about-faced. "I hope she tears you a new asshole." It took off.

"I hope so, too!" Geddy shouted after it. "The old one's been acting up!"

He got on the open elevator, which automatically closed and began to rise. It dumped him out into a long hallway with shiny black marble floors, a bright natural light at the end. Typical gaudy Semenov style. He cautiously made his way down.

The source of the brightness was a massive solarium with a ten-meter-wide cylindrical aquarium at the center. It teemed with the very sort of bizarre-looking fish he'd hoped to see earlier in the tube. It rose all the way to the ceiling, a high dome of glass and steel through which the planet's two distant suns burned, currently far apart in the hazy sky. He came around one side until he spotted the end of a giant desk that faced the middle of the room. Leaning against the front of it with her arms folded was Tatiana.

She was always hot, but now she was blazing. Her hair cascaded down her back in a shimmering waterfall that nearly brushed her legendary ass. She wore a flimsy cream-colored blouse that scooped low and a sort of chain belt encircling the top of a painted-on skirt — like any woman home alone.

Seeing her again had the same effect it always did, making his own pants a bit too tight for comfort.

— Listen, pal, I need you to keep me on track here. Whatever it takes. There's a reason they named a black hole after this woman.

— *You can count on me.*

"Hey, gorgeous," he muttered.

"Hi, Eddie." Her strappy heels click-clacked across the floor as she approached. "Or should I say, 'Geddy'?"

"You've got a million questions." He showed his palms in deference. "I only have one."

She allowed a thin smile. "My first question is, can I offer you a drink?"

— *Okay, this is a softball. Alcohol affects your judgment. Just say no.*

"Sure, why not?"

— *Um ...*

She turned on her heels and angled toward a wheeled cart beside the desk bearing an assortment of liquor. "Old Earth, I assume?"

"You know me."

She gave a knowing smile and poured him a finger of the brown liquid. He silently rejoiced, because he thought he'd had the last of it. His eyes kept drifting down to her flawless legs, smooth and polished as shellacked wood.

— *Stay strong.*

If if you managed to ignore the looming seawall, the long slope of fine, gray-brown sand and the green-tinged ocean could've passed for any one of the nice planets. Every brick and pane of glass in this palatial estate was flown in from somewhere, no doubt at staggering cost.

He meandered back to the giant aquarium and took in the technicolor profusion of bizarre life inside, some species resembling those on Old Earth. The Deuce had no aquatic life at all, only groundwater.

"Are these the last of the fish?"

She came up beside him, her bewitching scent enveloping him. "Unlikely. The vast majority of the ocean is still uncharted."

The fish were clustered in the upper two-thirds of the cylinder, separated from the lower third by a layer of nearly invisible mesh. But apart from a few gently swaying stalks of bright purple seaweed and chunks of coral, it appeared empty.

"What's the story here?"

"Look closer."

She nodded toward a faint shape on the aquarium floor about the length of his arm. It looked like a cross between an eel and an alligator, its bright yellow eyes locked on and boring a hole into his corrupt soul. Razorlike teeth poked out on both sides like there wasn't enough room for all of them. If not for the hollows of its eyes, it would've been indistinguishable from the sand and coral.

"Holy shit, is that ..."

"A baby mogorodon, yes. Like goldfish, their size is a function of their habitat. This one won't get much bigger here. We've learned a great deal about their anatomy, too. There's actually growing demand for their parts in gourmet circles."

Geddy shook his head and averted his eyes from the creature, allowing a smirk. Jeret owed him fifty credits. "Monetizing monsters. Leave it to you, Tots."

"Tots." She turned back with a bemused chuckle. "Haven't heard that in a while."

He followed her over to a corner of the room where two chairs and a couch were arranged around a low, ornate table that used to be in Ivan's office back in Semenov Tower. He settled onto the couch while she chose the chair nearby. For the first time, he noticed she didn't have a glass.

"Nothing for you?" he asked. "You may recall I make a mean martini."

"I'm in charge now. Day drinking's a bad look."

"Sorry to hear about your dad. He was a ... large figure. You look good, though."

She scanned him and wrinkled her nose. "You look like you're here to patch a hole in the drywall."

"How'd you find out about my name?"

"Is that your one question?"

"You know what my question is."

"Do I?"

He heaved a sigh. "Look, Tots, I've come too far to play this game. I'm here on an errand, and that's–"

"Your real name is Edgar Louis Kepler. Born to Captain Lucas and Deryn Kepler July 13, 2389. Orphaned at age 13 as a result of a tragic crash during an off-the-books joyride. Two months later, you stowed away on a ship bound for Kigantu.

"From there, you fell into a life of crime as the right-hand man for a notorious criminal, during which time you piled up a rap sheet a kilometer long and a mountain of unpaid debts to some very unsavory people. How am I doing so far?"

"That's ... in the ballpark."

"Then, for reasons unknown, you suddenly return to Earth 2 with a new identity and take a job working for my father's geothermal plant. We meet, start dating, and get engaged. My father thinks you're a loser, I think you're cute.

"Later that year, a catastrophic explosion collapses a tunnel and traps you inside. They can't find you, so we all assume the worst. Meanwhile, the atmosphere slowly fills with shit-smelling gas we can't stop. Six weeks later, we're planet shopping again."

Geddy's face felt hot. He took a sip of his drink and licked it off his lips. "How'd you know I was alive?"

"Interestingly, a purchase from the Laguna Luxe mall kiosk triggered a red flag on my credit. I sent some small probes to find out who the hell was still there to buy pants. Imagine my surprise when they found evidence of recent human activity, including some remarkably fresh DNA from the mall. Once I knew it was you, they tracked your movements for weeks. Apart from the mall, you only went to the penthouse, the tunnels, the foundry. ... and the spaceport museum."

Geddy slid forward on the couch until his butt was on the

edge. His eyes locked with hers. If scowling, hot-blooded party girl Tatiana Semenov had evolved into a more driven, even more ruthless version of her late father, this might be worse than he thought.

"Tatiana, listen … I'm sorry I let you think I was dead. That wasn't cool. And I had my reasons, but right now, what I need to know is–"

"I know why you did it. And why you built the ship."

His heart stopped. She couldn't possibly know. Could she?

"You do?"

Tatiana slowly uncrossed her exquisite legs, then switched them, tapping the tips of her slender, manicured fingers together as she squared up to him. He goes from not touching another person for seven years to this?

"You were ashamed of your past. Your lowly station. The closer we got to the wedding, the more you worried you weren't good enough for me. That you were a nobody, a schlubby, no-account scoundrel who would forever stand in my shadow."

"Um …"

Her bottomless aquamarine eyes drifted to her lap, where she discovered an invisible piece of lint. She flicked it aside like a parasite.

"I know how people look at me. They think, 'Oh, she's so stunning and successful and put-together and rich, and yet, approachable and profoundly humble.' It shouldn't be possible. I get that."

"Well, I think that's … I mean …" he stammered.

"But you never saw me that way. You didn't care about my flawless body or my immeasurable wealth. You saw my heart. I, on the other hand, only saw you as a well-endowed accessory who looked good in coveralls and had exceptional stamina. That wasn't fair."

She rose effortlessly from her chair and unbuttoned her

blouse, letting it slip off her shoulders. Slowly, she reached back to unzip her skirt.

— *Get out of there!*

— Let's see where this is going.

"Tots, listen, I think you've got the wrong …"

She tugged the peach-colored skirt down over her smooth, trim hips, revealing a pair of white lace panties that popped like neon against her smooth, tan skin. The blouse was next, which parted like curtains to expose her magnificent tits, yearning to be freed from the cruel restraints of her bra. Tears of joy welled in his eyes.

With her legs splayed, she bent down and placed her hands on his knees, kneading them like focaccia dough. Her breath was hot and minty, her hair redolent of jasmine. Her heavy, gently swaying boobs held him fast like a charmed cobra. The hair on his arms stood at attention, along with everything else.

— What did I come here for again?

— *The ship!*

— Oh, right.

"Not until I knew you were building a ship did I realize how far you would go, how much you would sacrifice, just to get back to your *Hot … Tati.*" She ran her fingers down the front of his shirt and placed her plump, candyfloss lips right next to his ear. "I can't imagine *anything* sexier."

— *Red alert! Abort!*

Electric heat flooded his body. His heartbeat quickened. Sweat beaded on his upper lip. This wasn't going at all like he'd expected. Somehow it was both better and worse. Wasn't he just lamenting the scarcity of blue balls?

"About that ship, I need to …"

Tatiana sinuously swayed her hips back and forth, staring through the tops of her elegant black eyelashes and into his very soul as she toyed with his buttons.

"When I thought I'd lost you, I took comfort in depravity.

An endless parade of lovers, sometimes two or … eleven at a time. Men. Women. Young adults. Much of it, I'm not proud of. Still, nothing could fill the *aching, empty hole* inside me. Like an itch I couldn't quite … reach." Her hand slid from his knee to his crotch and squeezed him hard. "Know what I mean?"

He squirmed under her tight grip.

— *Splash some water on your face. That's a thing, right?*

He gulped. "Did you say 'parade?'"

"When I saw your adorable little ship, I had to know how far you would really go to find your way back to me. You rode an elevator into space and crossed an ocean of stars just to find me and beg my forgiveness. You can't imagine how hot that makes me."

Just like that, he was in her grip again, both literally and figuratively. His mind raced to find some way, some combination of events that would satisfy both their needs — not just in the heat of the moment, but for all time. He came up empty.

— *Geddy, please! Don't do it!*

— But I've been dreaming of this for seven years. Cherie the hologram meant nothing to me.

Tati moved into his lap and straddled him, pressing her ample bosom to his face as her molten breath caressed the base of his neck.

One practiced flick of his hands and her bra would drop like a flower petal. He could live like a king here if he wished, a kept man, a sex slave to one of the most desirable women in the universe.

But then Eli would be trapped inside him forever.

Everything he'd done to get here — every trial he'd endured, every inhale of rotten-egg air, paled beside the thought of pushing Tatiana off him and standing. Where was a glass of ice water or an old-timey seltzer bottle when you needed it?

— If you're not gonna help me, Eli, I'll have to do it myself.

— *Seriously?*

Tati moaned when his hands encircled her waist, but when he only lifted her off him, she flopped back on the couch and stared at him with her legs splayed, her face twisted into an incredulous scowl.

"What the *fuck*??" she spat.

Geddy popped up and paced back and forth, patting himself hard on his cheeks and taking deep breaths like he was practicing lamaze. He couldn't look at her again. Not until he asked the question he came to ask.

"Tatiana, where's my ship?"

"*That's* what this is about? Your stupid little *ship?*"

"Just tell me where it is and I'll get out of your lair — er, hair."

Standing to face him, she said, "Who says no to this?" She ran her fingers down the sides of her hourglass body. It was a very fair question.

"I spent seven years building that ship. You can't imagine how much it means to me."

"More than me, apparently." She stood abruptly and put her skirt back on. She zipped it and turned it around, then, disappointingly, re-buttoned her flimsy blouse with her back to him.

"Look, I'm done hurting you. Once I have my ship, you'll never see me again."

As she re-tucked her blouse, she leaned close again and said, "Maybe *I'm* not quite done hurting *you*. In fact, maybe I haven't even started."

CHAPTER 18

TATIANA

"What's that supposed to mean?"

Tatiana whirled, her hair fanning out and slapping him in the face before she returned to her desk. "I dug a lot deeper than your Earth 2 biography, *Geddy Starheart*. Well … *I* obviously didn't go traipsing around the dirty parts of the galaxy. I hired someone."

Terror seized him. "Who??"

"I never learned his name. That was part of the deal."

"Look, I came a long way. I know you're upset, but this is very important to me."

"In lieu of credits, he asked if he could take something from Earth 2. I told him to knock himself out" She gave an indifferent shrug. "If your little ship's gone, then he must've taken it."

Venom flooded his veins, his dirty fingernails digging into his palms. "Who?"

She waved her hand dismissively. "Oh, you know these contractors. Half don't tell you who they are at all, and the other half lie. I must say, you got in with some very shady people, Eddie, or Geddy, or whatever your name is."

"Tots, it's very important that you–"

"Oh, no. No, no, no." She wagged her slender finger back and forth like a scolding mother. "You don't get to call me that anymore. It's Ms. Semenov, and I don't have to tell you shit."

— *Take that olive branch out of your ass and hit her with it.*

— Talk about your metaphor salad.

He took a couple of deep breaths and calmed himself, then forced a pained smile. "Look, I was an asshole, and I'm sorry. Is that what you want to hear?"

To his pleasant surprise, her face softened. He'd admitted fault but hadn't apologized. Maybe that was all she needed. "You are? Sorry, I mean?"

Geddy leaned against the railing surrounding the aquarium with his arms crossed, facing her directly. "Everything you said was right. I got in with some bad people, and I wanted out. I never saw you coming. I mean, I've seen you coming many times, but …"

Tatiana got up from her desk and slinked toward him, her bright blue eyes glimmering as he trailed off. "Tell you what. I'll tell you who took your ship if you tell me why it's so important to you."

— *Boy, she can turn on a dime, can't she?*

He took a deep breath that gave him time to think of a convincing lie. "You might say it's a part of me. I spent most of my life destroying things, but this … it's a new start."

She gave her head a slow shake. "Come on, Eddie. Don't bullshit a bullshitter." Her fingers walked down the front of his shirt. "You can tell me anything. If you show me yours … maybe I'll show you mine. For old time's sake?"

Geddy couldn't tell her the truth, and even if he did, she wouldn't believe it. But he didn't necessarily have to lie, either. There was another reason he needed a ship, though it hadn't occurred to him until that very moment.

He stuffed his hands in his pockets and shuffled back to the aquarium, trying to focus on the colorful fish instead of the dead-eyed monster lurking at the bottom. Its eyes still hadn't left him.

"After the transports left, I went out to my old house at the base. I thought maybe time would've helped me come to terms with what happened to my folks, but it didn't. I realized the only way I'd ever have closure was to go up to the Ice Castles and see for myself."

Comprehension washed over her. "That's what the ship was for."

He hadn't told Eli, but if the test flight to Trebek went well, he thought he might do exactly that. Maybe he still would someday. That made it only half a lie.

"In part. But I also knew I couldn't stay. Once your machines were done with Laguna, it would just be a smelly rock."

"But you had no intention of coming back to me."

The hurt in her voice suggested she wasn't made of stone. He turned to face her. "We were never gonna work. Not in any of the ways that matter. You might say we filled each other's voids."

Tati was unamused. Well, you decided for both of us then, didn't you?"

"Dying was easier than telling you the truth. I was a coward."

— *Ooh, that's nice. Give her the goods!*

— Not helpful.

Tatiana searched his face for signs of deceit, but she would find none. "I'd like to believe you."

"That's as honest as I've ever been with anyone. If it's still not enough, then–"

"Sammo Yann," she mumbled, cutting him off.

"What?"

"That's his name."

Geddy honestly expected to know, or at least had heard of, whomever had investigated his past on Tatiana's behalf. But the name didn't ring a single bell.

"Where do I find him?"

"Not my problem."

"How'd he wind up working for you?"

"His name was in Dad's records. I contacted him through backchannels. We never met."

With that, another piece of the puzzle clicked into place. Ivan, being immeasurably wealthy and ambitious, had a lot of powerful friends, not all of whom were involved in legitimate enterprises. There couldn't have been more than two degrees of separation between the people he did business with and those Geddy used to work for. Someone in Geddy's network would know who this Sammo Yann was, but as soon as he opened that door ...

It hardly mattered now. If Everett Hau knew he was alive, it wouldn't be long before everyone did.

"I'm not telling you because you charmed it out of me," she continued, looking over the tops of her eyes. "It's so what I'm about to say lands."

Well, this was intriguing. "You've got my attention."

She took a couple steps closer, but not in a sexy way. Her face was dead serious. "Whatever trouble you got into, I promise Sammo's in it *waaay* deeper. I gave you his name so you could steer clear of him."

Geddy gave her credit for seeing his determination to be reunited with the *Penetrator.* He'd dealt with shady smugglers most of his life, but she couldn't know that. Not everything. He had nothing to fear from Sammo Yann. Hell, if anything, it was the other way around.

"You know I won't do that. But I appreciate the warning."

A rueful smile crossed her lips and she held out her empty palms as though she'd done all she could. "Suit yourself."

Something in her tone made him wonder if that was self-absolution or a threat.

"So, who's your friend? I noticed you didn't come alone."

"He's just part of the crew that picked me up after your processing ship ejected me into space."

"Crew of what?"

"Deep salvage vessel." He paused, then figured he might as well call a spade a spade. What difference did it make? If she wanted to know where the *Dom* came from, she could find out. "A salvage trawler."

A sly grin crossed her glossy, pink lips. "How fitting."

Tatiana lunged forward, gathering his shirt into her fists, and kissed him, so deeply he thought her tongue might burst out the back of his skull. Her breasts pressed against him, burning through the fabric, hot as grill covers.

— *Was that a kiss or did she just deposit an embryo in your chest?*

Had he still been on the couch, it would've been too much to bear. But somehow, he saw her differently now. She wasn't Tatiana Semenov, smoke-show socialite any more than he was Geddy Starheart, emotionally stunted orphan-henchman. The equation had changed, and so had the result.

It wasn't just a goodbye kiss — it was a kiss goodbye.

"You really had me going for a while, Eddie."

He let her hands slip through his as he backed away. "Something tells me we'll meet again."

"Earth 3 is always open for business," she cooed after him. "And so am I."

— *Go now. Just keep walking.*

The baby mogorodon's unblinking eyes followed him the whole way out as though daring him to someday return.

CHAPTER 19

WHAT HAPPENS IN UNDERSEA VEGAS

Jeret and his minions dropped Geddy off near the main entrance to Earth 3's compartmentalized city under the sea, known widely as the Bubbles.

"Whatever your … business was with Miss Semenov, consider it concluded," Jeret warned, his jaw clenched. "I wouldn't come back if I were you."

"You should work at the department of tourism."

Jeret only scowled and took off in the railcar.

— *Now what?*

— Now we find Denk and get off Waterworld.

He turned around toward the beckoning pedestrian tunnel the width of a highway. Its arched entrance read:

Welcome to Earth 3
Third Time's a Charm!

Apart from a smattering of curious aliens, the vast majority of pedestrians were locals who lived in the ring of undersea high-rises, which were now clearly visible through the somewhat turbid, fish-free water. Hopefully, he didn't run into anyone else who might recognize him.

As he walked, his thoughts bounced back and forth between awe at the magnitude of this engineering feat and the obvious question of how long it would take before it all went to shit. Old Earth was a paradise his ancestors ruined. The Deuce was halfway decent until he inadvertently turned it into an airport bathroom. As a result, the last million or so of his kind were relegated to a wind-whipped nightmare of a water planet dominated by submarine-sized apex predators that got hungrier by the day.

What could go wrong?

A moving walkway transported him through the big tunnel as upbeat music played through hidden speakers. When it ended, he stepped off into the Bubbles. If anyone talked about going to Earth 3 — and not many did — this was what they really meant.

A ring of thick, transparent domes at least two hundred meters across linked to the even larger bubble at the center via short passages with massive bulkhead doors on both ends. Each one was dedicated to a specific function like farming or entertainment. The dildo-shaped towers where most everyone lived encircled it.

Since Earth 3 was originally intended as an undersea getaway for Earth 2's wealthiest citizens, the main bubble's focus was leisure. Multi-level restaurants were clustered around a little turf-covered park with a gaudy sculpture fountain in the middle depicting the three Earths. One section was called A Walk Among the Stars, replete with exotic cuisines from across the galaxy and a simulated night sky. Still another area paid tribute to Old Earth, including a much smaller version of the museum from The Deuce.

His mother would've been sad to know the Space Exploration museum's collections were still squirreled away somewhere, but space down here was at quite the premium. The day would come when nobody bothered to remember the old pioneers at all.

Denk might feel somewhat at home here. His people were forced underground long ago when Durandia's ozone layer dissolved. Though, since their cuisine consisted almost entirely of tough root vegetables and grubs, a Durandian restaurant seemed unlikely.

He stopped at an information desk to ask directions to the Vegas bubble, and the young woman pointed him to a brightly lit section on the far side.

Old Earth stood as its own monument to excess, but whomever planned out this complex apparently wanted to top it. The Vegas' bubble's design motif was to cover every visible surface with a blinking light, making it seem like everything was in motion. There was even a stand hawking sunglasses, which only humans could justify needing in an underwater city.

Only someone with bad eyes or a penchant for motion sickness could handle the central courtyard for more than a few minutes. A prominent stand of glittering neon palm trees protruded from a little island in the middle of a pond teeming with robotic fish, also neon.

— *One more light would've ruined it.*

—At least they stopped before it got tacky.

Sandwiched between a pair of small casinos was a watering hole called Deep Dickens Old Tyme Go-Go Parlor, which seemed like a good place to start. Two half-naked girls with dead eyes were perched on the glossy surface of the bar at both ends, listlessly gyrating to earsplitting house music that sounded like a cat trapped in a dishwasher.

Geddy nodded politely to the girl at the front and made his way toward the far end where the heavily muscled bartender was cleaning glasses. If memory served, he'd had the same job on Earth 2 at a place called Nebula Nick's, which Geddy didn't frequent.

"Howdy, pardner," he said, tilting his leather cowboy hat upward. "What's your poison?"

"I'm looking for a young kid about yea tall who looks like a happy mole rat with mutton chops."

The bartender leaned in conspiratorially. "That's pretty specific. Give me until this afternoon."

Geddy rolled his eyes. "I mean, I'm trying to find my friend."

"Oh." He jutted his chin toward the far side of the bubble, where an altercation had just spilled out into the open courtyard. "Is that him?"

It was Denk all right, jabbing his finger accusingly at a guy twice his size outside the entrance to a place called Tiki Tommy's. He couldn't make anything out over the music.

He thanked the guy and broke into a run across the sparkling expanse, arriving a moment after the bouncer shoved Denk away, knocking him flat on his ass.

"Whoa, whoa, what the hell, dude?" He helped Denk to his feet. "You okay?"

"Hey, Geddy." Denk brushed himself off. "This jerk needs a lesson in manners!"

"You know this kis?" growled the bouncer.

"Yeah, what's the big idea?"

Denk scowled. "They won't serve me."

Geddy's eyes narrowed at the bouncer. "Why not?"

He pumped his palms in calming motion. "His ID says he's only fourteen. You need to be at least fifteen."

"Fourteen in *Durandian years!*" protested Denk. "That's like twenty-seven. Tell him, Ged!"

"Okay, okay, let's lower the temperature here," said Geddy. "What if he's with me? Seems you could use the business."

He glanced behind him at the completely empty bar and pursed his lips. "All right, but sit at the back."

Geddy smoothed Denk's clothes and patted him on the back. "See? We call that a spoonful of sugar. Speaking of which, let's get ourselves some tropical beverages. Come on."

He purposely bumped into the bouncer as he passed. He was huge but doughy. If it came to it, Geddy liked his odds.

They settled onto stools at the far end of the dimly lit tiki bar. Geddy ordered two margaritas from the dour, middle-aged woman behind the bar, who eyed them disapprovingly.

"What's in a margarita?" asked Denk.

"Lime juice and regret. You'll like it."

Denk frowned and shook his head. "Sorry, Geddy. I've got a real bad temper sometimes."

"Nothing wrong with standing up for yourself."

"Easy for you to say," he grumbled.

The woman delivered their drinks in glasses the size of Denk's head. "Jesus," Geddy said. "We might need an insulin chaser."

"Fifty," she said flatly.

"Oh yeah? You don't look a day over forty-six."

Her puffy face reddened with irritation. "Fifty *credits*."

"For two tequila smoothies? High overhead, I guess." Geddy slapped down three twenty-credit squares and slid them across the bar. She swept them up in one of her meathooks and glared, muttering to herself as she walked away. "The tip's for your charm school application." They raised their fishbowl glasses and clinked them together. "To bitter women, for making the rest seem that much sweeter."

Denk took a tentative sip and grinned broadly. "Oh, that's good."

Geddy slurped from his and wrinkled his nose. Sugar water, as expected. "Just imagine how good it would be with booze in it."

His young friend regarded him with a strange smile, shaking his head. "I don't know how you do it."

"Do what?"

"Be so … fearless."

He frowned. "What are you talking about? You fly fearlessly."

"Flying's different," said Denk, his eyes darkening. "On the ground, I'm just a nothing. Durandia wasn't much better."

"Why'd you leave? If you don't mind me asking."

He got a faraway look. "There was this girl. Pyna. I asked her to be my mate, but so did this other guy, Ingo. When Durandian men vie for the same girl's hand, they fight."

"And? Did you stomp his stupid face?"

Denk gave a rueful shake of his head. "I was so sure I'd be humiliated that I stowed away on a supply ship the night before. I never went back."

"That's not why you left."

"How would you know?" he asked, mildly offended.

"You weren't afraid of humiliation. You were afraid of watching this Ingo asshole wind up with your girl. I call that pain management."

"Call it what you want, Geddy, but I'm a big coward."

"Then I guess that makes two of us."

He perked up. "What do you mean?"

Geddy's finger made slow laps around the base of the huge glass as he spoke. "Oh, I've mastered the art of running away. From grief. From responsibility. Even from love."

Denk frowned, confused. "But you're not running now."

Since he wasn't entirely sure about that, he gave a pained smirk. "All's I know is, you can't run toward something without running away from something else. That takes courage. The way I see it, you ran from a hole in the ground all the way to the stars."

— *Oh, Geddy. That was lovely.*

The kid's eyes turned glassy and he gave a sheepish grin. "I never looked at it that way."

He took one more sip of his drink and grimaced, then patted Denk on the back. "Come on. Let's get the parts we need for the *Fiz* before our sugar crash."

"But our drinks ..." he protested, sliding off the stool and following Geddy out.

The bartender's eyes darted back and forth between them and the barely touched margaritas.

"Those aren't drinks, they're cries for help," he said, giving her a sly wink. "Thanks, Smiley, but the circus of sadness is leaving town."

CHAPTER 20
PRETENSIA

Following their less-than-hospitable trip into the Bubbles, Geddy and Denk returned to the spaceport to see about parts for the *Fiz*. As he feared, though, prices were exorbitant, and there was no telling how long their Caloth money would have to last. Geddy felt badly for getting a lift from them.

"What do you think, Denk?" asked Oz from the *Dom's* screen.

"Geddy's right — parts here are just too expensive," Denk replied, checking for Geddy's agreement. "We could burn a novasphere to Thegus or something and still be money ahead."

Oz considered this briefly, then addressed Geddy directly. "What about you? Did your ex know who took your ship?"

"Yes, but not where to find him. I know a guy who might be able to help, but he's in Pretensia."

"Pretensia?" Oz asked, suddenly interested. "So, he's old and rich?"

"Those aren't the first adjectives I'd use, but yeah."

He was referring to Tev Joclen, a hustler who tried to sell counterfeit Zelnad weapons to his boss on Kigantu. Tretiak's orders were to kill him, but Tev showed him such a good time, he couldn't quite bring himself to do it. Geddy let him live under the condition he check into Pretensia and never leave. Tev appreciated the gesture and said he owed him one. The time had come to collect.

Tev had about ten years on Geddy and always fancied himself to be a big player in black-market goods. That wasn't necessarily true, but he did know an awful lot of people. If anyone could point him to Sammo, it was Tev.

"I've never been," Oz said.

"Me, neither," Denk agreed. "I wouldn't even know how to get in."

As heartening as it was to have their help, Tev wasn't exactly the kind of guy people were glad to know.

Geddy shook his head. "I can't ask you to take me there. Besides, they're not equipped for major repairs."

"Sure, but it's easy in and out, right?" asked Denk.

Pretensia was an artificial moon sandwiched between the binary gas giants Yedol and Lodey, virtually identical color-shifting planets on the doorstep of the amusingly named Two-Fist Nebula. Stopping there wouldn't put any added stress on the ship, but it only stood to help Geddy's own predicament, not theirs.

"I guess we're saying we don't have anywhere better to be," said Oz. "Besides, I'm ready to get off this boat for a while."

Geddy threw up his hands. "All right, Pretensia it is. We'll have them touch up the weld on that patch and head back to the *Fiz*."

"I'll leave the lights on," Oz said with a wink, and the screen blinked out.

A very long time ago, before the collapse of the Alliance, a wealthy Eyerian named Dewarnes bought a decommissioned research station and turned it into his own private paradise for retirees at the edge of charted space. The story held that he wanted to make it as hard as possible for his in-laws to visit.

Pretensia was positioned in a gravitational equilibrium between the two planets in what Dewarnes called a "resonant flux envelope." It was just technobabble, but he understood that there was a force in the universe more powerful and influential than gravity itself:

Marketing.

He convinced his investors that the so-called flux envelope dramatically slowed the aging process. In reality, he and his wife just ate right and exercised. But the more people who came to see for themselves, the more Dewarnes expanded the station. Over time, it grew large enough to be considered an artificial moon.

"Wow," muttered Denk as he decelerated. "I had no idea it was so big."

"That's what she said," chuckled Oz.

"I heard it's even bigger on the inside," Geddy added with a wink, "and that's what *he* said."

— *A woman who makes dad jokes? You must be smitten.*

— No comment.

The other ships docked around the main visitor entrance made the *Fizmo* look like a floating turd. Anyone who was here to gamble or get laid needed the time, money, and novaspheres to do it. They had precious few of these.

A young man appeared onscreen as the ship eased closer to its assigned dock. He had a thin face and a long nose that wrinkled as though he'd just caught a whiff of something foul. His nasally voice dripped with judgment, each sentence sounding like a question.

"*For Sale By Owner*, I'm showing that you're still using the super old V7 airlock connector? Is that correct?"

"Everything's original on this girl," Denk smugly assured him. "Except for all the parts we've had to replace. Well, and the hold. And the dropship. And the bidet."

He pursed his lips and gave his head a little shake. "Um, yeah, that's gonna be a little bit of a problem? Because we use the new V11 so we have to, like, get an adapter? And it's in storage, so … yeah."

Geddy stepped into his field of vision. "No problem. We'll just hang out here until you find it."

"Okay, but it might sort of be a while? We're, like, *super* busy. Assuming you just stopped by to grab some snacks or use the restroom, I think maybe the spaceport on Zorr might be more your style?"

"Relax, skinny, we're here to see a resident," said Geddy.

Irritation passed over his face. "May I have the name?"

"Tev Joclen."

He typed the name into a nearby terminal. "Mmm hmm. And is Mr. Joclen expecting you?"

"Nope."

"I do see that he is a resident here, but of course I'll need to ring him. May I have your name, please?"

"Starheart. Geddy Starheart."

"One moment."

The affected young man blinked out for a couple minutes then returned to say someone would be along with an airlock adapter shortly. Tev would meet them in the visitor lounge, beyond which only residents and invited guests could pass.

Geddy rifled through the closet in the crew quarters in search of more appropriate clothes, though Oz already told him he wouldn't find any. She followed him back and leaned against the door with her arms crossed.

"How do you know this guy, anyway?"

"I was sent to kill him."

Oz laughed, waiting for him to say he was joking. "Wait — you're serious?"

"He was an arms broker who tried to sell fake Zelnad weapons to my boss. He took a dim view of that."

One uniform looked newer than what he had on, but it was two sizes too small. He frowned and slid the door shut with a groan.

"Told you. So why didn't you? Kill him, I mean."

"He didn't know his stuff was fake, and we had too good a time together. I told him if he got out of the game and stayed here, then he could owe me one."

He shuffled past her, their chests briefly touching in the narrow corridor, and gave her a polite smile as he returned to the bridge. The docking crew was in spacesuits retrofitting the airlock with some clunky step-up adapter. It had probably collected dust for years.

Denk stood in front of a small mirror smoothing his hair.

"Hopefully Tev'll let us clean up at his place," Geddy said, dampening a washcloth at the bathroom sink to wipe a dried glob of nutrimush from his collar.

A red light over the airlock flipped to green. He opened the door and strode through with Oz and Denk in tow.

"No Morph?"

"It's not his scene," Oz said. "Besides, he usually prefers to stay with the ship."

Geddy wondered what that could possibly mean but could see how a dirty wad of phlegm might not fit in.

An attractive female android wearing a navy-blue skirt and jacket greeted them with a blinding white smile. "Hello, Mr. Starheart and guests. I'm Daia, one of Pretensia's visitor envoys. Please follow me to the lounge. I believe Mr. Joclen is on his way."

"Great," Geddy said, mildly disappointed she didn't bring hors d'oeuvres or sparkling water.

"So, how much?" asked the android.

"How much?" asked Geddy.

"For the ship."

"It's not really for sale."

"Then its name is for ironic effect?"

"Something like that." His eyes drifted down to her artificial ass as she sashayed away, and once again couldn't help but think of Tatiana.

A shocking number of visitors milled about the vast oval lobby. Some held drinks from the little bar in the corner as they perused the pop art on display around the perimeter. Others were queued at the Information Desk. A portly woman in the gift shop held a gaudy pink T-shirt up to herself that said *My parents retired to Pretensia and still can't afford this shirt* as her husband nodded yes, that's the one.

"Ooh, I want one!" said Denk.

Geddy snaked his way through the crowd to a doorway marked *Registered Guests* and immediately faced a security checkpoint. A burly bot stepped in front of him and held up its stout metal hands.

"Registered guests only."

"It's okay, we're on the list."

"Name?"

Tev appeared from behind the bot wearing khakis and a casual jacket with a checkered dress shirt underneath. He looked ten years younger than when Geddy last saw him. Either he'd gotten some work done, or there was actually something to this flux BS.

"Tev Joclen!" Geddy exclaimed.

The bot stepped aside and gestured them through. Geddy smiled and extended his hand, but Tev went straight for the hug. He was one of the few humans in the weapons trade back in the day, which might have been why they hit it off. Dealing with Xellarans and Screvari day in, day out got tiring. Humans were every bit as conniving and greedy, of course, but at least they knew how to have a good time.

Funny what you missed sometimes.

"What the hell, amigo? I heard you were dead."

"And you should keep thinking that. Listen, I want you to meet the crew of the *Fizmo*. This is Oz, the first officer, and Denk, the pilot. I hitched a ride with them."

Tev greeted them with hugs as well, lingering a bit too long on Oz.

"Any friend of Starheart's is a friend of mine. Come on, I'll give you the dime tour and let you get cleaned up. I'll have some clothes delivered for later. Oz, I'm guessing you're about a six?"

"Are you kidding me?" joked Geddy. "She's at least a nine."

She glared at him, her smile vanishing. "Six is fine, thanks."

"And Denk?" he scratched his chin. "I'm gonna say a thirty-two extra short for the jacket?"

"Jacket?" asked Denk, looking at Geddy with mild panic in his eyes.

Tev winked and flashed a toothy grin. "Don't sweat it, boss. Papa Joc's gotcha covered."

They rode an escalator up through a tastefully lit tunnel. As they passed through the opening, their ears filled with the sounds of a hangar-like space that Geddy recognized immediately from pictures and videos. He'd long dreamt of seeing it.

"The Grand Promenade," Tev declared, rolling the Rs as he swept his hand across the cavernous expanse. "Entertainment. Gambling. Food. Drinks. Carnival games. We just got something called Skee-Ball, some game they used to play on Old Earth. It's a hoot. If you guys come down here on your own, just put everything on my tab. Whatever you want."

A giant dome covered the Promenade, its view of the nebula partly obscured by towering roller coasters and at least two multi-level bars. Stone paths snaked between verdant sprays of flowering plants teeming with gawkers. Overhead, tiny ships zipped through a course of floating rings. Clearly, this was more for kids. Denk was mesmerized.

"Where's Grown-Up Land?" asked Geddy.

Tev chuckled. "That's where we're headed. Now, listen, I'll have to take you down a service corridor on account of your … you know." He looked them up and down then kept walking.

He led them through a side door and down a long hallway where they only passed employees. They regarded everyone but Tev with thinly veiled disdain.

Several minutes later, they arrived at a bank of elevators under a sign marked "Residences: Tower 4." A uniformed young man examined Tev's credentials and nodded. Tev leaned in and whispered, slipping a fifty-credit square into his palm as he did.

"Right away, sir."

They boarded the next elevator and rocketed up the side of the tower, giving them their first uncluttered view of the binary planets. A faint blue cloud enveloped the whole facility with long, bright streaks that reminded Geddy of melting cheese.

— *That must be the flux field.*

— I was starting to wonder when you'd weigh in.

— *This is where you want to live?*

— That's the plan. Why?

— *Doesn't seem like you.*

— Relax, we're not even to the good part.

— *Oz didn't appreciate your joke.*

— I meant it as a compliment.

— *She didn't take it that way.*

— Okay, Mom. Jeez.

The elevator dumped them into a short hallway. Denk was peppering Tev with questions about the facility, so Geddy dropped back a bit to walk abreast with Oz, whose lips still formed a straight line.

"Hey, I didn't mean to offend you back there."

She cocked an eyebrow. "You really think I'm a nine?"

He smiled warmly. "Inside and out."

"Well, here we are," Tev said as a door hissed open.

Tev's place wasn't palatial by any means, but it was very nicely appointed. He strode to the window and pulled aside the curtains. Unlike the elevator ride, his window faced away from the planets.

"Wow, great view of ... open space," Geddy said. "No planets or colors to muddy it up."

"Yeah," Tev said, absently scratching his head. "I started out in a planet-view suite, but I was hardly ever there. I didn't come here to stare out the window, right? Anyway, make yourselves at home. Geddy, maybe when you're ready we can go grab a bite and catch up."

"Sounds good."

Geddy couldn't get in the shower fast enough. Compared to the sad trickle of yellow water that passed for a shower aboard the *Fizmo*, it was like standing under a warm, tropical waterfall. Soft music played through hidden speakers as accumulated dirt and grime washed away.

— I could get used to this.

— *I get a weird vibe from your friend.*

— What do you mean?

— *I don't think he's entirely okay.*

— Ah, that's just Tev. He's always been a little rough around the edges.

As he dried off, he caught a glimpse of himself in the heated mirror, something he couldn't recall doing even once since the last transport left The Deuce. The penthouse was practically a hall of mirrors, of course, but he'd never stopped to look. He needed a shave and a haircut, but otherwise he was pretty pleased. Apparently sweating his ass off all day agreed with him.

— *So, that's what you look like.*

— What are you talking about?

— *You never so much as paused in front of a mirror.*

— Really?

— *Only as a child. In the home videos.*

Once the steam cleared, he noticed a set of clothes hanging on the back of the door, an ensemble strikingly similar to Tev's. He dragged a comb through his hair and got dressed, then offered the bathroom up to Oz, who was clearly eager to remove herself from Tev's admittedly creepy company. A black dress was draped over her arm.

She leaned in and whispered, "I don't like him. Or this place."

"It's means to an end. As soon as I get what I need from him, we're gone. I promise."

"Okay." Her bright eyes passed appreciatively over him. "You clean up pretty good."

He gave a wink. "A solid six, six and a half?"

"I'd go as high as eight. Unless you're talking."

"That's fair."

Tev appeared behind her, hitching up his pants. "Whoa, get a load of you, Starheart. Or should I say, Starheart-*breaker*? Heh, heh."

Oz's polite smile disappeared as her head swung back to Geddy. "See you downstairs."

CHAPTER 21

ENTRÉE NEW

The maitre d' at the restaurant called Coeur D'étoile was Kailorian, like the late Captain Bykite but shorter. He introduced himself as Belvinar and proffered heavy, leather-bound menus with an expert flourish of his dainty hands.

"Tonight's appetizer special is an exquisitely delicate preparation of fresh mogorodon polyps in a basil bubble on a white truffle parsnip fleur-de-lis with smoked blue algae dust. A colorful and verisimilitudinous interpretation of Earth 3 on a plate. It's very nice."

Geddy had quite enough of mogorodons, say nothing of eight-syllable words, but after hearing what Tatiana said about selling their parts to gourmets, his curiosity was piqued. He decided to play along and pretend he was the rich prick he always dreamt of becoming.

"I've only had polyps once. My proctologist told me to eat more vegetables."

Belvinar puckered his blue lips and sniggered nasally like he'd only seen laughing described in a book. "How delightfully droll."

This was just the kind of guy he liked to have a little fun with. He cleared this throat and looked down his nose at the menu. "Now these polyps ... were they humanely harvested?"

"Oh, yes. The creatures are treated well, and our diver-farmers receive years of training. The ones who survive must meet stringent continuing education requirements."

Geddy scratched the back of his head, smirking at Tev, who was enjoying this little flight of fancy. "I dunno. If you've had one mogorodon polyp, you've had them all, know what I mean?"

The waiter's eye twitched, his lips forced into a patient smile despite his reddening face. He looked like he wanted to punch something. "I assure you, sir, *our* polyps are second to none. They're brought in fresh each day from Earth 3 and slow cured in their own husks. The result is a more tender, buttery polyp. An orgy of taste and texture building to an explosion of flavor on the tongue."

— *That's what she said?*

– Easy layup. But, you're learning.

"You know what?" Tev said, slapping his palms on the table to put an exclamation point on Geddy's act. "It's a special occasion. Two tongue explosions for the table, garçon."

"Excellent, sir." He gave a tight nod and clicked his heels together before gliding off toward the kitchen.

"Well," said Tev, leaning back in his chair. "I know you didn't just come here for the polyps."

"I'm looking for someone named Sammo Yann."

"Sammo Yann ..." Tev's eyes darkened, and he chuckled to himself as he ran the tip of his finger idly around the rim of his ale glass. "Haven't heard that name in a long time."

"How do you know him, but I don't?"

"Ah, you know how it is with these freelancers. Never in one place for very long. He's a ghost."

"So I've been told. How do you know him?"

He let out a long sigh and took a swig of his ale. "Years back, I went to pick up a shipment of Gundrun armor. All's I got is a set of coordinates, which take me to the middle of the Elenian Belt."

— Hey, we were just there! Small world.

— Shh.

"The only way for me to physically get there is to do an EVA. The whole time, I'm thinking this can't be right. But sure as shit, one of these billions of asteroids has a cargo door."

"*On* the asteroid?"

"That's what I thought. Anyway, the door opens and in walks this older Soturian in a spacesuit and mag boots."

Hollowing out an asteroid for your stash was next-level dedication. But a well-hidden arms warehouse in the Elenian Belt was logistically ideal.

"And?"

He shrugged. "Dude was all business. I clipped the crate of armor to my belt and towed it back to *Allie*." He was referring to his souped-up smuggling ship, *Allegro*.

"I don't suppose you know how I'd find him now," said Geddy.

"Why you looking for him? Don't tell me you're back in the game."

"No, no, nothing like that," he said quickly. "He took something from me. A ship."

"What kind of ship?"

"The fast and impractical kind."

"Midlife crisis," Tev said knowingly.

Thousands of years ago on Old Earth, it was canoes or cars. Now it was spaceships. That's not what this was, but Tev didn't have to know that.

He held out his open hands and shrugged. "Is it that obvious?"

The waiter reappeared carrying a blue bottle filled with

liquid and gently cleared his throat. "Gentlemen, to start you off, I'd like to offer our house-made artisanal sparkling water." He caressed the bottle as though it was the baby in an ancient prophecy. "The water is made from pure elemental hydrogen and imported oxygen, filtered fourteen times through our exclusive process, and then distilled. Our chef personally exhales for three hours every day to make the bubbles."

"Which three hours?" Geddy asked.

"You should try it," Tev said. "It has a little different character each time depending on the chef's mood and what he had to eat."

"Sounds expensive," said Geddy.

"Don't worry about it."

"When on Pretensia ..."

Tev gave a little nod, and the waiter poured half a glass of the water for both of them, ensuring not a single drop was spilled. "Very good, gentlemen. I'll return shortly with your polyps." He disappeared with the bottle.

Geddy sniffed at the water and took a tentative sip. It tasted like any other sparkling water, albeit with a faint soupçon of morning breath. Is this how people ate here every day? What if you just wanted pizza and beer?

"Oh, that's *good.*" Tev smacked his lips.

"Best breath water I've had all day. Now about my ship ..."

"Ah yes. What is it? Freighter? Fighter?"

"Recreational. A twin-engine one-seater."

Tev leaned forward with a dubious smirk. "Why would Sammo come all the way to The Deuce just to steal some little kit ship?"

Geddy was about to answer when Belvinar returned trailed by three younger waiters who formed a semicircle beside the table.

"Gentlemen, your polyps." He and Tev leaned back as the

waiter set the covered platters down in front of them, handling the plates as though a jostle would ruin the artful presentation.

He jutted his chin toward the other servers. "I wasn't expecting an audience."

Belvinar gave a bemused snort. "They are here for emotional support and to congratulate you on your choice."

With that, he whisked the covers away in perfect unison, revealing plates so big they almost met in the middle of the table. Smack dab in the center was a tiny pink sac the size of a marble covered by a small, cloudy bubble and sitting on a leaf-shaped smear of pale-yellow puree. Grayish green dust was sprinkled around it that resembled something you'd scrape off a dry-docked sailboat.

Belvinar continued, "The basil bubble represents the Bubbles on Earth 3, of course. The puree, the ocean floor, and of course, the algae dust suggests the ocean."

"Such an inspiration," said one of the young servers, his hand over his heart. "Thank you for your order."

"I'll never forget where I was," agreed another, his eyes turning glassy.

Tev sat back again to allow the servers to team-spread his napkin over his lap. Geddy reluctantly did likewise, half expecting a tug job. They stood shoulder-to-shoulder with Belvinar and watched in reverent silence, their hands folded in front of them.

Tev popped the bubble with his fork, releasing a tiny cloud of vapor, and stabbed the glistening pink nugget. After swirling it in the vapor, Tev dabbed it in the puree before easing it into his mouth. The servers clapped politely.

His eyes rolled back in his head just before he closed them, slowly chewing. "Mmm … they really are the jewels of the colon."

"Maybe they should call it an assetizer," Geddy quipped.

"I think that's a marital aid," returned Tev.

Geddy reluctantly imitated what Tev had done, basil-tinged air and all, before taking the one and only bite. He expected it to be the nastiest thing he'd ever tasted, but it was exactly the opposite, slightly briny, with the texture of a perfectly creamy egg yolk. He really didn't know what a polyp was made of, but in the moment he didn't care.

"Holy shit," he muttered.

"See?" said Tev, raising his glass of breath-infused water. "Tell me I don't know how to live large."

The younger servers whisked the giant plates away and returned to the kitchen. Geddy leaned over the table.

"Listen, about Sammo, all I know is he took my ship as payment for a job. Now, if he was trying to turn it into cash, where would he …" An electric dread seized him.

He didn't need to say it out loud. Knowing Sammo Yann was a freelancer who would want top dollar for the ship, there was only one place to take it. He hadn't thought about it until now because he didn't want to think about it at all.

Kigantu.

"Fuck."

— *Kigantu. Isn't that where–*

— Don't say it. I'm not ready to hear it. I'm not even ready to think it.

Tev was about to say something when a crisply dressed man approached, flanked by two Saraks in tuxedoes.

"Mr. Joclen, yes?"

"Who's asking?" asked Tev, annoyed by the interruption.

"I'm Liam Dewhold, executive director of operations. May we have a word in private?"

CHAPTER 22

MINOR MONEY MISUNDERSTANDING

Geddy absently sipped his breath water, watching with great interest as the stern manager engaged in an animated, finger-wagging conversation with Tev. At one point, the two Saraks had to intervene to calm him down.

After a while, Tev held up his hands and nodded, smoothing his shirt and hair as he returned to the table, his face reddened by anger, embarrassment, or both.

"Sorry about that." He sat back down and huffed. "I'll have that little weasel sacked for this. Now, where were we?"

"What was that all about?"

He gave a dismissive wave of his hand. "Ah, some snafu with my account. You'd think these people would know basic accounting."

"Well, do you need to take care of it?" Geddy thumbed over his shoulder. "Because I can go and–"

Again, he batted the idea away. "No, no. You're my guest and we're having a nice dinner. Those pricks can blow me."

"If you say so."

Tev nervously ran his fingers along the edge of the table,

never quite meeting Geddy's eyes. "It's just that, y'know, until we get it sorted, I might need you to … cover dinner."

The restaurant's menu had no prices on it, but he'd assumed that meant Tev was on some all-inclusive plan. Apparently not. Imported mogorodon polyps had to be pricey. The funeral costs for the divers alone …

"Yeah, sure, no problem," Geddy said. "It's the least I can do. And you know me, I always do the least I can."

His old acquaintance laughed a bit too loudly at this, then he took a long drink of his water, so thirstily some trickled out the side. He wiped his chin and leaned forward.

"See, amigo, the thing is, I'm a little overextended."

As long as Geddy had known him, Tev lived at the outermost edge of his means. Running weapons was lucrative, but not enough to justify his flashy, extravagant lifestyle. He was always buying rounds or giving gifts like he was desperate for friends. Geddy was never quite sure where all the money came from.

"How overextended, exactly?"

The maître d' appeared again, rubbing his hands together. "Gentlemen, are you ready to look at some entrées? We have a walnut-crusted spignork loin that is simply–"

"Actually, we'll just take the check," Geddy said, his eyes not leaving Tev.

Belvinar's long face shortened as it fell. "Very good, sir. Mr. Joclen, is there a problem with–"

"It's fine," said Geddy. "We'll pay cash."

"Cash." He flared his highly arched eyebrows. "How quaint. I'll be right back."

"How overextended, Tev?" He asked through gritted teeth.

"Two hundred large, give or take," he muttered.

"What?"

"This place … they nickel and dime ya to death. These waters alone are fifty each. It's highway robbery!"

"Says the man who ordered mogorodon polyps like French fries."

As if on cue, Belvinar appeared with the check and set it down, clearly annoyed they weren't ordering any more. "Whenever you're ready."

Geddy slid the bill over to the edge of the table and reluctantly opened it just wide enough to see inside. Their water and polyp meal came out to almost nine hundred credits, not including gratuity. He had to cough to keep his throat from closing.

— Is that a lot?

— For two waters and an appetizer the size of a kidney stone? Yes, Eli. It is.

He dug into his pocket and counted out the cash, leaving twenty percent for Belvinar and Co., and downed the rest of his water as he rose.

"Sure you don't want a bottle of wine?" Tev asked. "Your friends should be down any minute."

Geddy gave him the stinkeye and pushed in his chair, hustling outside with Tev at his heels.

"Whaddya say, old friend?" Tev said. "Help a brother out?"

He spun around. "Do I look like I've got two hundred grand? What's the matter with you?"

"You don't understand, Ged. These guys play hardball. If I don't get square with them by the end of the month, they'll terminate my residency."

"Good! You clearly shouldn't be here. Nobody should except fat-cat douchebags who want to buy into an alternate reality." He said it a bit louder than intended, drawing a few displeased stares from tables nearby. "What? That's verbatim from the brochure!"

"What should I do?"

"I dunno, man, but you'd better get it sorted." He dug in

his pocket and threw a thousand credits on the table, which Tev eyed hungrily. "I'm gonna go find Oz and Denk."

He got up to leave, but Tev grabbed his arm. "Geddy, please. If I don't pay up, those Saraks'll put *me* on the menu."

He ripped his arm away. "Not my problem. Thanks for the tip on Sammo. Maybe I'll see you around."

Five steps later, Tev's voice came from behind him. "Then gimme back those clothes."

Geddy spun around. "Seriously?"

Tev's eyes were pleading and desperate. "Come on, man. Let's go back to the room, cool off, and figure something out over a cocktail like old times. Whaddya say?"

He'd dreamt of this place for so long. Visions of boisterous storytelling and cigars with fascinating old crooks had played over and over again in his head. At least, that's how he remembered it from his previous visit. But it wasn't like that anymore. Not by a long shot.

Geddy guffawed and shook his head. "You want your clothes back, Tev? Here. You clearly need 'em more than I do."

He whipped off the jacket and threw it at Tev but didn't stop there. The shoes, pants, belt, and shirt came next. A few seconds later, he was standing in his underwear right outside the restaurant and Tev stood in a puddle of clothes.

"There's about fourteen hundred cash in my pocket. Consider it payment for the information. Maybe you can even get dessert."

As horrified onlookers took a wide detour around them, Oz and Denk appeared.

Oz was wrapped in an elegant, form-fitting black dress slit high up the sides, with a set of matching pumps that made her tower even higher over Denk. Her ropy, blood-red hair practically glowed, her cheeks rosy and youthful. And she smelled like jasmine.

Denk, on the other hand, was wearing a sport coat with a

garish yellow Pretensia T-shirt underneath. Presumably it, too, had gone on Dev's ever-rising tab.

"Hel-lo, Beautiful," said Tev, giving a low whistle. "I never gave Temerurian women much credit, but *damn*."

She and Denk had been smiling brightly when they first appeared on the walkway, clearly looking forward to a night out, but Tev's leering comment and Geddy's state of undress quickly erased their smiles.

She cocked an eye at Geddy. "Can I punch him? Because I'd really like to."

The threat only seemed to excite Tev all the more. "And a sparkplug to boot," he said, grinning lasciviously. "That's a rare combo."

Geddy lifted his chin to Oz. "Make it count."

Tev opened his mouth to issue a phony apology, but he didn't get to say it because Oz's fist shot out and popped him in the Adam's apple. His eyes widened in panic as he stumbled back, trying to force air through his pinched trachea. The Saraks noticed the altercation and strode angrily toward them.

"Time to go." Geddy corralled her and Denk in front of him at a brisk walk toward the entrance to the Grand Promenade.

"Can I take off this jacket? It's hot," Denk said, looking back anxiously over his shoulder as his stubby legs struggled to keep up.

"Keep it," Geddy replied. "Oz, same goes for you."

"Why?"

"Because we're all going to the Double A."

CHAPTER 23

THE RED RAVEN

The *Fizmo* had barely disconnected from the dock before Geddy's inner conflict about his experience on Pretensia began eating at him again. His long, lonely time on The Deuce had hinged upon a very specific vision of what the retirement moon offered. But between mogorodon polyps, artisanal water, and entitlement, Tati might be right. It didn't suit him.

Still hungry, he worked the nutrimush lever over a clean bowl and sat alone in the galley, mindlessly shoveling the paste into his mouth and wishing it didn't bring him as much comfort as it did.

— *Your mind is unquiet.*

"It looks like my retirement plans might have to change."

— *Is it retirement you yearn for? Or is it the chance to stop running?*

"I know what you're going to say."

— *Oh?*

"That I need to face my past before I can embrace my future."

— *No, but that's actually pretty good.*

"What do you know? You're immortal."

— I'm not technically alive. Only a consciousness.

"What are you talking about?"

— I thought you understood.

"Understood what?"

— Until we reach Sagacea, you and I are are bound together.

"No, no … you're like a spark in my brain. If I die, you float into someone else's."

— That's not how it works. Your end is my end.

"You're telling me this *now*?"

"Who ya talking to?" asked Oz.

Geddy's eyes flew to the open galley door. He had no idea how long she'd been standing there, still in her slinky dress. Panic seized him.

"Just thinking out loud." He did his best to sound normal. "This whole Tev thing's got me in knots. Sorry you didn't get your night out."

Her eyes narrowed as though she was about to call him out on the lie, but she merely nodded. "Don't worry about it. I was just gonna hit the rack."

"You can stay," he said, a little too quickly. "I mean, if you want."

"Sure, why not?" She settled into the seat across from him. "Denk's got a vector to Kigantu, but it's a few hours away. He and Morph are running system checks on the warp shell."

"They need help?"

She waved her hand. "Nah, they're fine. So Pretensia wasn't all you imagined?"

"It's aptly named."

"It was fun to play dress-up for a night. Well, part of a night. Really just a trip down the elevator, but still."

"You look beautiful." He felt his face flush. There was only so much you could hide from a Temerurian woman. They were known to be deeply empathic. "And now you've got an outfit for the Double A."

"You weren't so bad yourself. I don't really care about putting on a show."

"You read my mind."

"I can't do that."

He gave a sheepish shrug. "Figure of speech."

"You don't need to hide your thoughts from me. I pick up on vibes sometimes. There's not much more to it than that. Whatever's going on in your head is your business, but if you ever want to talk, I'm here for you."

Even if she couldn't read his thoughts, she could read his emotions. Thinking about his mother stirred plenty.

"Well, hopefully my ship's still on Kigantu and I'll be out of your hair soon."

Denk burst into the galley wide-eyed and breathlessly excited, with Morpho perched on his shoulder like a tarred parrot. "Guys, you've gotta come see this!"

"What is it?" Oz sprang up from the table, hurrying out as fast as her dress allowed.

Geddy followed her and Denk out and turned toward the bridge as Denk explained over his shoulder. "I left the scanners running while Morph and I were working. They found this."

He dropped into his seat at the front and pulled up the display. It filled with the image of a Zelnad vessel about half the size of the *Fizmo*.

"There's not much out here. No telling how long it's been adrift."

"How do you know it's adrift?" asked Oz.

"No electrical activity, no drive signature, no transponder, no nothing. I hailed them, but no response. It's moving, but not that fast."

"Could be a trap," Geddy said.

"Can you tell where it came from based on its heading?" Oz asked.

Denk hemmed and hawed before answering. "The core systems, maybe. There's no way to know for sure."

Geddy pointed to a large bubble at the top of the ship's smooth, sleek surface, tapping it with his finger. "That looks like a sensor array. I don't see any obvious weapons. I'd wager this is some kind of deep-space recon ship. Basically a flying scanner."

"Damage?" Oz asked.

"Not from this angle. Should I send a drone to check it out?"

He threw a look back at Geddy as though seeking permission to proceed. Even Oz looked to him for a decision. An intact Zelnad ship would be worth millions.

— *He looks up to you, you know.*

— It's not just you and me anymore, Eli. You can't talk to me all the time. I can barely follow one conversation.

— *Sorry.*

"It's not my call."

"What if it was?" Oz asked.

Geddy wasn't unsympathetic to Denk and Oz's situation. Even with the late Captain Bykite and Morpho, they must've run themselves ragged keeping up with the big old ship. Sure, he could play captain for a while. But not before he got Eli home.

"How would we bring it in without a net?" asked Geddy.

"There's a tow cable. It's designed for rescues, but we can use the rear shield as a buffer. At least get it to where we can take a closer look," Oz explained.

That was a tempting option for such a big score. But after what happened with the Myadan-bound ship and the ranse, it gave him pause.

"Deploy the drone. If she's really out of commission, we'll tow it out of here."

"Aye, aye, C– Er, I mean, roger that."

Denk punched some controls and an old drone emerged from under the ship's nose, its round metallic shell scarred by blaster marks. Its little jets fired, and it drifted toward the disabled vessel.

"Little guy's taken a few hits," Geddy said.

"Yeah, and that's one of the good ones," said Denk. "Parts from the other three are still back on Caloth."

"Just be ready with one of those blue balls in case things go sideways. Something smells about this."

"At least it's not you anymore," Denk offered.

"I just can't imagine ... " he trailed off. From the corner of the display came a tiny glowing streak headed straight for the Zelnad ship, growing brighter as it went. He spun anxiously to Denk. "What's that?"

Through the front shield a trawler twice the size of the *Fizmo* had seemingly blinked into existence. It was a deep rust color but shiny and new.

"Shit, it's the *Red Raven*!" said Oz.

"Where the hell did it come from?" asked Geddy, incredulous. "Have you ever seen tech like that?" The question turned out to be rhetorical. "What's the protocol here?"

"Whoever nets it, gets it," said Oz.

"He's hailing us," Denk said, opening the frequency.

The Kailorian who appeared onscreen looked more or less like Captain Bykite and the snooty waiter.

"Well, well, if it isn't the *Jizzmo*," he sneered. "Maybe you should change your name to *For Trash, By Trash*."

— *That's actually a pretty good burn.*

His jaw set determinedly, Denk said,"This is our claim, Tompanov."

"That's where you're wrong, rodent face. I've been looking all over for this."

"Look!" Oz thrust her index finger at the ship. A bright yellow tractor beam shot out from a port beneath the *Raven's* bridge and started pulling the Zelnad vessel toward it. "He's already bringing it in."

"Better luck next time," Tompanov said. "If I were you, I'd be on my merry way."

"His weapons just went hot," Denk said. "What do we do?"

— *Can I say something?*

—Depends. Is it better than what I'd come up with?

— *Fire a novasphere, then use the warp shell as a shield and push it through the jump gate. Do a proper retrieval on the other side.*

Eli's idea was neither great nor elegant, but it could work. The *Fizmo* could do a quick burn and capture the derelict ship before the *Raven* hauled it in. The impact would easily break the tractor beam's hold.

"Denk," Geddy whispered. "How's the warp shell?"

"Strong and steady. Why?"

"Tell him he can have it and bring back your drone, then power up the warp shell. Gently run into it then launch a blue ball."

Denk cocked his head in confusion, then understanding washed over him. "You want to push it through a jumpgate?"

"Unless you've got a better idea."

"But technically, Tompanov beat us to it."

"So what? You see the salvage police anywhere?" Geddy turned to Oz. "Whaddya think?"

"It'd buy us time."

"That's all we need."

"Morph?" Oz said, looking upward. "One novasphere, if you please."

A little swinging noise came from among the wires and

brackets in the ceiling, then the little blob dropped down and flung open a storage panel in the wall. He retrieved one of the expensive, baseball-sized novaspheres and again dropped it into the launch tube.

Denk activated the comm. "*Raven,* we don't want any trouble. We'll be on our way in a jiffy."

"Too bad. I thought we might duke it out like the old days. Speaking of old, where's your so-called captain?"

"He's ... uh ... in the shitter."

Geddy smacked his face with his hands and shook his head. These two were way too nice for this business. Denk nudged the stick toward the motionless ship as the wheezy old drone made its way back.

Tompanov gave a self-satisfied smile. "I'm surprised you have two novaspheres to rub together. I figured you'd be burning coal by now."

"What if they're really stranded?" Oz whispered.

"Then I guess they'll feel a jolt and wake up in another galaxy. I used to call it Friday night."

"It's a big risk," she warned.

"It's a big get. Risk comes with it."

"Denk, what are you doing?" asked Tompanov. "You're on a collision course."

"We've, um, temporarily lost directional thrusters," Denk said. "Resetting now."

He tapped a few screens and the drone returned to its place under the ship. They were seconds from impact, the derelict vessel nearly filling the screen. Geddy and Oz settled into their seats and tightened the restraints.

"What kind of stunt is this?" demanded Tompanov. "Reverse course or I will fire!"

"Everybody hang on!" said Denk.

The translucent warp shell collided head-on with the Zelnad ship, the impact thundering in Geddy's chest as he slammed forward into the straps. Denk recovered and expanded the shell around their quarry, then quickly accelerated.

"You were warned!" said Tompanov.

Denk said, "Ha! I'd like to see you– Whup, he just fired at us."

"Launch it, Denk!"

"We're not quite on our vector yet!"

"We're close enough. Just get us the hell out of here!" Geddy yelled.

He threw the switch and launched the novasphere into space. When it burst, the aperture peeled open straight ahead. At the same time, a pulsing red torpedo rocketed toward them.

"It's gonna be close!" Denk hollered, wincing.

He gave a banshee scream as the *Fiz* barreled through the jumpgate a blink before the torpedo hit. When they emerged into a powerfully sunny afternoon, they were face to face with a mountain.

CHAPTER 24

KIGANTU

Entering a jumpgate at any point other than the one precisely calculated by a ship's nav system was a dicey proposition. Since the vast majority of space was, well, space, usually the worst that could happen was exiting the gate much further from your destination than you intended. Sure, there were stories about ships that jumped straight into stars or planet cores but they were just stories.

Geddy didn't even know it was possible to jump into atmosphere, yet there they were, hurtling toward a mountain.

— *Life sure has thrown you some curveballs lately.*

At least the atmosphere they'd jumped into appeared to be Kigantu's.

If they decelerated or changed course, the Nad vessel would wrench free of the warp shell and likely slam into the ground. But then they'd clip the jagged peak.

Fire peeled off the edges of the shell. It was designed to handle the forces of an event horizon for a millisecond, not an uncontrolled entry at a bad angle. They had seconds.

"I'm firing the retros!" Denk reached for the button.

"No!" The whining engine and the thundering turbulence

swallowed his voice. "We'll lose the Nad ship and crash anyway! Take out the mountaintop! Everything you've got! Fire! Fire! Fire!"

Denk's hands flew expertly over the controls as he launched all the *Fizmo's* torpedoes and fired all disruptors at once. There was a sharp *pop-pop-pop* as their full arsenal, such as it was, launched from the belly and sides. The torpedoes whizzed underneath the Nad ship in front of them and converged with the disruptor blasts on the peak. The old ship shook so violently, Geddy thought his teeth might shatter.

— *I h-h-h-ope this w-w-w-w-orks.*

— M-m-me t-t-t-ooo.

Their full payload exploded, and for a short time, the mountain looked like an erupting volcano. Car-sized chunks of rock exploded skyward, trailing dust like daytime fireworks. The shockwave expanded at the speed of sound until it slammed into them like a wall, causing a dozen different alarms to sound as the ship threatened to snap in two.

"Warp shell integrity at twelve percent!" Denk warned.

"Just hold her steady!"

A massive dust cloud obscured the mountaintop. Between it and the ship blocking their vision, there was no way to tell whether they'd shaved off enough of it. The scanners had been jarred offline. They'd know for sure in a moment.

The *Fizmo* plunged into the dense veil of smoke and dust. Geddy closed his eyes and gritted his teeth, hoping like hell they didn't die today. Pebbles from the explosion pelted them as they skimmed over the flattened mountaintop by what couldn't have been more than a few meters, emerging into clear skies and a dune-rippled desert that stretched to the horizon.

All three of them whooped. Morpho flattened into a puddle as though heaving a sigh of relief. Denk feathered back on the engines little by little, the flashing screen indicating the warp shell was about to fail. Finally, they settled into a hover just above the rolling dunes.

"All right, now ease us down before the–" The warp shell gave out and the Nad ship dropped like a stone, landing with a jarring *thunk* in the sand. "Never mind."

"Look for a rocky spot to land," Geddy warned. "This sand is treacherous."

Denk deployed the skids and they touched down on a spot where winds had swept the sand from a table of bedrock. He sank back into his chair as he powered down the engines. "Everyone okay?"

"I think I ruptured a tit," Oz said, releasing her restraints.

Geddy did the same and rubbed his sore chest. "I'm no doctor, but I'd be happy to–" Oz silenced him with a glare.

"Well," Denk began, "we now have no weapons besides disruptors, no salvage net, no cargo, one slow-ass drone, and one last novasphere, which we can't use until we fix the warp shell."

"At least we have each other," Geddy quipped.

Oz rolled her eyes. "Where the hell are we?"

"Kigantu," Geddy said. "Never imagined that could be good news."

"You're sure?" she asked.

"Very."

Geddy rose and went to the bridge's weapon locker. A couple of rusting swords were parked in the corner, and a single antique blaster in its holster hung from a hook.

"Are you kidding me with this crap? Where are all your weapons?"

"Traded away," Oz said from over his shoulder. "Lost in bets. Stolen. You name it." She swung her own holster around her waist with practiced ease and buckled it. "In case you haven't noticed, we aren't exactly flush right now."

He jutted his chin at the blaster. "Does that thing shoot lasers or dried peas?"

"Come on, the Exeter D6?" she asked. "It's a modern classic."

"I'd be surprised if it could light a stove."

She shrugged. "Then don't take it."

It was better than nothing. Geddy checked the balance, wiped the dust off the barrel, and cinched the holster around his waist. Then he retrieved a short sword — a melee weapon was never a bad idea.

"All right. Let's see how badly that ship is damaged. Watch where you step because there's dry quicksand everywhere out here. And you'll want to cover your mouth and nose. Morph, stay with the ship."

Morpho gave a quick salute before slinging himself up into the vent. Geddy and Oz wrapped their heads in towels, while Denk decided to use his Pretensia T-shirt. Once they were ready, Oz opened the ramp. A blast of dust instantly turned them beige. They hurried down and closed it behind them.

Oz set her arms akimbo and swept her eyes across the flat, endless horizon as the ceaseless wind turned the very ground into a river of blowing grit.

"Real garden spot you've got here, Starheart."

"I know it ain't much," Denk said, nodding down to the blaster at Geddy's side. "but it's better than harsh language."

"Let's see about that."

Geddy pointed the blaster at a nearby sand dune and fired, surprised by the kick as a crater opened in the side. A burning smell briefly met his nostrils before the wind whipped it away.

"Told ya," Oz said.

"Not bad. Come on."

They struck out from under the protection of the ship, giving the Nad vessel an appropriately wide berth as they circled it in search of a door. The sleek, iridescent skin looked more like an organism than a ship.

When they reached what they agreed must be the back of the craft, they spotted a hatch. As luck would have it, the ship caught a rock when it fell those last few meters, twisting the airframe just enough to leave one corner exposed. Geddy half expected well-armed Nads to burst through and turn them to dust, however, it was a recon vessel. Its occupants would be nerds.

Oz ventured forward and gave the door a couple sharp raps with the butt of her pistol, then stepped back and leveled it at the ship. Nothing happened.

— *If there are Zelnads inside, would that make you pirates or kidnappers?*

— That's actually a good question.

Denk shrugged off his backpack, which had a handful of tools. "Let's crack it open."

He worked a pry bar into the corner of the twisted door while Geddy and Oz pulled. A little piece of the iridescent armor broke free and plunked into the sand. The void it left filled in before their eyes like a liquid.

Denk gasped with delight. "Wow, did you guys see that?"

Oz and Geddy exchanged worried looks. This was next-level tech. Curious, Geddy stepped forward to touch the strange skin. When he did, it rippled outward from the spot as though activated. It peeled back from the edge of the hatch until its shape was revealed, and then it slid aside into the fuselage. He jumped back in surprise, and they leveled their weapons at the dark opening. Nothing came out.

"How'd you do that?" Denk asked.

"I have no idea."

Oz ventured over the threshold and activated a small flashlight she'd taken from her pocket. She swept her blaster across the inside as Geddy and Oz came in behind her. Four workstations sat empty and dark, mirrored by four more overhead. The bulkhead door to the crew quarters was slightly ajar and not a single light illuminated. It wasn't conventional by any stretch, but at least it resembled a regular working ship inside.

She turned around, her face a mask of confusion.

— *I get a weird vibe from this place.*

— Bad weird or just weird?

— *I'm not sure.*

"Oz, do you sense anything?"

"Nothing," she whispered. "I'm gonna check the bridge."

She tiptoed toward the ajar bulkhead door and threw it open. It, too, was empty. Nothing was out of place or damaged. No signs of a struggle or an obvious malfunction, either.

Denk dug a small, glowing instrument from his pack and passed it over various electronic components. The readout remained perfectly flat.

"No electromagnetic activity," he muttered. "This thing's a brick."

"Then how'd the hatch open?" Geddy muttered.

A noise from the back seized their attention. They whirled in time to see the hatch slide authoritatively shut.

Oz heaved a sigh and turned the light on Geddy. "Well, at least we have each other."

CHAPTER 25

VOPROT

"There's gotta be a latch or a button somewhere," Oz asserted, running her light over the edge of the smooth hatch. Much like the workstations and the bridge itself, there were no obvious controls.

"Computer," Geddy said in his most authoritative voice. "Open door." Nothing happened. Oz gave him a *Really?* look. "It was worth a try."

Leave it to the Nads to get rid of buttons and access panels. No buttons? On a spaceship? Was nothing sacred to these monsters?

"Okay, okay, we're smart people," said Denk. "Let's put our heads together and figure this out. The ship's part biosynthetic, right? How do you get something living to do what you want?"

"Marry it?" said Geddy.

"Give it a guilt trip?" Oz quipped.

"Fine," huffed Denk. "I'm not afraid to try." He touched the wall as gently as he would a woman and closed his eyes as though he was trying to bond with the ship or something. "Ship, I know you're hurting right now. In fact, you may even be dead. But we'd sure appreciate it if you opened for us."

"Would you two like some privacy?" Geddy asked.

"Man, screw you guys."

The only sound was the faint *whoosh* of the incessant Kigantu wind howling outside. He patted Denk on the shoulder. "I think we all knew that wouldn't work."

Denk wrenched away and scowled. "I don't hear you offering any solutions, Mr. Computer-Open-Door."

— Any bright ideas, pal?

— *Not exactly, but our situation sparked a theory.*

— Lay it on me.

— *I believe the ship's biosynthetic systems respond only to Zelnads.*

– You may be on to something.

Geddy emerged from his reverie to find Oz staring at him like she was trying to peer into his soul. Could she have sensed the conversation he'd just had?

He looked away and cleared his throat. "What if the ship only responds to Nads? Like a lock and key?"

Denk's eyes grew big. "Whoa, that would make sense. No crew, no power."

"If you're right, we're pretty much screwed," said Oz.

After spending seven years going back and forth between the tunnels and the smelter, Geddy wasn't exactly crazy about confined spaces. He took a couple deliberate, manly steps toward the sealed door and aimed a kick at it. Another. Another.

"Gee, why didn't I think of that?" Oz asked drolly, shaking her head. "Men."

"I'm a little claustrophobic." Another kick. He felt their eyes on his back but didn't care. "Trapped in a Nad ship in the middle of the Kigantu desert isn't exactly how I want to go."

He paused his labors, panting, his hands on his hips. Oz

stood there shaking her head. "Smart use of our limited air, Starheart. How about a running start?"

"Good idea." Geddy backed up and ran at the door, aiming a flying side kick at it. It might as well have been a boulder, but he backed up again.

"Geddy, come on, man, you're just gonna hurt yourself," said Denk.

"I'm pretty sure I felt it move. One more good hit oughta do it."

— *Touch it.*

— Here? Wouldn't that be weird?

— *I mean the area around the door, you juvenile.*

— Whaddya think I just did?

— *That was your boot. I mean your bare hand.*

Doubtfully, Geddy splayed his fingers and touched the hatch near the seam. At first, nothing happened, but as he ran them down the edge, something clicked, and the hatch slid open. Light flooded the interior along with blowing sand.

He laughed in spite of himself and re-covered his mouth and nose as he turned to a very surprised Denk and Oz. Before he could say anything, though, a giant clawed hand roughly grabbed his jacket and yanked him outside like a doll.

Geddy's feet immediately left the ground. The powerful arm of an eight-foot-tall reptilian giant effortlessly lifted him up so their eyes were level. Its head resembled that of an iguana, sharp teeth lining its jaws along the length of its thick and bony snout. The slits of its orange-yellow eyes stared at him through a second set of eyelids.

Behind him, Oz and Denk emerged, their blasters trained on the creature.

"Let him go!" Oz commanded, but it did no such thing. "Now, or I'll shoot!"

The shock of the situation had thrown Geddy, but as his legs flailed ineffectually beneath him, it finally dawned on him that this was a native Kigantean, a nomadic race many didn't believe still existed.

"It's okay," he said, though he couldn't know. "Lower your weapons." When the Kigantean's eyes glanced down, Geddy drew the Exeter and pressed it into his chest. "Put me down."

It bared its teeth and hissed at him, its eyes narrowed to murderous slits. But after a moment's hesitation, it set him back down, and he backed away. Once he'd put a few meters between them, he slowly holstered the blaster. The big lizard was clad head to toe in ranse-scale armor, which was even more mythical than the Kiganteans themselves. Anything that could kill a ranse and harvest its indestructible scales deserved their respect.

For a time, back when Aquebba was little more than an encampment of exiles, criminals, and pirates, the nasty, centipede-like creatures owned the planet. They would burrow into their tents and huts and paint the insides red. He'd heard stories of people being torn in half when they shot up out of the sand with their toothy mandibles spread open. That's why modern-day Aquebba was built on a layer of concrete with a thick wall around it.

Like its distant cousin, Gundrun, Kigantu was so colossal that its gravity continually tugged asteroids out of orbit. As a result, it was pummeled by meteorites, sometimes leaving stadium-sized divots in the sand. Most disintegrated before reaching the ground, but sometimes they fell as a storm of hot iron and nickel. Being out in the elements risked getting turned into a whiffle ball. Hence, the armor. Nomads weren't nomads unless they could travel as needed.

An electric crackle emanated from a whip on his belt,

though he made no move to grab it. For a few pregnant seconds, they just stared at each other.

Nearby, the Kigantean's sad little caravan had paused its travels. A sand barge of rope-bound junk was lashed to a wide turtle-like creature like a kotatsu with legs. Trailing behind that was a group of three in shackles — one man wearing a thick scarf who might have been Ornean and two knee-high, leathery-skinned creatures that resembled dried brown string beans. None of it made much sense, especially the Ornean.

"Who are you? What you want here?" the creature boomed. Considering his forked tongue and lack of lips, his diction was halfway decent. Either Geddy's implant understood Kigantean or it was speaking English.

The Kigantean's eyes, set to the side as they were, made it hard to tell where he was looking. "Easy, big fella. We have a legitimate claim on this ship. As soon as we scoop it up, we'll be out of your hair … er, on our way."

"Ship is Zelnad but you are not. Explain!" His scaly fingers inched closer to the whip.

"How do you know we're not Zelnads?" Denk asked.

"You are too stupid and clumsy to be Zelnad!"

Geddy gave his hands a calming pump. "You're right. We're not Zelnads. We're the crew of that big ship right there and this vessel is our salvage. It's empty."

The brute's long, sharp claws curled into a defiant fist. "Then maybe Voprot claim it for Kigantu!"

He was so close to getting his ship back now. Once, he would've drawn his blaster and taken care of this in two seconds. Maybe there was another way out of this where everyone could walk away happy.

"Okay, big guy. Voprot, is it? I'm Geddy, and this is Oz and Denk. Let's say you claim the ship and we go our separate ways. What're you gonna do with it?"

"I take to Aquebba and sell."

"Okay. How?"

The relentless suns had turned the vertical pupils of the Kigantean's giant yellow-orange eyes into black slivers. They roamed back and forth between Geddy, the others, their ship, and the caravan.

"Voprot … not think that far ahead."

"Look, there's plenty of room aboard our ship there. We could take you."

— *What're you doing?*

— Buying us time.

He cocked his head, intrigued. "You offer Voprot transport?"

— *Why's he referring to himself in the third person?*

"I'll do you one better," Geddy said. "I can broker you a deal. Without me, you'd get swindled. That's a fact."

"Why you help Voprot?"

"Because if I get you top dollar for that ship, we can split the take fifty-fifty and part company. Set us both up really good."

The lizard's side-facing eyes narrowed. "Enough to get off planet?"

"Off-planet, hell. How does anywhere you want sound? Help us get the ship into the hold. We'll take you to Aquebba and everybody gets rich. Whaddya say?"

"Maybe Voprot steal ugly ship and fly away."

"Ugly?" Denk growled.

"You know how to fly a Ghruk freighter?"

He paused to consider this, then shook his head. "No."

"Who's the Ornean?"

"Exile," he said. "I sell him, too."

Orneans were legendary scholars, scientists and philosophers. Their entire culture was built around knowledge and insight. Many were officers back in the days of the Alliance. What did he have to do to get exiled?

The wind freshened, delivering clouds of stinging hot dust to his eyes and hands. He turned away until it cleared, then noticed the low-slung turtle thing was slowly being covered by blowing sand.

"How's about we get this thing loaded in and negotiate on the way? FYI, I think your turtle might be dead."

He whirled, saw the inert turtle thing being covered and dashed over to it. He fell to his knees and wailed, "Tippy!! Voprot sorry!"

On his knees, he was pretty close to Geddy's height. He approached the grief-stricken Kigantean and put his hands on his hips, peering solemnly down at the fallen creature.

"He seemed slow but steady," Geddy offered. "So whaddya say?"

The best place for his ball of odds and ends was right here, because they wouldn't even let him through the gate with that junk. All he had was his armor, his whip, and three slaves at the end of a chain.

Voprot's head dropped and his shoulders sagged, as they do when your choices fall away. "Voprot accept."

CHAPTER 26

DR. TARDIGAN

The process of getting the Zelnad vessel into the back of the *Fizmo* was somehow both more and less sophisticated than Geddy expected. Denk opened a large compartment in the floor of the hold to reveal six slow-moving bots that reminded him of the ones that mined his shinium ore on Earth 2. They slipped a set of straps under the ship then affixed them to the bots, which team-lifted it up out of the sand. A dune had already climbed halfway up the side.

Their tracks got stuck several times during the agonizingly slow journey back to the ship, the underside of which was streaked black from the heat of their reckless entry. The Ornean and the two creatures called globzoiks remained obediently silent while Voprot led them up the ramp and into the back of the hold.

Denk fired up the engines only to realize their nav sensors were still offline and dispatched Morpho to troubleshoot. Without them, the only way to find Aquebba in the featureless desert was to allow Voprot to guide them from the bridge, though he had to get down on all fours to fit. Geddy left Oz and Denk to do the flying so he could have a chat with Voprot's Ornean captive.

The globzoiks prodded and sniffed at the bowls of nutrimush before gorging themselves. Geddy watched them bemusedly and ate his own while leaning against the mostly empty shelves of scavenged junk. It gave him time to consider his next move.

They didn't owe Voprot a damn thing, but striking a bargain prevented a violent confrontation, and Geddy could sense their scaly adversary's desperation. Besides, they needed him to navigate. As for Aquebba, he'd figure the rest out when they got there. In any event, they weren't about to split the take fifty-fifty.

Once he finished eating, Geddy got up and approached the stoic Ornean, who ate in silence with his back to the Nad vessel as far from the globzoiks as his chains allowed.

"Mind if I sit?" Geddy asked.

His eyes rolled up and he shrugged. "It's your ship."

Only it wasn't. He wasn't the captain, and Oz and Denk weren't his crew. He let the comment go and slid down beside him, resting his elbows on his knees. "Did you get enough? Nutrimush isn't exactly gourmet, but I figure you've been eating mostly sand."

"This the most civilized I've felt in three weeks."

"That's how long you've been with ol' lizard lips?"

He flared his arched eyebrows. "It feels much longer."

Geddy extended his hand. "Geddy Starheart."

He took it, his hand surprisingly soft. "Tardigan. Doctor Krons Tardigan."

Geddy blinked in surprise. "Doctor? Voprot said you're an exile."

He lowered his eyes to the floor, a dark look crossing his face. "Sadly, yes. But considering my crime, exile is a price I was happy to pay."

Tardigan didn't look it, but he clearly had demons like everyone else. "Jeez, what'd you do? Murder? Rape?"

"Worse."

"Necrophilia?"

"Academic misconduct." He sniffled, wiping a tear from his elongated orange-brown face. "I fabricated experimental data to support my conclusions just to get published in a peer-reviewed journal. Oh, god, the shame!" He planted his face in his hands.

— *This guy's bad news. Maybe talk to the globzoiks instead.*

— Right? First Voprot and now this guy?

His thin, bony body heaved with sobs. Geddy patted him reassuringly on the arm. "There, there ..."

"A jury of my peers convicted me and shot me off in a rocket. It randomly delivered me here. The Kigantean found me at the brink of death. I owe him my life."

Geddy gave a subtle nod toward the chatty creatures, whose conversation sounded like a pair of maracas in a dryer. "What's their deal?"

"Kiganteans keep globzoiks to lure ranses into their traps. Their language drives them insane with rage."

"Bait, eh? On Kigantu, that's a white-collar job."

He pulled back in disbelief. "You know this planet?"

"Only Aquebba. And I wish to hell I didn't."

"Rough place?" Tardigan asked sheepishly.

"You've never heard of the Double A?"

He shook his head. In Geddy's circles, the Aquebba Auction, better known as the Double A, was a household name. Apparently Orneans didn't follow the criminal underworld. It was starting to seem like few people did.

"It's sort of a high-end auction for criminals. Your savior intends to sell you."

He waved that off with a laugh. "It would not have taken

much cunning to avoid that situation, Mr. Starheart. May I inquire as to why are you bound for Aquebba?"

"I'm looking for someone."

Tardigan leaned into him and muttered, "Perhaps we can help each other."

"How's that?"

"Voprot, too, is an exile, a juvenile in years who was cast out by his people for his determination to see the galaxy. He hopes to trade his possessions for passage off-world. If he fails to do so, he will be stuck in Aquebba with nothing and no one."

The Double A was no place for a naïve kid. Having something of actual value, fetching a good price for it, and getting out alive was dicey enough for veterans. Giant lizard or not, Voprot would likely wind up dead through no fault of his own, and his ranse armor would be on the auction block before he turned cold. Getting him off-world was already part of the plan. What did he care about money, anyway?

"What's in it for me?" Geddy asked.

He cocked an eyebrow. "This is a large ship for such a small crew. I could be useful."

"Not my call. I'm only a passenger. Once I get what I came for, I'm gone."

"All the more reason to bring me on. I can translate. Offer counsel. Provide medical care. Planetary dossiers. History. My needs are meager."

Geddy shrugged. "Pitch it to Oz and Denk. They're bleeding hearts."

"Oh, but they look up to you, Geddy. Surely you see that."

— *He's right. Maybe you could you some third-party advice.*

— You *are* a third party.

— *Of course.*

A scenario popped into his head where everyone, including Voprot, got what they wanted. Nothing said it had to be fair.

The Nad vessel was worth millions, but Voprot wouldn't know that. Once he was out of the picture, Geddy could either use it as a bargaining chip with Sammo Yann or auction it himself and use the cash to buy his ship back. Then he, Oz, and Denk could split the remainder and go their merry ways.

Once, he would've figured out the best way to kill Voprot and dump his body out the back, but that wasn't him anymore. He couldn't help but sympathize with the big reptile. They were fellow exiles of a sort. The difference was, Geddy chose his.

"Okay," Geddy whispered. "Here's what we'll do."

Once the engines shut down, Denk lowered the hold ramp and they followed Voprot out, the chain tethering his slaves wrapped tightly around his scaly arm. The upper deck of Aquebba's spaceport thrummed with activity. The place had grown up since Geddy left for Earth 2, but by the looks of the characters streaming toward the main part of town, gentrification was still a long way off.

"Morph, see if you can get the sensors working again," Denk said over his shoulder. "We might need to bug out of here in a hurry."

Morpho swung into view at the top of the open door and dropped to the floor with a thick *splat*. He gave a little salute, or so it appeared, then slithered up to the controls. The ramp was painfully slow to close. Hopefully no one caught a glimpse of their priceless cargo.

"What is *that*?" asked Voprot, staring at Morpho.

"A sentient lint remover," said Geddy, smirking, as he turned back to them. "Now listen up, 'cuz there are some ground rules here. First, don't look anyone in the eye. Second, don't trust the street food, especially not the vegan options. As for the brothels, you pretty much get what you pay for. However — pro tip — if you fill out a comment card on your way out, they'll give you ten percent off your next visit. Any questions?"

Oz leaned forward expectantly. "That's all there is to know?"

"Just stay close and let me do the talking. Come on."

He gave Dr. Tardigan a tight nod and led them across the deck to the wide steps that descended to Turduranto Street, Aquebba's aptly named main drag. On any given day, it was the main route of a degenerate parade.

Nobody was here on legitimate business. Even the street performers were bit players in some bigger grift. Most came to sell something illegal, buy something illegal, or fight over the scraps. Some were here to simply immerse in the grimy spectacle of it all.

If it wasn't weapons on the block, it was stolen artifacts. The rarer the better. And if it wasn't either of those, it was people. A despicable place to the core. On the plus side, it was largely free of judgment.

The Double A itself took place inside a hollowed-out mountain at the edge of town with tight security. If you weren't known or couldn't prove you had something worthy to sell or buy, you'd be turned away at best. More likely, they'd shake you down so you were scared to try it again.

One of Geddy's first jobs had been door security, and plenty of people who got stonewalled there never made it back to their ship. How many Voprots had he consigned to the desert in his day? When they got shoved outside using a device not unlike a pinball launcher, they had a choice: Keep going and become ranse food, or run back and be gunned down. That was what passed for justice in Aquebba.

Not far from where the stairs spilled onto the street, the crowd thickened, slowing their progress to a dirge-like shuffle.

Everyone they passed either had their arm around someone or their hands clutching a mug of ale. Usually both.

Oz caught up to him and leaned in as they wound between the drunken revelers. "You mind letting us in on the plan here?"

"It's honestly best if you don't know."

"You really don't trust me?" she asked.

"It's not about that. We need this to go a certain way. You guys are variables, and I can't afford those."

She stuck her hip out and crossed her arms. "Variables. Well, aren't you sweet?"

"Ugh. You know what I mean."

"At least tell me where we're going in case we lose each other in this ..."

"Wretched hive of villainy?" he asked. When she didn't react, he continued."To see an old acquaintance of mine named Kriggy."

"What about Voprot?"

Geddy stole a glance behind him to make sure the lizard wasn't in earshot. He and Denk were chatting amicably as the crowd parted for them. It was very safe to talk. "The Ornean said all he wants is to get off -world. We use that."

"How?"

"He has no idea what that ship's worth. I just need Kriggy to advance us some cash so we can convince Voprot it's a done deal. We make a show of splitting it, put him on the next transport out and go to the Double A like we planned. Everybody wins."

"Except Voprot."

"Hey, that ship is ours. He's lucky to get anything at all. Besides, I can't risk him getting in the way." He chose not to tell her what Tardigan said about his being an orphan. She was a bleeding heart for sure.

Oz gave a big sigh, her voice tinged with guilt. "Fine. But we stick together."

"What're you guys talking about?" Denk asked as he caught up.

"Oz'll fill you in."

Voprot was trying to manage his chain, his tail, and his slaves while the party people struggled to make room. Species came in all shapes and sizes, but after a while, you saw a lot of the the same ones. Not so with Kiganteans. Most people didn't know there was anything beyond the wall but ranses. It must've been like seeing a mermaid.

— *You don't feel a little guilty?*

— Why?

— *For cheating Voprot.*

— Geddy not cheat him. Geddy save him from becoming boots.

Voprot caught up to them just as a drunk guy hollered, "Hey, if I sliced off your tail, would it grow back?"

"Yes," said Voprot. "Would your arm?"

CHAPTER 27

KRIGGY

The only thing different about the tattoo parlor was a new sign, which could only mean the original had been stolen or crumbled into dust. Krigor "Kriggy" Ranimus was old even by Nurithean standards — old enough, at least, to recall when Aquebba was a prison colony, which was pushing two hundred years ago. If he didn't know about it, it never happened or was too long ago to matter. And if he didn't know *you*, you didn't exist. Not here.

As a tattoo artist, though, he was shit. Any design he hadn't already inked on a thousand different shoulders, calves, or tits was a roll of the dice. Of course, Kriggy's true canvas wasn't skin but Aquebba itself. His gift was putting things or people together to make something new. And, if necessary, to take them apart or make them disappear.

Geddy gripped the handle of the creaky door, took a deep breath, and opened it. Before he entered, he turned to Oz and said, "Why don't you guys grab a drink somewhere close. I'll come find you."

She tried to look past him into the dim light. "You sure?"

"Yep." He offered his most reassuring nod and slipped

inside, making the little alarm on the wall ping. Oz turned and led the others across the street.

"Be right wit' ya," came the familiar voice from in back. Shuffling steps grew louder until he appeared in the doorway of the supply room and froze, his jaw hanging open.

Geddy held out his arms and shrugged. "Long time no see, Krig."

He looked basically the same as ever, like a partially deflated ball riding a chicken. His soft, droopy nose hung inert unless he got really animated, when it would wiggle in precisely the same manner as a flaccid penis. Distractingly large ears sprouted shoots of wispy gray hair, but in Kriggy years, he hadn't been away all that long.

"Starheart?" He shook his head in disbelief as he drew further into the parlor, swinging the reclining client chair out of the way. Before Geddy could react, Kriggy raised the blaster he'd slyly grabbed from behind the counter and scowled, leveling it at his heart. "You've got some brass balls on you, kid. Gimme one reason why I shouldn't make you dead right now."

Geddy held up his hands defensively, angling sideways to make himself a slightly smaller target.

"Look, I know I didn't leave on the best terms, but hear me out. I've got a plan, and if all goes well, I can pay my debts and we can both walk away very, very rich."

His grip tightened on the blaster, leveling it at Geddy's face as he took another step forward. "These days, anyone pulls a fraction of the shit you have takes a walk outside."

"Kiss my ass, you pustulent wart-nibbler!"

— Are you crazy? Don't you–

Kriggy's thin-lipped stare transformed to a grin, then he burst into raucous laughter and plunked the blaster on the counter, slapping his leg as he doubled over, hacking away like he was clearing a hairball. Small wonder a lung didn't come flying out.

— *That was a joke?*

— You have to know Krig.

The round little man lurched forward and wrapped Geddy in a sweaty hug that smelled like ink and pipe smoke. "Come here, ya big shithead! I couldn't fill Geddy Starheart full of holes if I wanted to. And I really do!"

"You haven't filled a hole in fifty years!" Geddy quipped, and Kriggy laughed again.

"Come on back," he said with a sly grin, motioning for Geddy to follow. How many hours had they sat on his fart-impregnated couches, drinking Kailorian gin and swapping war stories? It was the best thing about this hellhole.

"What if a customer comes in?" Geddy said, and Kriggy doubled over once more.

The blue room, as the two of them called it, hadn't changed much, either. The sheets protecting the couches might be new, though they probably just covered up the stained ones. It smelled like Kriggy, only dirtier.

Such wonderful memories.

Kriggy sank into his old spot in the middle of the now V-shaped couch, so low he had to spread his spindly knees just to see Geddy.

"Love what you've done with the place." Geddy eased himself onto the other couch. Sometimes the right rear leg broke if you sat in it too hard.

"Tough times, my friend." He gave his head a rueful shake, again setting his sad penis nose a-swinging. "There are at least three better artists than me here now."

"Oh yeah? How many shops in all?"

"Four, I think." He laughed again.

"Didn't you always say a legitimate business is no way to make a living?"

"Ah, I say lots of things!" He batted the idea away and shuffled his body toward the edge of the seat. "Where are my manners? You must be thirsty."

After the day he'd had, a drink would be perfect. But he had to keep his eyes on the prize. If he didn't, he might wake up in this very spot the next morning with cottonmouth, acid reflux, and a very unamused Oz and Denk.

"Maybe later. Look, pal, I want to catch up, but there's something I need to move fast on."

His eyes twinkled. "Now we're talking. Whatcha got?"

Geddy related the short version of how and why he came to Kigantu and that he had a completely intact Zelnad ship to sell.

Kriggy's eyes widened into saucers. "You mean to tell me you wrapped a disabled Zelnad ship in a warp shell and pushed it so crooked through a gate that it dumped you out into our atmosphere?"

Geddy grinned at his old friend's fiendish delight. It did make for a pretty good story. "We had to torpedo a mountaintop so we didn't crash into it."

Again, he doubled over in laughter and slapped his thigh, which was nearly at eye level. "Son, you must have nine lives. So, what're you looking for? The standard package?"

"Not exactly. We picked up a stray. A Kigantean kid the size of a house. Long story short, I need him out of the picture."

"You mean ..." he made a gun shape with his fingers and pressed it to his temple.

He shook his head emphatically. "No, no, nothing like that. All he wants is a ride off this dump. He doesn't have to know what that ship's worth."

"You want to bamboozle him. Take him off the board before the Double A tonight."

He smiled broadly. "You read my mind."

Kriggy stuck out his bottom lip and stroked his chin. "How much are you thinking?"

"I was thinking two hundred. Half to him, half to us, and he walks away. That kind of dough would set him up pretty good."

"He's that dumb?"

Geddy barked a laugh. "Dumber. Talks about himself in the third person."

"Why you wanna help some prepubescent ... did you say Kigantean?"

"I've turned over a new leaf. Now are you gonna help me out here or what?"

Kriggy acquiesced with a shrug. "The money's no problem. Neither's a ride for the kid."

"I hear a 'but' coming."

"You know what I'm gonna say, Ged."

Up until now, Geddy hadn't even wanted to think the name, as though merely doing so would conjure him or somehow give away his precise location. But he could avoid it no longer.

He heaved a sigh, his eyes drifting to the filthy couch. "Tretiak."

Tretiak Bouche, better known as the Auctioneer, was a human who had run Aquebba since well before Geddy's time. He started pushing a broom, then worked his way to doorman and eventually the boss of everything. A savvy, ruthless, and deeply connected businessman whom everyone was right to fear.

Geddy first worked the coat room, then the door for several years. When Tretiak's main man in collections hung up his blaster, Geddy took his place. Most of the time, bidders settled up right away and got out of town, but sometimes they were swept up in the excitement and got in over their head, winning auctions they couldn't afford. If they were lucky, they'd just be banned and the lot would go to the next-highest bidder. But anyone who flouted the rules or tried to swindle the Auctioneer took the walk.

If the Auctioneer didn't get paid, nobody got paid. But Kriggy came next, because his people always knew who was in the room, what they were worth, and who they associated with. There was no law to worry about, but by and large, everything on the block was stolen or otherwise ill-gotten, and people who came looking for their stolen shit tended to cause trouble.

Tretiak didn't like trouble.

Just as his reach extended far beyond Kigantu, the demand for new inventory at the Double-A grew to a fever pitch. Toward the end, Geddy was traipsing the galaxy with a list of prominent bidders, threatening to expose them if they didn't come up with something juicy to put on the block. He'd return to Tretiak bearing the fruits of his exploits and take his paltry five-percent cut.

Over time, it added up to a decent haul, but by then Geddy had finally had enough. Convinced he didn't have enough money to leave Kigantu and set himself up on Earth 2, he started placing big bets at the uguinok tables. Most didn't pay off, and he found himself deep in debt. Tretiak got wind of it and warned him to get his affairs in order or else.

That was always Geddy's intention, but he sensed his window of opportunity closing. By the time he worked long enough to pay back everyone, he'd lose his nerve. One night, he stole Tretiak's favorite ship and fled back to Earth 2. During the course of that long jump, Eddie Kepler the henchman became Geddy Starheart the unassuming tunnel worker. His old friend, Jeledine, set him up with all the right credentials.

"How do you expect leave this planet alive?" asked Kriggy.

"That depends on you."

He cocked his head. "So, this isn't just about a phony transaction."

"I'm been looking for someone. If he's not here, I'm pretty much screwed."

"I'm all ears."

Geddy masked his convulsive laughter by coughing into his hand. Even Eli couldn't help himself.

— *Wow. And without a trace of irony.*

"Sammo Yann."

His eyes narrowed suspiciously. "What business do you have with him?"

"Is he here?"

"Oh, he's usually around. He's Tretiak's star supplier of the moment."

"Yeah, well, he's got my ship and I want it back."

Somewhere behind Kriggy's cold, beady eyes, the pieces of the puzzle fell neatly into place. "So *that's* what this is about. You have something going up on the block, and it's something Sammo stole."

Geddy nodded. "And I need the money from the sale of the Nad ship so I have enough to buy it if I can't get it back the hard way. But Tretiak can't know I'm here."

"Keeping secrets from Tretiak's a slippery slope. What's in it for me?"

"Besides a pile of money?"

"Bah! I've got money. You just can't tell by looking."

"Then do it for me," Geddy said, drawing closer to his old friend. "I built the ship to honor my dad."

It was meant to be a useful lie, but even as he said it, he realized it wasn't entirely untrue. Kriggy knew all about his parents. In a way, he felt like an uncle.

Kriggy heaved a long sigh and scratched the inside of his conch-sized ear, burying his finger to the hilt. "I can't control the bidding. If someone decides they really want this ship of yours …"

"I know the deal, Krig. This way, everybody gets what they want. Once I've got my ship, you'll never see me again. Neither will Tretiak."

He pondered this for a moment, then rose with considerable difficulty. Geddy did likewise and extended his hand.

"Whaddya say? For old time's sake?"

Kriggy smirked and used the same hand that had been digging in his ear to seal the deal. "I must like you more than I thought, kid."

CHAPTER 28

A PEEK UNDER THE HOOD

Kriggy made a slow lap around the Zelnad vessel with Geddy at his heels. Oz, Denk, Voprot, and the globzoiks remained near the closed door of the *Fizmo's* hold. As they circled back, Dr. Tardigan met his eyes with an anxious gaze that said, *Any day now.*

Kriggy ran his stubby fingers along the iridescent armor and whistled softly. Out of the light it appeared gray but still had a mesmerizing sheen. In any event, his hand was right where the hatch should be, but it didn't respond to him.

"I gotta admit, Ged, I had my doubts about this."

"What do you think?"

He nodded toward the sealed door. "Let's have a look inside."

"Small problem there," Geddy said. "Their armor forms an impenetrable shell around it. We almost got trapped …" He ran his fingers along the rear of the craft. As he did, a greenish ripple pulsed across its gleaming skin. He instantly pulled his hand away. "… inside."

"Whoa, what just happened?" asked Krig, drawing closer.

"I don't know. I'm just showing you how it opens."

Geddy shook his head. Obviously, it wasn't so simple as that, plus he'd foolishly hoped Kriggy would be so dazzled by the ship that he wouldn't care what was inside. But a Zelnad ship wasn't much good to anyone if they couldn't crack it open.

"Do it again," said Kriggy.

— A little help?

But Eli didn't respond. Eli always responded whether he wanted him to or not. Geddy again brushed his fingers against the ship's skin, and again, the light radiated outward in soft, overlapping waves, like pebbles in a pond.

As his mind raced for an explanation, he realized Voprot had somehow opened the door from the outside.

"How'd *you* open it, Voprot?" he asked the big Kigantean.

"Voprot work claws under gap and pull."

Kriggy eyed him suspiciously, like Geddy had omitted a key detail that changed the nature of their arrangement. Geddy gave him a look that said, *I'm as surprised as you are.*

"Open it up again so Kriggy can see," he said to Denk.

Geddy swallowed hard and took a tentative step forward. He wasn't a Zelnad, but Denk's theory that it would only open for them was the only reasonable explanation. He ran his fingers lightly around where he guessed the seam might be, all the way up the left side and across the top, as light rippled across the shiny skin. About halfway down the right side, the shimmering pattern shifted, revealing a distinct, small circle.

— Was that there before?

— *I'm not sure. It was too bright out there.*

He touched it, and the seal around the edge of the door melted away. Something inside engaged, and it pulled into the fuselage with a gentle hiss. This time, the inside lit up like a Christmas tree.

— *Guess you found the light switch.*

Maybe whatever made the lights come on was on the fritz.

He couldn't shake the feeling that the ship somehow *decided* to turn them on.

Kriggy drew his blaster and leveled it at him. Oz's hand flew to her weapon, but he stopped her with a firm shake of his head.

"What the hell are you trying to pull, Starheart? Don't tell me you're one a' *them*."

"What? No, no. Listen, Krig, I have no idea–"

"I don't believe Geddy's theory is quite correct," came Dr. Tardigan's voice from behind them, cutting Geddy off. They spun around to face him.

"Who's this fuckin' guy?" asked Kriggy, his phallic nose calling to mind a morning jog at a nudist colony.

"Dr. Tardigan," Geddy explained. "He's an Ornean exile."

"Ornean?" said Kriggy, bemusedly looking him up and down. "You're a long way from home, smarty pants. You help Dinosaur Jr. here with his homework or something?"

"I've studied Zelnad technology," Tardigan replied. "This coating is too advanced to merely be biometric."

"Then why's it respond to Geddy?" asked Kriggy.

"The ship is a marriage of mechanical parts and synthetic organism. You might say it *knows* it's injured to the point where it cannot repair itself. Something about him makes the ship believe he can … heal it. In other words, it trusts him."

— Could that be true?

— *It's not you the ship is detecting.*

— Huh?

— *It's me. I'll explain later. Take the lifeline he's throwing you.*

Kriggy's brow furrowed, his eyes darting back and forth between Geddy and Tardigan. "How do I know he isn't under the spell of those Zelnad weirdos? For that matter, how do I know you all aren't?"

"You can't know that," said Tardigan. "We still do not fully understand what the Zelnads really are or what they want. But

I assure you, this is just a trash trawler and this is just their salvage. I give you my word."

After a moment's consideration, Kriggy lowered the weapon. "You said you built a whole ship yourself?"

He nodded. "From scratch."

Finally, he holstered the blaster and his face softened. "Well, now I've seen everything. Lead the way, master mechanic."

Geddy gulped and led him inside the now-glowing vessel. Dazzling holographic displays hovered everywhere, pressing in on him. He could handle small ships, but only if they had windows or open spaces. This work area reminded him of the double-decker bus at the Old Earth Museum of Cultural History.

"You know what any of this shit is?" Kriggy asked.

Geddy turned back and shook his head. "No idea. My best guess is it's a research vessel."

"But you're the only guy who can open it. How are we supposed to sell it?"

— A little help here?

— *Walk slowly. Pause at each display. There must be a way to disable the security protocols.*

Geddy knew his way around the average ship, meaning buttons, gauges, and screens. None of this made a lick of sense. Slowly he moved up and down the aisle, studying each glowing terminal for some clue.

— *Okay, stop. See that sphere floating to the left of the display? Grab it and open your hand.*

Geddy wrapped his fingers around the glowing ball of light, which had no substance but still pulsed with a kind of tactile warmth. He opened his hand and a schematic of the ship appeared along with a language he didn't recognize.

— *That symbol shaped like an umbrella with three dots underneath. Touch it.*

He did, and a soft *whuuum* came from the ship, like something powering down.

"Hey, something just happened," Denk said from outside.

— How did you know to do that?

Geddy followed Kriggy out. The faintly shimmering armor had seemingly sucked back into the ship itself, revealing a dull silver metal beneath. Tukrium, the toughest stuff in the galaxy next to shinium, which nobody else knew about. *Fizmo's* love tap wouldn't have left a scratch, nor would dropping it a few meters onto sand. Whatever damage it sustained must have come from the off-vector jump.

Kriggy slapped him on the back and laughed. "Well, kid, looks like we can do business after all. Let's talk turkey, shall we?"

"Thought you'd never ask," Geddy said, and nodded to Denk to reopen the rear door of the hold.

— You and I need to have a chat.

— *I know.*

CHAPTER 29
NYAPTOMURK POPPERS

Upon collecting Kriggy's cash advance for the Zelnad ship, Geddy and the others decided to celebrate at an overpriced tourist trap called Spaklop's Tavern, rightly the least popular on Turduranto. No one would recognize him there, which was the point.

Despite the small hiccup with Kriggy, everything was now on track. The only thing left to do was give Voprot his cash and get him on the next ship out.

"Voprot not understand. Why no auction?"

"Too risky," Geddy said. "The less people know there's a Zelnad ship in Aquebba, the better, if you know what I mean."

His giant eyes popped open, panicked. "Zelnad come to Kigantu?"

A few patrons overheard that. In a cautioning tone, Geddy whispered, "That's what we're trying to avoid." He felt badly deceiving the kid, but they both wanted the same thing, which was to get him off-world.

A young waiter appeared with a tray of ales, nervously eyeing Voprot as he set them down. The sight of him at one end of the bench and his slaves at the other looked like a seesaw that had given up.

"I'll check on your nyaptomurk poppers," he said apologetically. "The kitchen's slammed."

"No rush on those." Geddy grabbed a frothing mug and hoisted it toward the ceiling. "To our mutual good fortune!"

They tapped their mugs together and drank, the baleful stares of Dr. Tardigan and the bickering globzoiks spoiling the festive mood. Voprot sniffed suspiciously at his ale before taking a tentative sip, wincing at the taste. Meanwhile, Geddy took out the pouch of cash and checked to make sure no one's eyes were on them before sliding Voprot's hundred grand across the table with a smarmy grin.

"The deal's done. I don't like to pat myself on the back, but I got you the deal of the century. Here's your cut. You keep that out of sight. As soon as we're done here, turn right and walk five doors down to the Thirsty Thief. All the pilots hang out there. Negotiate yourself a ride. That there'll get you to Zorr with a little extra to set yourself up."

He again raised his mug, this time in Voprot's direction, and took another swig of skunky, room-temperature swill. How this place remained in business exceeded his understanding.

"What Voprot do with them?" He nodded toward his prisoners at the other end of the bench.

"Thanks for reminding me." Geddy counted out five thousand credits, sliding the short stack of squares across the table. "For the Ornean."

Voprot lowered his giant head to the stack.

"Just take it."

"Okay." He slipped both bundles into his vest, then unlocked Tardigan. "What about globzoiks?"

As though sensing a shift in the conversation, the pair of

wrinkly little stringbeans at the end abruptly stopped their nattering and stared hopefully in his direction.

"Well, I mean … look, I'm not quite up to speed on current market conditions, but I think it's more likely someone would pay you to keep them."

The globzoiks' faces fell and they bickered in their clickety-clackety tongue. Voprot cocked his head and asked, "Not even for their meat?"

"I'd say you'd be lucky to make a decent Philly out of them."

"What is Philly?"

"Never mind. Here, I'll prove it." Enough was enough. Geddy slid out of the booth, stepped up onto the bench and bellowed, "Hey, anybody want three globzoiks? Totally free. They excel at attracting ranses. Oh, and their language sounds like marbles down a fire escape. Going once … twice …"

A handful of gruff patrons either rose or leaned to the side to get a look at the globzoiks, but immediately returned to their conversations. Geddy stepped down and slid back into his seat.

"Sorry, pal. I tried."

The big Kigantean sighed, his shoulders sagging down into his heavily muscled frame.

"Besides, Voprot," said Denk cheerily, "if you're gonna make your way in the world, you can't go dragging slaves around at the end of a chain. It's not a good look."

Voprot nodded okay and unlocked the shackles from the tiny ankles of one little claw-footed creature, which gazed up at him with glassy-eyed gratitude. He then curled his fingers gently around the hapless thing, picked it up, and bit its head off like a corn dog.

Blue-green blood spurted from the stump of its neck, raining down on the remaining one as it shook in terror, its tiny mouth agape in a silent scream.

Geddy sprayed his mouthful of ale across the table as Voprot spat the head out onto the floor. "Dude! Not cool!"

"What?" he mumbled, the globzoik's still-twitching feet sticking out of his mouth as its bones crunched audibly between his powerful jaws. "Ech. Voprot not like the head. Not much brain meat." A handful more crunches and he tossed his head back, his neck elongating and contracting like a bird as he swallowed. A still-twitching, globzoik-shaped bulge slid down his pale-yellow gullet.

"Hey, can't you read, buddy?!" The ornery bartender jabbed his finger toward a sign over the door. "No outside food!"

"Voprot not read," said Voprot, chewing the last stringy morsel of globzoik. Dejected, he unlocked the other's shackles and it bolted into the street, darting between the legs of the inebriated.

The globzoik's severed head had rolled up against Denk's foot. Gagging, he gathered it into a wad of napkins and searched for a wastebasket while disgusted patrons from adjacent tables anxiously asked after their checks.

Volprot met their horrified stares, a stringy chunk of globzoik still wedged between his teeth, and mumbled, "Sorry."

Geddy exposed his teeth and pointed. "You've still, uh, got something ..."

He probed around with a claw and flicked the morsel out. It landed in a nearby drink, but nobody noticed. With considerable difficulty, Voprot extracted himself from the bench, his heavy tail sweeping some guy's chair out from under him.

"Voprot grateful for your help. Goodbye."

Geddy washed down the guilt at the back of his throat with a swig of ale and shook Voprot's clawed hand. "Thirsty Thief. Five doors that way." He pointed back toward the spaceport. "Good luck, buddy."

With that, Voprot nodded and left, his ranse-scale armor rattling as the door closed behind him.

Geddy mimed wiping sweat from his forehead and heaved a sigh. "Whew. Geddy feel lighter already."

"Well, I think we've worn out our welcome here. Dr. Tardigan, it's been real," Oz said, slapping her palms on the table as she rose. "Enjoy your freedom."

"Wait," said Tardigan, holding up one hand. "There's something I've been meaning to ask the two of you."

Oz sank back down onto the bench. "Okay …"

"I spoke with Geddy, and he agreed I might be of some use aboard the *For Sale By Owner*."

"Did he now?" asked Oz.

Tardigan was quick to deflect the blame away from Geddy. "Don't misunderstand. He wasn't offering on your behalf. I inquired, and he said to talk to you."

"Are you really a doctor or is that, like, a nickname?" Denk asked.

"I assume you mean a doctor of medicine. That is one of my degrees, yes, but I have several areas of more … practical expertise."

Denk and Oz flared their eyebrows, duly impressed.

Oz leaned forward, tapping her fingers lightly on the table. "What else?"

"I have deep knowledge of many civilizations. Customs. History. Politics and languages."

Denk asked, "What'd you do to get exiled?"

The stone-faced man's lower lip trembled as though recounting some deeply painful memory. "I was found guilty of academic misconduct and shot into space. My only salvation is in service."

"Geez," said Denk. "Ornea sounds kinda rough."

"You should see what they do to bad spellers. Please — I'll work for room and board. Anything to prove myself worthy."

Oz swung her head to Geddy. "What do you think?"

Geddy liked and respected these two. And Tardigan was right — they did look up to him. He'd feel better about parting ways if they had an extra pair of hands. The three of them plus Morpho would make a pretty decent crew.

He held up his hands in deference. "I only bought his freedom. Whatever you guys decide is your business."

Oz chewed thoughtfully on her lip and turned back to Tardigan. "Tell you what. You help us get Starheart's ship back and we'll give you a shot."

Sheer joy washed over him as he humbly lowered his head in gratitude. "I will give you all my very best every day."

"That's good enough for me," Geddy said, getting back up and stretching. "Let's get back to the *Fiz* and clean up for the auction." The waiter appeared with a heaping plate of nyaptomurks. "Oh, darn. I guess we won't be needing those. Denk, we'll wait outside while you settle up."

"Me?" Denk pleaded, but they were already out the door.

CHAPTER 30
THE DOUBLE A

The doorman guarding the entrance to the Double A was a Sarak Geddy didn't recognize. Every last jagged, triangular tooth crammed into his mouth was coated in gold. Maybe he and ol' Laszlo went to the same dentist. He studied the four of them with unmasked contempt.

"No tourists," he growled, jutting his chin back toward the city.

"We're not tourists," Denk objected, drawing himself up to his full height and smoothing his sport coat. "We're the crew of a salvage trawler."

Geddy was about to intervene when Krigor appeared from inside and placed his hand on the Sarak's brawny shoulder.

"It's okay, Terry, they're with me."

The Sarak growled his disapproval and took out a handheld scanner. "Leave your weapons. You can pick them up on your way out."

"Come find me," Kriggy said.

— *Geddy, the key!*

— Oh, shit, I wasn't even thinking about that.

— *Will he confiscate it?*

— Afraid so.

"Hey, uh, Oz?" He tapped her on the shoulder just as she lifted the side of her dress to retrieve the blaster strapped to her thigh. "I'm gonna hit the head. I'll meet you inside."

She nodded okay ,and Geddy went back down to the bathroom. Finding it empty, he opened one of the stalls and dropped his pants.

— *What are you doing?*

— Keeping the key safe.

— *Are you doing what I think you're doing?*

— I've done it before.

— *When?*

Once again, he thought of Tatiana.

When the deed was done, he washed up and returned to the door, surrendering his blaster to the Sarak as it regarded him suspiciously. It passed the scanner over him and paused when it beeped next to his buttocks. After a brief pat-down, it turned him around.

"You've got metal somewhere."

"Artificial prostate," Geddy said. "I can show you the scar if you'd like."

By then, a queue had begun to form behind him. The grumpy Sarak motioned him past, and he heaved a sigh of relief.

As much as he reviled being back here, returning to the Double A felt like a sort of homecoming. Viewed from above, it was just an ordinary mountain at the edge of town, featureless and barren. But inside was a cathedral of criminal commerce.

A short tunnel led to the main auction room called the Vault. It was a symmetrical dome with smooth walls, ringed with tastefully dim lighting that made it feel like an opera house. A thick central column of the original rock bore most of the ceiling's weight. Curved bars of brilliantly polished wood bracketed the sides like parentheses, where they charged three or four times as much for the same drinks you could get outside.

Along the far wall, an enormous rotating platform bore the auction items in and out. Shaped like a ring, it rested on giant stone bearings and was pushed around by heavily muscled slaves. The openings to either side could accommodate anything up to a small ship. All the inventory was squirreled away behind the wall of rock in another, heavily guarded chamber. Labyrinthine corridors connected the facility, including a few secret escape routes and cells in case anyone got out of line.

The others were waiting for him at the back of the Vault. As they made their way to the bar, Kriggy spotted them and waved down the bartender, telling them to order whatever they liked. While the others bellied up, he pulled Geddy aside.

"I assume you took care of your Kigantean problem?"

He winked. "He should be parsecs away by now."

"Good. Now listen, Tretiak is amped up about that Nad ship. It's the final auction of the night, and he's gonna run it personally."

A knot formed in Geddy's stomach. He had plenty to fear from his old boss. Everything he'd done to leave Kigantu and start over was a betrayal that had seven years to fester and deepen.

Tretiak lived in a lavish fortress even deeper inside the mountain. He rarely lowered himself to actually show up and run an auction, preferring to leave the day-to-day to his underlings. Geddy very much hoped their paths wouldn't cross, and as long as he stuck to the shadows, they wouldn't.

"He can't see me, Kriggy. I'm serious."

"I know, I know. But trust me, by the time he takes the

block, this place will be packed to the gills. We've already spread the word to some ... select clients."

The big auctions were truly exciting to watch. A part of him still thrilled at the idea of competitive bidding between rich, amoral patrons.

— *Can we stay focused, please?*

"What about Sammo Yann?" asked Geddy.

Kriggy scanned the crowd. "I don't see him yet, but once I do, I'll find you."

"Did you see the ship in back?"

"The shiny twin-engine one? Yeah, it's lined up for the block."

"Good," replied Geddy.

— *It's here, Geddy. It's really here!*

— Don't get too excited. We still have to figure out how to win the damn auction and get out of here.

— *You don't have a plan?*

— My plan is to have the winning bid. Kriggy'll take it out of my share of the Nad ship. As soon it's back in our hands, we'll be off to Sagacea.

— *But remember what Tatiana said about Sammo. He knows everything about you. What if he sees you?*

Just as his friends reached them with fresh drinks in hand, Krigor said, "It'll be among the last few items. Until then, I say kick back and relax."

Oz idly stirred her fruity cocktail and locked eyes with Geddy. "You guys talking about the Zelnad ship?"

"That's the final auction of the night," Kriggy said, noticing the Sarak at the door motioning to him. "Excuse me."

"Any idea what it'll go for?" asked Oz as Kriggy hustled away.

"Hard to say. High seven figures for sure."

She exchanged a frown with Denk, who lowered his eyes to his feet.

"What?" asked Geddy.

"I feel bad for Voprot," Denk said.

Geddy stared at them in disbelief, desperately searching their expressions for some sign of a ruse. "Okay. First of all, he had no claim to the ship.We did. Second, we don't owe him jack. We gave him a ride, he navigated. That alone would've been a fair trade. I didn't have to give him a hundred grand out of my cut, but I did. That's the end of it."

"Perhaps it's not my place," said Dr. Tardigan, "but I believe the issue is emotional in nature. Scavenging is an inextricable part of Kigantean culture. To Voprot, finding an intact ship in the desert was nothing short of a miracle. This kind of money could lift his people out of–"

"You're right," Geddy snapped, his ire rising. "It's not your place."

— *Isn't that what Captain Bykite said to you once?*

— It's not the same.

"As long as you're weighing in, *Professor*, I don't recall you thanking me for buying your freedom."

"But you didn't."

He blinked and shook his head as though to clear it. "What are you talking about?"

"You slid your money across the table to him and said, 'For the Ornean.' You then insisted he take it."

"You were his slave."

He cocked his head quizzically. "I never said that."

"You were in shackles. He was coming here to sell you!"

"But he didn't take your money, therefore he simply let me go."

Geddy rubbed the bridge of his nose, unsure what conversation he was even having at this point. All he knew was that he'd given Voprot an extra five grand for no particular reason. If so, then it more than made up for the little white lie about the auction.

His fingernails dug into his palms as he tried to calm himself. "It doesn't matter now, because a mutant superlizard that eats live globzoiks and refers to himself in the third person is never getting past the–"

A commotion came from the main entrance, likely whatever Krigor had been called away to deal with. To his dismay, the hulking figure being stonewalled at the door was Voprot.

— What were you saying about curveballs?

Without explaining himself, Geddy ran to the door, where Kriggy was trying to calm the Kigantean down.

"There he is!" Voprot bellowed excitedly. "Geddy, it is me, Voprot! Geddy!"

"Oh, for fuck's sake ..." he muttered.

"Tell your pet he's not welcome here!" Kriggy hissed.

"Voprot, settle down, okay? And stop saying my damn name."

"Sorry, Geddy." He visibly relaxed and shrugged off the Sarak's hands.

The others had come up behind him. "Hey, Voprot!" said Denk.

Voprot waved excitedly. "Hello, Rat Boy!"

"What's going on?" Oz asked.

Geddy's jaw clenched. "I think our friend came to explain why he's not halfway across the galaxy by now."

"I do what you say. Voprot too big. Have to pay for two seats. Come to sell ranse-scale armor."

Kriggy's eyes practically popped out of his head. "Ranse scale? How'd you manage that?"

Voprot nodded and thumped his fist against the breastplate. "Voprot kill many ranses."

He practically shoved the Sarak aside to inspect Voprot's armor, running his fingers over the shiny black plates with greedy glee. "I know people who would give their left nut for this."

"Voprot prefer money."

"And money you shall have, my eloquent friend," Kriggy said, removing the velvet rope to usher him inside. "Welcome to the Double A. Make yourself at home while I write up the sales contract."

"Come on, big fella," Oz said, offering him her hand. "Oz and Denk buy Voprot overpriced drink." She shot daggers at Geddy and guided Voprot toward the bar.

— *Forgive me for saying so, but your plans haven't been working out.*

— So I've noticed.

Once they were out of earshot, he turned back to Kriggy. "This is a terrible idea."

Kriggy smirked and patronizingly smoothed Geddy's shirt. "Relax, Starheart. You know the rules. We can score a king's ransom for that armor. Besides, I thought all you cared about was your ship."

Geddy's anger cooled. In his haste to get Voprot out of the picture, he'd lost focus. He took a deep, cleansing breath and felt his tension ease. It had been quite a stressful journey to this point, but the so-called brass ring was nearly in hand. The big auctions wouldn't start for another hour or so. Might as well have a cocktail and smooth things over with the others while he still could.

"You're right," he said, chuckling at how amped up he'd gotten. "Guess I'm a little wound up."

Kriggy smiled warmly and patted his cheek. "Atta boy. But listen, before you go, there's someone I'd like you to meet." He jutted his chin toward someone standing behind him, and his nose flopped from side to side.

Geddy turned to his right and found himself face to face with a Soturian in his late fifties dressed in a gray bespoke suit that accentuated his fit physique. Perfectly coiffed white hair lay atop his head like a contented cat, his neatly trimmed beard framing a square jaw and gleaming white, pointed teeth. Were it not for those and the raised pattern on his forehead, he could've passed for human. One hand was curled around a tumbler of delicious-looking whisky.

"Geddy Starheart," he said, his voice smooth and confident. "What an unexpected pleasure. My name is Sammo Yann."

CHAPTER 31

SAMMO YANN

"Well, I'll let you two get acquainted," Kriggy said to Geddy and Sammo, then wandered off to rub elbows with a circle of patrons.

Sammo's steely blue eyes pierced him like a hot needle. "Looks like we've got a while before the main event. Buy you a drink?"

"Sure."

Back in the day, guys like this were a dime a dozen. Impossibly confident rogues who combed the galaxy for items of value and dubious provenance just to sell them at the Double A. Sure, there were as many black markets as stars, but this one burned brightest. An opportunity for the moneyed elite to live dangerously and rub shoulders with people who might otherwise rob them blind.

The auction boiled everything down to a simple equation. No matter what you had or how you got it, its value would be judged for all to see. Mostly, it was a transparent transaction, no different than buying from a very expensive store. But sometimes, an item would attract multiple suitors, driving bids into the stratosphere. Often, it would come down to two bidders, batting exorbitant figures back and forth in a breathless brew of greed and desire that stiffened the hair on your arms.

Something told him Sammo Yann felt the same way.

"What's your poison?"

"Rusty Nail," the android bartender answered for him. His eyes never left Geddy as he made the two-ingredient drink. "Good to see you back at the Double A, Mr. Starheart."

Of course Greg recognized him, long beard and all. How many times had he sat at this very bar with Kriggy and Tretiak after the auction closed, swapping war stories and getting fall-down drunk? Too many. "I'm not really here, Greg. Just passing through."

"Understood," he said with a wink.

Sammo grinned. "I should've guessed you had a soft spot for Old Earth cocktails. Considering your mother's fondness for history and all."

The mention of her stabbed him in the heart as Sammo likely knew it would. "Don't pretend you know me."

Greg handed the drink to Sammo, who passed it on to Geddy and tossed a hundred-credit square at him. "Keep the change." Greg gave a gracious nod and slipped the square into the pocket of his white tuxedo jacket. Sammo raised his glass. "To the free market."

Geddy reluctantly clinked his glass against Sammo's and took a sip. The sweet and smoky combo coated his grateful throat as Sammo strolled toward the central column. A handful of bidders were gathered in front of the platform, halfheartedly raising their paddles in response to a set of disruptors that looked old enough to be in the space museum back on Earth 2, which by now had likely been swept clean by the destructors.

— *Ask him about the ship!*

— Patience. This is a dance.

Sammo set his glass on the narrow table encircling the

column and heaved a sigh. "It appears I can't rely on Miss Semenov's discretion after all."

"You're hardly the first guy she's screwed."

Sammo gave a knowing grin. "Perhaps neither of us are as mysterious as we think."

"Our paths would've crossed either way."

"Is that right?"

He nodded and took another sip. "I don't know what your plan was here, but I'm getting my ship back no matter what."

"Straight to business." He lifted his glass appreciatively. "I respect that."

"Sell it to me. I can have it taken off the block right now."

"Twenty-five thousand," intoned the auctioneer, his amplified voice wafting over the growing crowd. "Do I have twenty-six? Twenty-six, madam, thank you."

He considered this, seemingly intrigued. "What are you offering?"

"What do you want?"

"Why's it so important to you?"

"That's not your concern. Just give me a number."

Sammo chuckled, bemused. "I see the work you put into your ship, Mr. Kepler. Can I call you that? So few men know how to make things anymore."

"You could've taken anything you wanted from Earth 2. Why my ship?"

"I'm not at liberty to say."

Geddy slammed down his drink hard enough to spill some of it. "Look, pal, if I wanted to get jerked off by some silver fox, I'd move to Pretensia."

"Pretensia ..." said Sammo, his eyes drifting away. "Ah. Tev Joclen." A knowing grin formed on his lips. "That explains it."

— *Oh, shit.*

"I don't know what you're talking about."

"How is he, anyway? I never would've pegged him for early retirement. I mean, considering his tenuous financial situation." Sammo clearly had his number. No point denying it. "Y'know, though, there's one question about you I never managed to answer. Why 'Starheart?'"

"What do you mean?"

"Eddie to Geddy isn't a big stretch, but Starheart … I don't get it. I just know it can't be random."

He chewed his lip for a moment, his eyes drifting to his mostly empty glass. The truth was that Starheart was a hero character he played in a school play when he was around eight. His dad called him that sometimes, and it made him feel like a superhero. But he wasn't about to tell Sammo anything of the sort.

"I just liked the way it sounded."

Sammo sighed heavily and took another drink, looking Geddy up and down. "Here's the deal. You want your ship back, you'll have to win it."

Geddy's free hand gathered into a fist, more out of impatience than a sincere desire to pop Sammo in his smug mug. Though he did want to do that. The thought of buying his own stolen goods back galled him, but plenty of AA patrons had done exactly that over the years.

"Then that's what I'll do."

"Best of luck, Starheart." He winked and sauntered away, adding over his shoulder, "Hope you brought your wallet."

— *I really don't like him.*

— You and me both, Pal. You and me both.

CHAPTER 32

LAST ON THE BLOCK

The crowd at the Double A always swelled during the last couple of hours, especially if word got around that something big was on the block. While the Vault filled in, Geddy fluffed his beard, mussed his hair, and stuck tight to the shadows around the central column in case Tretiak showed up.

As the evening wore on, his friends continued to enjoy themselves at the bar on the far side of the Vault. Wary patrons gave Voprot a generous berth, making them sort of an island. Eventually, one of Kriggy's minions led him off through the side doors to relieve him of his armor and prepare it for sale.

For his part, Sammo never left a tight huddle with a pair of nattily dressed men, a Xellaran and a Screvari, who remained stone-faced throughout the proceedings and never once raised their paddles. Were they there for his ship or the Zelnads'?

Loose Zelnad tech, even small components, got everyone very excited. They knew it would end up in the hands of some warlord or dictator, but when you came to the Double A, you checked your morality at the door.

As much as Geddy hated the thought of shelling out his

hard-earned cash to a shady operator like Sammo Yann, he had little choice now. With any luck, he'd still be money ahead after returning Eli to his home world, though his strange experience on Pretensia made him less confident about what should come after.

— What if the bidding gets too high for us?

— It won't. We'll clear seven figures from the Nad ship, easy. *Penetrator* shouldn't be more than a few hundred g's.

— I'm very excited to see it again.

— Me too, Bud. We'll be on our way to your home world soon.

There was a short break before the marquee items so everyone could refill their drinks or hit the bathrooms. Nobody wanted to miss the big show. During the break, Dr. Tardigan wound his way through the crowd and sidled up to him near the column.

"Is this column holding up the ceiling or are you?"

Geddy smirked. "I suppose they sent you to check on me?"

"In fact, you've hardly come up."

"Looks like Voprot's enjoying himself."

The giant lizard was clearly visible from everywhere in the room. He seemed to have found a drink he liked and was animatedly sharing a story with a group of fascinated patrons. Impressive, considering his aversion to adjectives.

Tardigan shrugged. "I think he is just going with the flow. Everything here is new to him."

"What'd you tell him about the ship?"

"That you decided it would fetch a higher price on the block."

Geddy grimaced. The AA got half, which meant they'd have to split the other half with Voprot now. "Damn."

"When's yours coming up?"

"Soon, I'd imagine."

Tardigan nodded toward where Sammo was in a huddle

with those two stoic onlookers. "I saw you talking to him earlier. Who is he?"

"The thief who took my ship."

"He doesn't look like a thief."

"Half the people in here are thieves."

The lights dimmed and banks of stage lights took over, swaddling the platform in purple and yellow. It made whatever was under it appear all the richer, which of course was the point.

A woman's silky voice came over the PA system. "Ladies and gentlemen, we are ready to begin the auctions for this evening's marquee items. To commemorate the occasion, the Aquebba Auction is pleased to welcome The Auctioneer!"

Conflicting emotions flooded him. Tretiak had been like a father in some ways, a boss in others, and negative influence across the board.

"Is he some kind of big deal?" Tardigan asked.

"You've never heard of The Auctioneer?"

He shook his head. "Should I have?"

"Probably not." Up to the moment they stuffed him into a ship and shot him alone into space, the Ornean only knew the life of the mind.

Enthusiastic applause greeted Geddy's old boss as he glided out of the shadows, his long black coat swishing about his legs. Under the lights, Tretiak couldn't see past the first couple rows of patrons, but Geddy still felt exposed.

His palms began to sweat, his throat tightening. He went to take a drink but found he'd already emptied it.

Unlike Krigor, Tretiak had visibly aged since the last time Geddy saw him. His features were more severe now, with hollow cheeks and deep creases across his high, polished forehead. His slicked-back hair was flecked with gray, as was his neatly trimmed beard. Sharply arched eyebrows suggested an old-timey, mustache-twirling villain.

A deep scar ran from just above the corner of his mouth almost to his shoulder blade, supposedly the result of a ranse attack the very day he arrived on Kigantu. He liked to boast that his great-great-grandfather was the last surviving original settler to Earth 2, though Geddy didn't know if that was true.

For many years, Tretiak was the only other human who actually lived in Aquebba, but that wasn't why they got along. Tretiak's philosophy was that anything he didn't take would just be snatched up by someone else. That resonated with young Geddy, who'd just lost everything that mattered to him.

"Patrons from across the galaxy, the moment you've been waiting for has arrived. Three exceptionally unique items grace our auction block tonight, beginning with a last-minute entry that may set a new bidding record for our humble auction."

He nodded to the row of oiled slaves who pushed the old ring-shaped platform around on its heavy bearings, bringing Voprot's armor into the light. Lacking a mannequin large enough to display it, they'd hastily erected a wooden stand in the shape of a stick figure. Whispers rippled through the crowd as it came into view.

Tretiak teed it up with his trademark theatrical flair. "Discerning collectors may recognize this as the stuff of Kigantean myth. A full suit of armor crafted by hand from one of the most fearsome and hardy killing machines in the universe — the dreaded ranse."

Gasps and explanatory whispers followed. Tretiak had a knack for whipping bidders into a frenzy.

"I'm told at least ten of these savage creatures had to be killed in order to make this remarkable armor, which renders the wearer nearly invulnerable to attack. Imagine such a rich conversation piece gracing the entrance to a home, or perhaps hanging in one's bedchamber to provide … masculine inspiration."

— *Really?*

— I mean, maybe?

"Never in the history of the Double A have we offered such a fascinating and unique slice of Kigantu's indigenous culture."

Patrons buzzed as they realized the armor could only belong to the seven-foot tall, upright-walking, half-tanked mega-guana holding court at the bar. For his part, Voprot appeared wistful and glassy-eyed, though that could've been the booze.

"Shall we start the bidding at one hundred thousand? One hundred right here, thank you, one twenty? There you are, madam …"

The longer Tretiak dragged out the bidding, the more uncomfortable Geddy became. Once the gavel came down on Voprot's armor, the *Penetrator* would be next. He couldn't raise his paddle without having all eyes on him — including Tretiak's.

"Doc, I need a favor." Tardigan cocked his head and moved his ear closer. "I need you to do my bidding. Literally."

"What?"

"The Auctioneer can't see me."

"Um ..."

He removed his paddle and placed it in Tardigan's hand. "I'll tell you what to do. Just raise that high when I say and repeat the bid I give you."

"That's it?"

"That's it."

Tardigan examined the numbered paddle while Geddy inched further behind the large column. Meanwhile, Tretiak continued to squeeze as much juice out of the armor as possible. To Voprot's amazement, the bidding had already passed two hundred.

"Two ten right here, thank you, do I have two fifteen? The

bidding stands at two ten." No one made a move. "Two ten going once ... twice ..." He brought the gavel down with finality, the sharp impact bouncing off the rock walls. Oh, did Tretiak love to ham it up. "Sold to the lady in the beautiful blue dress."

Enthusiastic applause filled the room as the woman, who Geddy didn't recognize, acknowledged the applause.

— *Who's she?*

— I don't know.

— *Oh, Geddy, I can't believe we're here.*

— Don't get too excited just yet. We still need to win it.

Once again, the muscled platform pushers did their thing, and the armor disappeared through the wall for delivery prep. Denk and Oz gave an audible cheer and raised their glasses to Voprot. At least someone was enjoying their evening.

The high price commanded by Voprot's armor worried him more than it probably needed to. It suggested this was a loose and enthusiastic crowd that might be willing to push bids through the roof.

A few seconds later, the *Penetrator* appeared through the big arched door on the left side, the brilliance of its shinium skin winking at them under the colored lights. Eli's design had one purpose — get Geddy safely through the barrier around his home planet. Otherwise, it was a simple one-seater with no practical applications. Aesthetically speaking, it looked like any kit ship a wannabe mechanic could build at home over the course of a summer.

The sight of her made Geddy's heart sing. A tear came to his eye as derisive sniggers propagated through the crowd.

"I know, I know," said Tretiak, showing his palms. "It doesn't look like much."

— *Hey!*

"But looks can be deceiving. As it happens, the exterior of this ship appears to be tukrium."

That changed the crowd's tune immediately. It wasn't tukrium, exactly, but Eli said shinium was basically a tukrium alloy. In any case, that was enough to convert most of the skeptics because tukrium was getting harder to come by. Geddy tapped Tardigan on the shoulder.

"Be ready."

"The bidding shall begin at three hundred thousand."

"Now?" Tardigan asked.

"Not yet."

"Three hundred, thank you, sir. Three-fifty right here, thank you. Do I hear four hundred thousand?"

The Xellaran beside Sammo raised his paddle. At four twenty-five, the Screvari raised his.

"Whatever he says next, raise your paddle," he whispered.

"Do I have four-fifty?"

Tardigan raised the paddle. Tretiak shielded his eyes to spot it as Geddy shrank into Tardigan's shadow.

"I have four-fifty by the column, thank you, sir. May I see four seventy-five?"

The Screvari went again. The bids kept increasing by increments of twenty-five and fifty thousand as the three of them volleyed bids, climbing to six hundred thousand.

Geddy had Tardigan raise his paddle for six-fifty, drawing the irritated stares of Sammo's companions. Sammo's eyes sparkled with greedy glee.

Tretiak's eyes darted between them and Tardigan as though daring them both to keep going.

"I have six-fifty. Do I hear six-sixty?"

The two scowling men's eyes narrowed at Tardigan, and they fell into a heated, but whispered argument. The Screvari with the paddle finally shook his head.

Tretiak banged the gavel, though not with his usual gusto. Squinting, he peered again into the darkness. Geddy slid back behind the column.

"Sold, to the … Ornean gentlemen." He gave an exaggerated bow. "The Double A welcomes you, sir."

Nearby patrons applauded and patted Tardigan on the back for his success. He nodded politely, his hands folded in front of him, and waited for the clamor to subside. Meanwhile, Tretiak signaled to the platform slaves to wheel the ship out.

That was that. It would take a big bite from his share of the Zelnad ship, but considering the alternative — having Eli in his head 'til death did them part — it was a bargain.

— Oh, boy! Sagacea, here we come!

CHAPTER 33

TRETIAK

The two men with Sammo were likely hired by him to drive the price up. It was bad form, even for the Double A, but hardly out of bounds for career criminals. If Sammo was as good a producer as Krigor said, then Tretiak was probably willing to cut him some slack. Especially if …

— *What are you thinking?*

— Nothing.

The already packed crowd pressed toward the platform to see the coup de grâce from up close. When the Nad ship rolled out, there was such a commotion that Tretiak had to calm everyone down. Most everyone except for Geddy and Tardigan pressed forward to get a better look.

"This evening's final lot speaks for itself," boomed Tretiak. "An intact Zelnad research vessel, jam-packed with technology so advanced we don't even know what it does. But safe to say, this beautiful marriage of the organic and the mechanical can probe the deepest depths and navigate uncharted oceans of stars."

He went on like this for some time, priming the pumps by

making it seem like the damn thing was crapped out by some kind of deity. The biggest-ticket single item Geddy ever saw at the auction went for eight and a half million. Within minutes, the bidding was up to twelve.

Eventually, only three bidders remained. The Screvari with Sammo kept pushing the other two higher and higher. One dropped out at thirteen five, the other at fourteen seven, which ultimately took it. Sammo's pals remained stone-faced throughout and left the instant the gavel fell. Maybe they weren't just there to drive up the price after all.

Fourteen seven, less twenty percent to the house, split four ways …

— *Two point nine-four million.*

— Dayum.

He gave Eli a mental high-five and finally allowed a smile to cross his lips. Sammo may have forced him to buy back his own ship, but to borrow a turn of phrase from Voprot, *Geddy have last laugh.*

At about eleven, Tretiak thanked the patrons and bid everyone good evening as the sweaty slaves moved the Nad vessel into the warehouse. A big party on Turduranto always followed the auction, so the energized crowd funneled toward the exit.

"Well?" asked Tardigan, inching away. "Shall we see if the others are ready to forgive you?"

Geddy was about to answer when he felt a hand on his shoulder and spun to find Kriggy alongside the scowling Sarak.

"Hey, Krig … what's up?"

His face was pinched in concern. "It's about your ship."

— *Oh, no!*

"You can skip the gift-wrapping if that's what you–"

Kriggy cut him off. "Can we speak in private?"

Tardigan had begun to come back to him. "Geddy? Is everything all right?"

He waved him off. "Yeah, I'll be right back." He gave Tardigan a reassuring pat on the shoulder and followed Kriggy out the side door between the bar and the platform. The others' eyes tracked him curiously as he passed, but he just gave a reassuring wink. Tardigan would fill them in.

Once the door closed behind them, Geddy asked, "Hey, you mind telling me what's going on?"

Kriggy slowed to a stop and pivoted, then nodded to the Sarak that had brought up the rear. "It's okay, Terry."

The Sarak nodded and went back out into the Vault, leaving him alone with Kriggy. Geddy held out his arms, anxious to know what this was all about. "Well, here I am."

He looked apologetic. "Listen, I'm sure it's just a mix-up, but we ran some inquiries, and ..."

"And what?"

"And you ain't got that kind of money, kid. Not even close."

Relief washed over him. A mix-up is exactly what this was. He laughed and exhaled. "Yes, I know. But I'm getting almost three mil from my share of the Nad ship, so it's there, it's just not *there*. Right? Remember, we did the phony sale for Kevin McScale out there?"

Kriggy lowered his head and looked away. "I know, Ged, but the ... equation has changed a bit since then."

His blood froze. If Kriggy couldn't hold this bargain together, there could only be one reason. The real reason he was here in the empty hallway, away from his friends.

"Tretiak."

"Sorry, Ged. He still calls the shots."

No sooner had he uttered the words than the Sarak slipped back in through the door behind him. At the same time, up ahead, four other Saraks marched in behind the lanky figure of Tretiak Bouche.

He stopped a few meters short of Geddy and studied him up and down, giving his head a slow, disappointed shake. "I always wondered what I'd do if I ever saw you again."

"So, should I drop my pants now, or …?"

Tretiak smirked. "Ever the comedian. Unfortunately, nothing about your situation is very funny."

"Look, I was just explaining to Krig this is a big misunderstanding."

He arched one eyebrow even further. "Oh?"

"I have a twenty-five percent stake in the Nad ship. Take what I owe out of that and we can all grab a drink and catch up."

Tretiak clicked his tongue and contorted his face into a look of phony sympathy. "I wish it was that simple. Unfortunately, when you stole my ship and disappeared, you still owed a lot of money to a lot of people. Someone had to clean up your mess."

"Fine. Take that out, too. All I care about is my ship."

"Ah, yes. The mysterious homemade ship procured by Mr. Yann. As you well know, Geddy, or Edgar, or whatever your real name is, my technicians perform a thorough inspection of every item that goes on the block."

—I don't like where this is going. Not one bit.

"What's your point?"

"It's clad in tukrium. I'd like to know where it came from."

"None of your business," Geddy said. "I won it fair and square. As for my debts, I'll pay you back. Just give me my take from the sale of that Zelnad ship, and you'll never see me again."

Tretiak let out a long, pained sigh. "Unfortunately, you didn't have a legitimate claim on the Zelnad vessel, therefore you're not entitled to any of the proceeds from its sale."

His heart leapt into his throat. "What?"

"Video from Beebit Tompanov's ship clearly shows he claimed the vessel before you."

After everything that happened, he'd almost forgotten that their high-tech rival trawler, *Red Raven,* had activated its tractor beam and was in the process of hauling in the Zelnad vessel when they ripped it from his grasp.

This Tompanov character either happened to spot the ship like Denk did or somehow knew it was there. If Tretiak had already determined it was his to sell, then half the money would go to that weasel and they'd get nothing.

Geddy's forehead radiated heat. His hands curled into fists. It didn't matter what he said now. "*We* found it, *we* got there first. We sent a drone to check it out before he even showed up."

Tretiak held out his palms and shook his head. "As you well know, the rules concerning salvage are thousands of years old. Drone or not, once it was in Captain Tompanov's tractor beam, it became his possession."

"Oh, cut the crap, Tretiak. This isn't about some bullshit technicality. This is about that ship. And mine."

Tretiak's face was a mask of pure innocence. "I don't know what you're talking about."

"The two guys with Sammo Yann who bought that ship must be Nads themselves. You need to find out where it came from and what they want with it."

He grimaced, shaking his head like a disappointed father. "Tell you what, Geddy. I'm willing to let bygones be bygones. Simply transfer six hundred fifty-thousand credits to me right now for your ship, plus half again that much to settle with me, and we can have that drink before you take off in your little ship. Call it an even million. Do that, and the first round's on me."

Geddy gritted his teeth. "You know I can't."

Tretiak tsk-tsked and let out an exasperated sigh. "Too bad. Unfortunately, the price of defrauding the Double A is rather steep, as you well know." Tretiak nodded sadly as though the words caused him physical pain and motioned to the Sarak thugs.

They advanced on him, too many to fight off. He whirled to run, but the Sarak named Terry still blocked the door. Before he could make another move, the others Saraks wrapped him up and dragged him down the hall as he struggled against their iron grip. They paused by Tretiak.

"Just give me my ship!" Geddy protested. "I won it fair and square!"

"In the case of insufficient funds, the option to buy falls to the next highest bidder. The Screvari gentleman has graciously agreed to acquire it in your stead." He waved his hand casually to the guards. "Take him to holding. I'll decide what to do with him later."

— No! You can't let them do that!

"Tretiak, wait!" Geddy pleaded as they dragged him, thrashing, down the hall. "Kriggy! That ship is mine! Sammo stole it from me and you know it!"

He gave Geddy a grim, apologetic look. "Sorry, kid. It's just business."

CHAPTER 34
HOUSEKEEPING

A crackling mesh of white-hot energy formed the outer wall of Geddy's cell, a major upgrade from the rusty old bars they used to have. Business must be very good. Unfortunately, the other appointments weren't nearly so fancy. A dirty mat lay on the floor and there was a honey hole in the corner that hadn't been cleaned in a very long time. The stench emanating from it was so strong, he could almost taste it.

The straight-backed metal chair against the wall was bolted to the floor and faced a metal sheet into which the Double A rules were etched. Apparently, it was to remind prisoners what they did to wind up there.

Tretiak had no legal authority to incarcerate anyone, but laws in this armpit of the universe were as loose as the women, if not perhaps as much as the sanitation standards.

— *What are we going to do?*

"I dunno, I'm thinking."

— *Krigor betrayed you.*

"He seized an opportunity. I would've done the same once. My question is why. Assuming the guys with Sammo were

Nads, then it makes sense they'd want their ship back. But why the *Penetrator*?" Geddy got up and paced back and forth, chewing hard on his lip. "You said shinium let us through the barrier around your planet, right?"

— *Yes. It is special like that.*

"What happens if it's not shinium?"

— *I'm not entirely sure.*

"How can you not be sure?"

— *No one's ever tried.*

"Could that research ship have tried to cross the barrier?"

— *It's possible. In fact, reaching Sagacea may have been its mission.*

"Could it have vaporized the crew? Maybe it was sent back as a warning."

— *That is possible as well.*

"You still haven't explained why the Nad ship responded to me."

— *I believe it actually responded to* me.

"Huh?"

— *Sagaceans are scattered throughout the universe. We are the seeds of knowledge. Where we go, civilization follows.*

"And you did this by launching millions of your own kind haphazardly into space?"

— *Our timeline was pretty flexible.*

"Wait … so does that mean that Old Earth …?"

— *That Old Earth civilizations were influenced by Sagaceans? Almost certainly.*

"How does that explain why the ship opened for you?"

— *Because I believe Zelnads are Sagaceans. Of a sort, anyway.*

"Say what now?"

— *I could sense it in the other bidders. The ones with Sammo. They have entities like me inside them, but … not like me. Their energy is different. More … angry.*

No one knew where Zelnads came from. The most popular

theory was that they were a quasi-religious cult that brainwashed people. From what he'd heard, otherwise ordinary people would just drop what they were doing and leave without explanation.

"I don't understand."

— In theory, a Sagacean could take control of its host.

"Really? So like, you could take control of me?"

— I believe so, but it is not my way. We are a team.

"Then why? What do you think they want?"

— I do not know. But I suspect they would have paid any price to get that research vessel back.

"What about the *Penetrator?* Did they actually want it, or was Sammo just trying to drive the price up to piss me off?"

— That is a good question. If they suspected it was made of shinium, it would've been worth the price to know for sure.

"What would they want with shinium?"

— Same as us. To reach Sagacea. But I do not know why.

"Maybe they just want to get back home like you."

— Maybe.

A wet, slithering sound came from the direction of the hole in the floor.

Geddy leapt from the chair and backed up as close as he dared to the glowing, humming bars of the cell. "What the hell was that?"

Visions of vengeful shit monsters played across his brain. All the bad burritos he'd eaten. All the hangover mornings when his legs fell asleep on the toilet. Maybe there was a price to pay.

The thing that came out of the hole was slick with raw sewage, a shit-slug with revenge in its smelly heart. Waves of muscular contractions rippled through its elongated body as it hauled itself out. For a few tense moments, it just lay there like it was taking a breather.

— *Step on it.*

— You step on it! These are my only shoes.

After a minute or so, the thing stretched itself into a glistening brown rod, twisting its body over and over like a … rubber band.

— *Wait. Is that …?*

Geddy beamed and took a step forward. "Morph? Aw, man, am I ever glad to see you."

— *Geddy, I think he's getting ready to–*

As he drew closer, Morpho released the tension in his stretchy body and let himself uncoil like a spring, showering the entire cell in raw sewage.

— *Clean himself, is what I was going to say.*

Geddy looked down at himself, finding his clothes speckled with foul liquid. It dripped down his forehead, off the tips of his ears. Some even got in his mouth.

— Thank you, Eli, for that timely warning.

Not two seconds after Morpho turned Geddy's cell into a toilet bowl, a man-sized shadow fell over him. He didn't need to turn around to know who it was.

"You're back." Geddy said.

Morpho instantly compressed himself into a wet, black, soft serve-shaped pile at the edge of the hole.

"Hello, Geddy."

He turned slowly around. Tretiak sniffed at the air, grimacing, as his eyes connected the myriad brown dots. "I see you've … made yourself at home." His eyes traced the spray pattern to the hole in the floor and the inert pile beside it. "Have you considered a fiber supplement?"

Geddy shrugged. "What can I say? Shit happens."

"I was troubled by how we left things," said Tretiak.

"Just now or back in the day?"

He smirked and gave his head a slow shake. "I don't wish you ill, Geddy. I did, at first. I've always had a hard time reconciling bad investments. But life went on. I got a newer, better ship and the Double A has never been more profitable. You know what the hardest thing was about your abrupt departure?"

"Writing the job posting?"

A pained smile flashed across his face. "It was that I regarded you as family. I grieved your departure as though you'd died."

Oh, that was rich. "First off, I *was* dead. To you and everyone else. And if your butt buddy Sammo hadn't stolen my ship, I still would be. And second of all, I have no family."

— *Geddy? Are we not family?*

— Of course we are. I'm just trying to piss him off so he leaves.

Tretiak leaned against the opening to the cell, his face illuminated by the humming shield. "But that's not true, is it? Sammo uncovered some very interesting facts about you." He narrowed his gaze and paused. "I wonder …"

"Where the sun goes at night?"

"Whether you know all the facts yourself."

"I think I'm pretty clear on my own backstory, thanks."

"Are you sure about that? Because I understand there are many unanswered questions, particularly with respect to your parents."

Geddy felt the color drain from his face. His expression went flat. "What the hell are you talking about?"

"Not a single piece of wreckage? No charred corpses or pieces of jewelry? How did you ever find closure?"

He reflexively lurched for him, momentarily ignoring the

shield. "Don't you dare pretend to– Ah! Fuck!" The searing heat painted a dark burn across his palm and he sucked in air through his teeth, wincing from the shock of pain.

"Ouch," Tretiak said, wagging his finger as he backed away. "That's gonna leave a mark."

"Then shut it off so I can leave a mark on you."

His thin lips curled into a smug grin. "I'm not heartless. Since you didn't take me up on my earlier offer, I'd like to sweeten the pot. Pay me what you owe, and not only will I buy you a drink, but I'll tell you what really happened to your parents."

— *He's lying!*

Geddy glared murderously at him over the tops of his eyes. "Bullshit."

Tretiak shrugged. "Only one way to know for sure, old friend."

His nails bit into his palms as he clenched his hands, ignoring the throbbing pain of the burn.

"You know I don't have the money."

Tretiak pointed his slender finger at the excrement-astic placard on the wall. "Auction rules state you have until the next business day to complete the sale. If you fail to do so, I'll have no choice but to do to you what we do to all frauds at the Double A."

"Put them on the first freighter out with a little spending money?"

After heaving a sigh, he turned back whence he came and gestured around him. "Such a shame. All this could've been yours. Goodbye, Geddy."

It crossed his mind to try and charm him into a deal, but the knife in his old boss' back was buried to the hilt. He listened to his footsteps until they faded into silence.

— *Just out of curiosity, what do they do to frauds?*

"Pretty much what Voprot does to globzoiks." He turned around and cocked an eyebrow. "Morph, get me the hell out of here."

— *What would you do without him?*

"I dunno. But he's a good shit."

CHAPTER 35

FINAL BOARDING CALL

As Morpho carefully slipped through a square in the energy mesh, putrid smoke rose up from where it burned the remaining sewage off of him. Once through, he rolled stickily up the wall across from him to the recessed terminal that controlled access then flattened to slide behind it like a butter knife. A couple seconds later came a loud *pop* and a puff of smoke, and the humming mesh flicked off.

Geddy gratefully stepped out into the hallway as Morpho dropped back to the floor, still smoking a bit himself.

"Thanks, pal. I owe you one."

— *One?*

"Okay, several."

The distant sound of running footsteps drew rapidly louder. Geddy backed away down the hall, preparing to run, but Morpho stayed in a pile on the floor.

"Morph, come on!"

Any moment, he feared a dozen angry Saraks would appear and beat him to a pulp. Instead, he saw Oz followed closely by Tardigan and … Voprot?

Geddy's heart just about leapt out of his chest. He'd never been so happy to see anyone.

"There you are!" Oz said, panting. "This place is a damned maze. I bought you a present."

She removed a small blaster tucked into her waistband, no doubt purchased from one of the many, many gun shops along Turduranto. It looked decent enough, but there was no guarantee a spring-loaded flag reading *BANG!!* wouldn't pop out when he pulled the trigger. Tardigan wielded one just like it and checked nervously over his shoulder. Voprot held his whip in one clawed hand.

"How'd you find me?"

"We can track Morph's unique biosignature. He found a way in through the ..." She sniffed the air and noticed the wreck of his cell. "Holy hell, what happened here?"

"Bad oysters. Voprot, what're you still doing here?"

"Voprot help friends." He brandished the whip. "Also like action."

"I owe you an apology, big guy."

He patted his heart. "Voprot know healing power of forgiveness."

"Did anyone see you?" Geddy asked.

Oz shook her head. "I don't think so, but we should hurry. Denk's keeping the *Fizmo* warm. Where's your ship?"

"Prep room. This way."

Morpho hopped up on Oz' shoulder and they took off down the hall. Even though the stone walls all looked the same, Geddy knew these catacombs like the back of his hand. Two lefts and a right later, they stood before the heavy, locked doors of the prep room.

The cavernous warehouse on the other side of the door was about twice the size of the Vault. Inside, purchases received final inspection and were prepared for delivery or pick-up.

That process generally took place the morning after the auction. Some upset bidders, and more than a few sellers, had tried to break in and steal back what they felt had been stolen from them. It never ended well.

"Look, there's gonna be a small army of Saraks behind this door. I can't ask any of you to go through it."

Oz drew her own blaster and cracked her neck. "Are you kidding? I dream about this shit."

"Listen, about everything, I–"

Oz cut him off. "You were an asshole. But we said we'd get to your ship, so that's what we're gonna do. When the shooting starts, run. We'll cover you."

As she stood there before the door with her blaster drawn preparing to unleash her badassery on whomever waited on the other side, he saw her in a new light. Under other circumstances, they might've been more than friends. But with any luck, he'd be rocketing away from this dustbowl in a few minutes and would never see her again.

Geddy gave her his best smile. "Guess you'll have to thank Denk for me."

"I'd hug you, but ... you know." Her nose wrinkled distastefully at his smell.

"I understand." He turned to Tardigan. "Doc, go back to the ship. This isn't your fight."

"I'm a crewman of the *For Sale Make Offer* now. It *is* my fight."

"Oh, I almost forgot." Oz reached into her vest pocket to produce a single glowing blue novasphere. "I figure you'll be needing this."

Warmth surged into his face. "Your last one."

"Meh. Blue balls are never far away when Osmiya's in town," she said with a wink. "Morph, do your thing."

Morpho hopped off her shoulder onto the wall and

prepared to crawl into the control unit, but before he could flatten himself again, Voprot pushed between them and punched a hole through the metal door. His scaly fingers curled around it and he ripped it free of the hinges like a toy, then grinned before barreling through.

Across the floor, between them and the evening's auction items, a group of at least eight Saraks had overturned a card table, using it for cover as they fumbled for their rifles.

Two dropped before they even touched their weapons. While they concentrated their fire on the door, Geddy broke free and bolted toward the *Penetrator,* a gleaming jewel nestled amid the assorted wares.

Energy bolts scorched the floor by his feet and singed the packing crates. He returned fire as he dashed past, but a sizzling bolt caught him just above the hip, opening a charred crater in his flesh. Hot, electric pain surged through him as he cried out and tumbled to the floor, quickly rolling behind one of the crates for cover.

Ten meters remained between him and the ship. A Sarak wailed in pain as it went down.

"Geddy, run!" shouted Oz.

A blast shredded the upper half of the box, exposing his head. He crawled behind another as a Sarak charged at him, firing and turning that box to splinters. He popped up long enough to blast it in the chest, but it ignored the wound and kept coming, gun blazing.

— *We're trapped!*

The pissed-off Sarak uncorked a fierce battle cry as it charged. In that moment, Voprot dropped to all fours and covered the distance between them in two lightning-fast leaps, lowering his shoulder and ending the hapless Sarak sailing into the Zelnad ship with a bone-crunching *thwack.*

The remaining two Saraks turned their fire on him but only got a couple shots off before Voprot lashed out with his whip.

As it unfurled, it came alive with sizzling blue energy like Zeus wielding lightning. It coiled about their legs and he yanked, neatly slicing their lower legs off as they toppled back. He pounced immediately and tore them to ribbons.

Geddy clambered to his feet, wincing from the searing pain in his left leg as he limped toward the ship. A moment later, a fresh shot came from behind him, whizzing so close to his right ear he smelled burning hair.

Tretiak's reinforcements had come.

Oz and Tardigan whirled and returned fire. "Morph!" Oz screamed. "Get Geddy in the ship!"

Morpho leapt from her shoulder and sprang across the room to him, stretching himself into an oblong shield just as a fresh hail of blaster fire reached him. Geddy lurched painfully toward the *Penetrator*, glancing to his left in time to see Tardigan, Oz, and Voprot take cover behind the Nad ship.

The shots hitting Morpho seemed to absorb into him, but the way he twitched with each impact suggested it wasn't entirely painless.

Geddy reached the ship and threw open the door, struggling to crawl inside the tight cabin while Morpho continued to shield him from the bolts. He flicked on the banks of switches and the engines rumbled to life. Dozens, if not hundreds of shots slammed into Morph, who was stretched so thin Geddy could see at least ten Sarak guards spread out, all concentrating their fire on him.

"Morph, get in!"

Morpho fell inside, remaining flattened out to protect Geddy as he yanked it closed. He immediately collapsed into a blob on the floor, his gelatinous body shaking with exertion, if not pain.

When he and Eli were building the ship, Geddy had a choice whether or not to add weapons. But doing so would've taken another year at least of meticulous smelting, casting, and machining. He wished like hell he had something now.

All he had — all he really needed — was the key. *Shit.*

— *Hurry!*

Merely fitting himself in the tiny cabin was difficult, say nothing of removing his pants and extracting the key from its hiding place. It required such a monumental effort that it winded him, but he got it done. Pulling his pants back up was out of the question.

He slipped the key into the port and turned it.

The *Penetrator* hummed to life, rising off the floor.

"Holy shit, it works! Eli!"

— *Of course, it works. We built it together.*

Blaster rounds bounced harmlessly off the ship's shinium skin as he lifted off. Meanwhile, behind the Nad ship, Voprot was fastening his suit of armor about his gargantuan frame, seemingly unconcerned about the scorch marks on his body and ready to fight for his life.

The Saraks advanced, half focused on his friends while the others fired uselessly at him.

— *How are we getting out of here?*

The walls and ceiling were solid rock, which left only the thick cargo door. They could blast through if they had enough speed, which gave him an idea. He didn't have weapons, but he had a pair of AS-322 MPD engines and needed to turn around.

Time for a barbecue.

Geddy nudged the stick left and aimed the ship directly at the advancing Saraks, then gunned it toward them, drawing their fire as they backed away in a panic. As they neared the door, he spun a hundred eighty degrees and punched it. The rear camera blazed pure blue-white as exhaust spewed from the thrusters at three hundred meters per second, turning them to ash.

The thrust pinned him so hard to the seat he couldn't breathe. Ahead, the cargo door loomed. He activated the shinium blast shield, leaving him momentarily blind save for the cool blue glow of the scopes and instruments.

"Could be a short trip, bud."

— *Have faith, Geddy. Have faith.*

CHAPTER 36

FLIGHT OF THE PENETRATOR

The *Penetrator* punched through the stout cargo door like a can opener. Geddy slung the ship around the mountain and accelerated as they climbed toward the heavens. She handled like a dream. How awesome would it be if it left a perfect cutout of its shape behind?

He worried about Oz and the others, but they'd be fine. Not only had he shown them the way out, but he'd turned their pursuers to ash. Hell, by the time he reached open space, they, too, would be en route to their next adventure.

It was surreal to think he'd parted ways with the crew of the *Fiz*. After all, they'd been through a lot together in a pretty short stretch. And, as much as it pained him to admit it, it was nice to feel like he had real friends for once. But the whole episode had sidetracked him from his objective, which was finding the way to Sagacea.

He slipped through a wispy cloud in the upper atmosphere, a haze of ice crystals melting away to the infinite void, beautiful desolation, and boundless reaches of–

— *Where are you going?*

"You're kidding, right?"

— *Look down.*

"What do you–? Oh, shit." Between his bare legs, still in a pile on the floor, was Morpho."

— *I think he is very depleted.*

"What do you want me to do? Give him some trail mix?"

— *You must return him to his crewmates somehow.*

"How the hell am I supposed to do that? This thing doesn't have an airlock."

— *Don't you think I know that?*

"They can't net me because there's no net. No tractor beam, either. And I can't even do an EVA 'cuz I don't have a suit."

— *Fly it in.*

"Fly it into what? The *Fiz?* But they haven't even–"

The scopes chirped an alert. Two ships in close proximity had just left atmosphere directly over Aquebba like bats out of hell. The one in back was gaining. After a moment, the transponders registered their names. *For Sale By Owner* and *Auctionaut Two.*

"Aw, fuck. Tretiak's sent his goons after the *Fiz!*"

Morpho still hadn't moved. He'd been through an awful lot back there. Maybe he wasn't exactly indestructible after all.

— *I say it's Morpho's call.*

— You want to leave it up to a … depleted loogie?

— *That loogie saved your life multiple times.*

Geddy grumbled in protest, then grimaced as he gave Morpho a poke. His finger sunk into the faintly warm black-green goo like something that had washed up on the beach. But before he could pull it out to examine it, a tiny jolt of electricity stung his fingertip, and drowsiness overtook him.

— *Geddy? What's happening? You're fading from me.*

— So … sleepy …

—*I don't understand. Why are you suddenly–*

— **Don't panic.**

A burst of adrenaline yanked him out of his little nap. The

voice in his head was neither his nor Eli's. It was calmer somehow. Flatter.

— Um, hello?

— I'm the one you call Morpho. I only require a small amount of energy from you. I can draw the rest of what I need from the ship itself.

— Don't tell me you're in my head now, too.

— Apologies for the intrusion. I only entered your consciousness to reassure you.

— Yeah, well it ain't working.

— Who is in here with us?

— *Hey, Morpho. I'm Eli.*

Far away, bright green disruptor bolts whizzed past the *Fizmo* as it dodged back and forth, taking a few hits to the rear shield. He would never have guessed the shields still worked on the old Ghruk freighter, but they wouldn't last long against a modern ship. Oz gave him their only novasphere, so they couldn't jump away. Whatever he was going to do, he'd better do it damned fast.

— I am very confused.

— That makes two of us, but we've got bigger problems right now. The *Fiz* is in trouble.

His head swam as though he'd just given blood before a marathon — not that he would ever do either. Morpho's energy drain couldn't continue much longer. Not on an empty stomach, anyway.

Morpho leapt past Geddy's face and plastered himself to the front shield, yanking his finger along with it. From the outside, it would've looked like an idiot without a spacesuit glued his finger to the window.

— We must engage them.

— We don't have any weapons.

— *That's not exactly true.*

— What are you talking about?

— *The ship, Geddy. It's indestructible.*

— Eli is correct.

— But I'm just water and meat, so ...

— You will have to eject.

— Come again?

— I can protect you from the vacuum for a time.

— Um ...

— I will absorb the air in the cockpit and form a bubble around you.

— Are you nuts? You'll inflate like a balloon. Say nothing of the temperature. And the radiation. And our velocity.

— I can convert radiation to heat. And I can use some of the air to maneuver. It will work. You must trust me.

— You got a corkscrew in there, too?

— *Morpho is right. This is the only way you can save them.*

— Morpho, not to change the subject, but I'm about to pass out.

— Oh, sorry.

Morpho released his finger, and the electric sensation instantly vanished.

Geddy had done a lot of things in his life. Terrible, strange, depraved, unforgettable things. But using his own ship as a missile would be a first, as would ejecting into open space.

The only reason the *Fizmo* was in this situation at all was because its crew had taken him in and treated them as one of their own. They'd risked their lives to get him to his ship, and now, through no fault of their own, they were fleeing in a rickety ship that couldn't jump out of danger. If he didn't do something, he was going to watch it be destroyed.

In the end, it wasn't a difficult decision at all. If he somehow survived — which was roundly improbable — the *Penetrator* would tumble out into space. Kigantu's gravity would suck it down into the desert, where even the Zelnads couldn't find it. If he couldn't have it, at least they wouldn't, either.

— Are we really doing this?

— *It is not for me to decide.*

— There's a good chance we'll both die.

— *Yes, but it is still just a chance. Your friends' death is certain.*

— If this is it, I'm sorry I didn't get you back to Sagacea.

— *You did your best. I'm proud of you.*

Geddy calculated a collision course and hit the thrusters, streaking toward Tretiak's ship as it focused its entire arsenal on the *Fizmo's* weakening aft shield. Its torpedo doors opened. One good hit and the old ship would be dust.

He transferred full power to the forward shield and re-closed the shinium blast shield over the window.

The *Auctionaut* spotted him and trained its starboard battery on him. The *Penetrator's* shield was meant for space junk or meteoroids, though, and not a Potzie-class interceptor. The disruptor blasts exploded around him, shaking the poor little ship like a paint can. He removed the key and zipped it into his pocket. At least he'd have the satisfaction of knowing no one else could fly it.

"All right, Morph. Hope you've been absorbing that air."

Morpho stretched himself into a thin sheet and began to envelop him. Geddy undid his restraints and hovered his shaking finger over the hatch release. A few seconds later, Morpho closed over his hand and squeezed. Maybe it was just his state of mind, but it felt like a hug.

A fresh barrage of disruptor fire slammed into the ship, the collision alert ringing in his ears. He blew the air from his lungs, opened the door, and pushed out into space.

As expected, Morpho instantly expanded to a balloon five meters across, his body stretched so thin that Geddy could see through it. The cold hit him like an icy fist. Mucus froze in his nostrils, and the saliva coating his tongue bubbled like a freshly poured beer. His penis retreated into his abdomen, never to return.

Tumbling inside the Morpho-bubble, he only caught a flash of the *Penetrator* ripping a hole through the interceptor's hull like a bullet, and a brilliant burst of light, and then nothing. An orgy of violence began and ended in complete silence.

When the sparks faded, the ruined hulk of Tretiak's ship fell aside, cleaved in two. As the chunks drifted slowly apart, they revealed his own ship tumbling lazily away from the wreckage in the general direction of Kigantu's nearest moon. Geddy wished he could've taken it across the cosmos with Eli, but it wasn't to be.

Sharp hisses of air released from somewhere around him. Bits of exploding debris from Tretiak's ship glanced off Morpho as he steadied them. The sudden deceleration threw him against the front of Morpho's precariously thin membrane, the only thing between him and instant death. They were more or less following the same path the *Penetrator* had, taking them toward the debris field.

Terrifying as it all was, and despite the fact his eyeballs seemed frozen in his sockets, he could still breathe, expelling thick white clouds of water vapor with each labored exhale. A faint warmth emanated off his strange and marvelous new friend, though it was only a matter of time before he succumbed to the cold. Violent shivers racked his body.

It all happened so fast. He'd survived ejecting, but what came next? Against the infinite blackness of space, he would be invisible. Oz and Denk, and even Tardigan would never imagine he'd ejected. They would go after the *Penetrator,* and by the time they realized it was empty, they'd have no idea where he was.

— Eli?

— *I'm here.*

— It's not looking good.

— *No.*

Scopes weren't designed to pick up tiny lifeforms like him. They were for asteroids and planets and other ships. They'd have to damn near run into him to find him, and that was if they even realized what he'd done. The smart move was to do a full burn out of there and hope the *Auctionaut* gave up the chase. Besides, he only had a few minutes of air left.

With his tumbling stopped and his face pressed to the Morpho-bubble, he had an uncluttered view of the *Penetrator* as it grew smaller and smaller. Were it not for the sun glinting off it, it would've been invisible.

— Well, there she goes.

— *I'd say her maiden voyage was a success.*

— It was, wasn't it?

Around the time he started congratulating himself on being so magnanimous, a vertical slit of light opened on the far side of the *Penetrator*, directly in its path. A blink later, the *Red Raven*, from which they'd essentially stolen the Zelnad vessel, birthed through the gate like a hideous interstellar baby.

— Aw, hell, no. No, no, no, no!

— *Wait … is that …?*

The big salvage ship's bright yellow tractor beam activated, instantly freezing the *Penetrator's* uncontrolled tumble. Its cargo door opened like the mouth of a predatory fish, slurping it down in seconds.

The moment the *Red Raven's* hungry maw closed on the *Penetrator*, another shimmering slit opened in the same place, and it jumped away before Denk could get off a shot. The gate shrank to a pinpoint of light, and then it was gone.

Geddy's jaw dropped, but he immediately closed it. The cold made his teeth hurt. Tears began to well, but he forced them back in. He couldn't face the end with eyes open if they were frozen shut.

— Huh. Was not expecting that.

— *Me, neither.*

— Not our problem now, is it?

— *No.*

He felt a bit warmer but wasn't sure if it came from Morpho or if he was freezing to death. Supposedly, a burst of warmth came near the end.

— Is this what it was like? Floating through space alone?

— *You are not alone. Neither was I.*

— Because you could sense the others.

— *Yes.*

Maybe there was something to that. Accepting his own situation was like wiping the grime from a window. Through it, he could only see Oz the Warrior, Denk the Dreamer, and Dr. Tardigan the Wise. He even saw Voprot the Inarticulate. They wouldn't find him, but they were looking, and that was all that mattered. There were still a few people in this world who didn't want him dead. That wasn't nothing.

— I think I would've liked being their captain.

— *You would've been a great one.*

— Why do you think so?

— *Because you are my captain, and you are a great one.*

That coaxed a smile to his cracked lips. With the sudden flood of delicious warmth came drowsiness. Still, he fought to keep his eyes open, because suddenly he understood that all things were beautiful. Even Kigantu and its nasty-ass ranses. Even Elenia and its ghosts. And if all things were beautiful, then so was he.

— You know, I always wanted to die without regrets. Guess I blew that.

— *You can tell me if you'd like.*

— There's not enough time to confess them all. But now that I'm here, only one is front and center.

— *What is it?*

— I probably should've peed before we left.

NEXT IN THE REASSEMBLY SERIES

vinci-books.com/trawler-trash

Hungry crew. Empty hold. Stolen ship. Geddy Starheart's only hope is the galaxy's deadliest race. Buckle up for Trawler Trash!

Turn the page for a free preview…

TRAWLER TRASH: CHAPTER 1

ALONE TOGETHER

If the crew of *For Sale Make Offer* was smart, they'd have jumped away by now. Circling back for him, a black bubble in the eternal ocean of stars over Kigantu, was suicide. Geddy Starheart just used his ship as a missile and turned his former boss' spectacularly expensive cruiser into space dust. One way or another, that would have repercussions. Reinforcements were already scrambling to return the favor to the *Fizmo,* and without shields, their only option was burn ass out of there and hide.

He'd just have to trust that that's what happened. It would comfort him in his final moments. Was it selfish of him to want this ending? To actually be the captain who sacrificed himself and his most prized possession to enable his crew's escape? Of course not. That was the kind of story told around campfires in hushed, reverent tones. *Have I ever told you boys about the bravest, most selfless captain to ever sail the infinite sea? His name was Geddy Starheart, and you'd do well to know it.*

Still, the moment felt bittersweet, tainted as it was by the fact that the *Penetrator,* the one-of-a-kind vessel he and Eli built together, was a direct casualty of his actions. He knew she was a tough ship, but it ripped the *Auctionaut* in half and kept going. Such a delicious moment for it to come through unscathed, only then for it to be swallowed by Beebit Tompanov in the *Red Raven*. Anything would've been better. Exploding with the *Auctionaut*. Tumbling into Kigantu's atmosphere and burning up. Not becoming someone's *salvage*.

But man, if there was ever a time to let go of shit you couldn't control, it was right fucking now.

It briefly occurred to Geddy that he should pull up his pants, but celestial beings had little need for such things. Now that the *Fizmo* had escaped Tretiak's ship, and the *Penetrator* was swallowed up by the rival trawler *Red Raven*, there was nothing left to do but enjoy the uncluttered view of Kigantu and its nearest moon, Balox.

Exposing himself to such stark beauty just felt right, like he was saying, *This is me. This is my body. Human. Fragile. Balls half frozen.*

It was much warmer now inside the Morpho-bubble, though that was a low bar. Somewhere in the vicinity of minus twenty, he guessed. Whatever process his biosynthetic savior used to convert electromagnetic radiation to convective heat had reached equilibrium with the punishing cold of space.

Crystals of frozen urine surrounded him like a cluster of sparkly yellow stars. Somehow, peeing out into the vacuum was among the least interesting things he'd done that day.

For a guy who wanted nothing more than to be forgotten, this should've been the perfect exit. But all he could think about was Eli, his longtime companion, and Morpho, the Zelnad booger that had saved his life several times over. A very weird little family of three, alone together at the end.

— Will I freeze first or run out of oxygen?

Normally, he'd talk out loud to Eli if they were alone, but his tongue had swelled to where he had to breathe through his nose. They'd chat in their quiet way. The only way for Eli.

— *Don't trouble yourself with such thoughts.*

— Not like I can save them for later.

— *This moment is about acceptance, Geddy.*

— I reject that theory.

— *Want a story?*

During those first several weeks after Eli revealed himself as a literal voice in his head, Geddy fought it. He had more than enough internal conversations, thank you very much. But as he came to see that Eli meant him no harm and that his plight to return to Sagacea was now Geddy's as well, they reached a sort of truce.

Eli enjoyed providing color commentary on Geddy's sad little life on Earth 2, but building the *Penetrator* together focused their interactions on the task.

He knew the broad strokes of Eli's home world, but precious few details. It was at the center of the universe, which could only be a metaphor, and his race had existed since the Big Bang. Its mission was to disperse the seeds of intelligence far and wide, giving any number of species the insight and inspiration to evolve into civilizations.

It now appeared that the Zelnads, the shadowy cult that spread faster than Vyephian blue fever, were little more than disgruntled Sagaceans that decided to go way, way off-book.

Eli could, and did, talk for hours about Sagacea and all the questions he thought about while floating through space for seventeen million years, but to that point, he'd never heard Eli tell a single story.

— I'm kinda busy dying, but sure. Let's hear it.

— *Once upon a time, an immortal being named Neil Armstrong found himself alone. The only one of his kind.*

— Wait. As in *the* Neil Armstrong?

— *The being's name is irrelevant. I thought it would make it easier to conceive if I used that of your favorite historical figure.*

— Neil Armstrong it is. Apologies in advance if I die before you get to the end.

— *Neil became so lonely that he forced his soul to split in two, like a cell, so he would have a friend.*

— Can we call that one Armstrong?

— *Of course. This other half of him – Armstrong – was an exact copy. For a time, Neil and Armstrong were very happy. But as the years rolled on, Armstrong turned bitter and resentful, opposing Neil at every turn and belittling him. What began as simple disagreements degraded into spite, and finally to cruelty. And so it went for all eternity.*

— Great story. Ending needs work.

— *Don't you see? Rather than accept his circumstances, he split in two. As a result, he was forever at war with himself.*

Geddy paused to consider the story's meaning. There were worse things to occupy your mind at the end. But it was asking too much of his oxygen-starved brain. He kept losing the threads. Oblivion beckoned. Kigantu and Balox were little more than blurry shapes now, frozen in the ether like ghosts.

His eyes were useless, so he closed them. It melted the crystals forming on his eyeballs and helped focus his thoughts just enough to understand why Eli shared this particular parable at this particular time. The other half of Geddy Starheart was little Eddie Kepler.

That doe-eyed kid who loved spaceships and Old Earth stories was still in there somewhere, but Geddy felt no more connected to that boy than a bird to its eggshell. Nothing about his ridiculously easy, absurdly happy life before his parents died struck a chord.

His long and distinguished career as a henchman wasn't a path. It was a retreat. But he didn't leave it behind because he *wanted* to. He left because he *needed* to. Somehow, that kid from Earth 2 reached clean through time and shook Geddy awake. *Come back,* he said. *You're better than this. Let me help.*

And so that's what he did.

What the boy with the pilot dad and docent mom wanted more than anything was a best friend. Someone worthy of trust and fully in sync with him. There were kids at the Planetary Defense Force base, of course, and he made a lot of friends, but never like he imagined a best friend being.

Eli became that friend. After all this time, the kid finally got what he wanted. Geddy Starheart would still be fighting the voice in his head, but Eddie Kepler? Eddie was just grateful for someone to talk to.

— I'm not at war anymore.

— *Nice feeling, isn't it?*

That was Eli's point all along. Of all people, Geddy Muthafuckin' Starheart was going to rest in peace after all. Who'd have guessed?

His right cheek pressed against the Morpho-balloon. The warmth felt luscious. A tingling, electric sensation pulsed through it, and again, Morpho joined the party in his head.

— You're too late, Morph. I don't have any energy for you.

— I have all I require.

— Then why are you here?

— To get your attention.

— Sorry, but it's important I let go. That's how my journey ends. Thanks for everything.

— Open your damn eyes!

The same electric tingle in his cheek surged through him with increased power, a jolt of adrenaline that made him gasp as his eyes popped open. At first, all he could see was the dim outline of Kigantu and a nearby chunk of Tretiak's ship, but a tiny puff of air from Morpho pivoted the balloon around. Morpho released him, and the flow of energy stopped.

Lights, not stars, in a symmetrical pattern.

— *Geddy? What is th–*

From the center came a supernova, a brilliant and blinding

explosion of light that burned a hole through his foggy eyes. Either he'd just witnessed the death of a star or this was the light, as in *the light*. The closer it drew to him, the more he wanted to be in it. He was ready.

— This is the end, pal. It's finally here.

— *I'm not so sure.*

Quite suddenly, the light disappeared. Something was blocking it. But what? Had it judged him unworthy, or was it just another piece of debris from the *Auctionaut?*

A moment later, the shape obscured all lights in the pattern, allowing it to reflect the bright glow of the moon. It was a chunky, artificial object that moved, one claw closing around the Morpho-balloon. And atop its strange form was a shiny bubble with a face inside that, at least to Geddy's addled brain, bore a striking resemblance to Oz.

AFTERWORD

Toward the merciful end of 2020, when we were all sick of everything and everyone and dreading the widely forecasted Winter From Hell, I was putting the finishing touches on the last book of my debut series, *The Cytocorp Saga*. They aren't any darker than other dystopian fiction, but to write it while a real-life dystopia was unfolding ... well, it got to me after a while.

After a short break, was ready to dive into something lighter and with fewer moving parts. I had this idea years ago about a guy with a one-of-a-kind spaceship who wakes up to find it stolen and, eventually, chopped up or otherwise sold off for parts. How fun would it be to follow this guy around as he tried to literally get his ship together, and in the process, figuratively get his shit together?

First, some critical backstory.

I had excellent friends growing up, especially in high school. Against all odds, we achieved nerd-vana — just enough cred to not get shoved into lockers but not so much that we ever had to worry about deciding which party to attend. Our interests overlapped where it mattered, particularly when it came to movies, books, and stories in general.

One of our favorite activities in study hall and on the band bus (trumpet, in case you wondered) was passing a sheet of paper back and forth in order to write the foulest, most violent, sex-filled story we could possibly conjure in the moment. Two voices, one goal, one sentence at a time. Here's an example of what our 15-year-old selves might have written using italics for the other author:

One day, while walking home in a frilly little dress and humming a happy tune, Anna encountered a hole in the ground.
From inside came a child's voice. "Help! I'm trapped in this hole!"
She stuck her hand in, but something latched on, yanking her down so hard that her skin peeled like a banana. *She landed in a cavern filled with hot blood.* Only it wasn't blood, but acid.
"Oh no!" cried Anna. "I thought it was just hot arterial blood, but it's actually acid! Aieee!"
Suddenly, a tree fell over the hole and trapped her in the subterranean room full of acid. *Only it was a very weak acid so she realized she would dissolve slowly like a nail in Coke.* But it didn't matter because she was on her way to dive off a cliff onto jagged rocks.
So, when you think about it, Anna got what she wanted. Just not *how* she wanted. *And that was the lesson the kid wanted her to learn.*

THE END

I can't tell you what twisted, dorktastic fun that was. Pure creation. Two friends, stewed in the same pot as Troma movies, Monty Python, the National Lampoon, and *Fangoria* magazine, writing down whatever popped into their heads and *dying* laughing, especially when there was a tug of war over which way it should go. (See acid/blood issue above.)

These sloppily constructed slabs of pulp formed the undergirding of my tastes, such as they are.

Around that time, I really started noticing the elements of story — especially the ones I responded to. I liked wisecracking heroes like Jack Burton from *Big Trouble in Little China* and Ash from *Evil Dead*. Space, aliens, weird stuff, so much the better. I especially enjoyed unexpected swerves into humor or camp, and even the occasional hint of romance, e.g. "Gimme some sugar, baby!"

But I also wanted to be like Stephen King or my then literary hero, Clive Barker. Guys who didn't mind going really dark but were also writing on just another plane entirely. I was drawn to the fun stuff, but I didn't want to be the guy who wrote just fun stuff.

Okay, backstory complete. Now let's fast-forward thirty years.

After *Cytocorp*, I was ready for a palate cleanser of sorts. To go back to my roots and try to recapture that same feeling of fast, fun writing. To write the kind of story I needed, and maybe what everyone else needed while applying the many, many storytelling lessons learned while writing the trilogy. *Rocket Repo* was the result.

Long story short, this is me in book form. If you made it to the end, then maybe you had nerdy friends yourself. *Rocket Repo* is for you as much as them.

C.P. James
April 2, 2021

ABOUT THE AUTHOR

C.P. James writes cinematic sci-fi with humor and heart. He lives in the magical country of Ecuador. His first novel, The Perfect Generation, was published in February 2018. A dystopian trilogy, The Cytocorp Saga, was released in 2020. Reassembly, a humorous space opera, was launched in April 2021.